CH

The
BLACK
MARKET

ALSO BY KIKI SWINSON

The Playing Dirty Series: *Playing Dirty* and *Notorious*
The Candy Shop
A Sticky Situation
The Wifey Series: *Wifey, I'm Still Wifey, Life After Wifey,*
Still Wifey Material
Wife Extraordinaire Series: *Wife Extraordinaire* and *Wife*
Extraordinaire Returns
Cheaper to Keep Her Series: Books 1–5
The Score Series: *The Score* and *The Mark*
Dead on Arrival
The Black Market

ANTHOLOGIES
Sleeping with the Enemy (with Wahida Clark)
Heist and *Heist 2* (with De'nesha Diamond)
Lifestyles of the Rich and Shameless (with Noire)
A Gangster and a Gentleman (with De'nesha Diamond)
Most Wanted (with Nikki Turner)
Still Candy Shopping (with Amaleka McCall)
Fistful of Benjamins (with De'nesha Diamond)
Schemes and *Dirty Tricks* (with Saundra)
Bad Behavior (with Noire)

Published by Kensington Publishing Corp.

The
BLACK
MARKET

KIKI
SWINSON

Kensington Publishing Corp.
www.kensingtonbooks.com

DAFINA BOOKS are published by

Kensington Publishing Corp.
119 West 40th Street
New York, NY 10018

All Kensington Titles, Imprints, and Distributed Lines are available at special quantity discounts for bulk purchases for sales promotions, premiums, fund-raising, and educational or institutional use. Special book excerpts or customized printings can also be created to fit specific needs. For details, write or phone the office of the Kensington special sales manager: Kensington Publishing Corp., 119 West 40th Street, New York, NY 10018, attn: Special Sales Department, Phone: 1-800-221-2647.

Library of Congress Card Catalogue Number: 2018944169

Dafina and the Dafina logo Reg. U.S. Pat. & TM Off.

ISBN-13: 978-1-4967-1280-6
ISBN-10: 1-4967-1280-3
First Kensington Hardcover Edition: December 2018

ISBN-13: 978-1-4967-1283-7 (e-book)
ISBN-10: 1-4967-1283-8 (e-book)

10 9 8 7 6 5 4 3 2 1

Printed in the United States of America

1

MISTY

I'd been in this world too long to just now be finding my way. But here I was, feeling grateful and shit about being healthy and having a roof over my head, thanks to the steady pay from my latest employer.

For the last five and a half months, I'd been collecting a check working as a pharmacy tech. The job was easy and my boss, Dr. Sanjay Malik, was a dream to work with. Not only was he a nice guy, he was very generous with the monthly bonuses he paid me and he would occasionally let me get off work early. The bonuses were for the extra work I did delivering prescriptions to senior citizens who weren't mobile or couldn't pick up their medication. Sanjay would have me deliver their meds to them, and after I completed the deliveries, he usually told me to take off work for the rest of the day, which I found awesome.

But three weeks ago, I noticed that Sanjay had me delivering meds to dark and questionable neighborhoods. I never said anything to him about it because who was I? And what was I going to get out of questioning him? He owned this place, which meant that he could fire my ass on the spot. So, I left well enough alone and minded my own damn business.

Sanjay wasn't aware of this, but I'd taken a few pills here and there for my cousin Jillian. Jillian got into a bad car accident over a year ago and hadn't fully recovered from it. Her doctor cut off her prescription meds six months ago, so I stepped in and threw a few pills at her when I was able to get my hands on some.

The first time, I stole two Percocet pills and two Vicodin pills. Each time I stole from the pharmacy, I took a few more pills. My nerves used to be on edge for about a day after each time I pocketed those pills, but since cops never showed up to cuff me, I knew Sanjay hadn't figured out I'd been stealing from him. I hoped he never would.

As soon as I walked into the pharmacy, I noticed that there were only three customers waiting for their prescriptions. I said good morning to everyone waiting as I walked behind the counter, clocked in, and went to work.

It didn't take long for Sanjay and I to ready those customers' prescriptions and get them on their way. After ringing up the last customer, I turned to Sanjay. "We got any deliveries?" I asked him while I searched through our online refill requests.

"I think we have six or maybe seven," he replied, before turning to answer the phone.

Sanjay was a handsome man. He resembled Janet Jackson's billionaire ex-husband. But unlike Janet Jackson's ex, Sanjay wasn't wealthy, at least to my knowledge. He owned this little pharmacy on the city limits of Virginia Beach, near Pembroke Mall. There was nothing fancy about the place, just your basic small business. But I often wondered why this doctor, who was doing well enough to own this place and have employees like me, wasn't married? From time to time I'd jokingly tell him that I was going to set him up with one of my friends. And his response would always be, "Oh, no. Believe me, I am fine. Women require too much."

Not too long after I started working here, he told me that his family was from Cairo, Egypt. From the way he talked about their homes and travel, I knew they were doing well for themselves. He also told me that education was a big deal in his country. And arranged marriages too.

"Think I could get me a man over in Cairo?" I'd teased. But his answer had no humor in it.

"You wouldn't want a husband from my country, because the men are very strict and the women they marry are disciplined. The things you say and do here in the US wouldn't be tolerated where I'm from."

Damn! "Yeah, whatever, Sanjay!" I'd chuckled.

Working at Sanjay's pharmacy was fairly easy. Time would go by fast. The first half of the day, it would be somewhat busy, and after two p.m. the traffic would die down. This was when I'd take my lunch break. If I didn't bring in my lunch from home, I'd leave the pharmacy and walk over to the food court in Pembroke Mall. This day was one of those days.

"I'm going to lunch, Sanjay. Want anything from Pembroke Mall?" I asked him.

"No, I'm fine. But thank you," he replied.

I walked over to the computer, clocked out, and then I left the building. On my way out, I ran into Sanjay's brother, Amir. As usual, he said nothing to me.

I'd always found it odd that Amir would stop by to see Sanjay during my lunch break. And if I was there when Amir walked into the pharmacy, Sanjay would send me on my lunch break or even send me home for the rest of the day. Now, I wasn't complaining because I loved when he let me leave work early, but at the same time, there aren't any coincidences. Something wasn't right with that guy and I knew it.

Sanjay had spoken to me about his brother, but I didn't

know much. He lived close by and was married with three children. And just like Sanjay, Amir was also very handsome. But Amir never said a word to me. If I hadn't heard Amir greet Sanjay, I'd wonder if he could speak at all. He'd wave at me when he'd come and go, but that was it. I never asked Sanjay how old his brother was because you could clearly see that Amir was younger. He was never flashy. He always wore a pair of casual pants and a regular button-down shirt. He had the look of a car salesman.

I grabbed some Chinese food from the food court in the mall and then I took a seat at one of the tables near one of the mall's exits. While I was eating, I got a call from my cousin Jillian. Her father and my mother are siblings. My uncle committed suicide when we were kids, so she lived with her mother until she turned eighteen. From there she'd been back and forth from having her own apartment to sleeping under our grandmother's roof. Jillian was a pretty, twenty-six-year-old, full-figured woman. She wasn't the brightest when it came to picking the men in her life, but she had a good heart and that's all that mattered to me.

She'd barely said hello before she asked, "Think you can bring me a couple of Percocets on your way home?"

"Jillian, not today," I griped.

"You're acting like I'm asking you to bring me a pill bottle of 'em," Jillian protested. "And besides, you know I don't ask you unless I really need them."

I let out a long sigh and said, "I'm gonna bring you only two. And that's it."

"Thank you," Jillian said with excitement.

"Yeah, whatever. You're such a spoiled brat," I told her.

"So. What are you doing?"

"Sitting in the food court of Pembroke Mall, eating some Chinese food."

"What time do you get off today?"

"I think I'm gonna leave at about seven since it's Saturday."

"Has it been busy today?"

"Kinda . . . sorta," I replied between each chew.

"So, what are you doing after work?"

"Terrell has been harassing me, talking about he wants to see me," I told her. Terrell was my on-and-off-again boyfriend.

"That sounds so boring."

"What do you want me to do, sit around all day like you and get high off prescription drugs?" I said sarcastically.

"Oh, Misty, that was a low blow. You know I don't do this shit for fun. If I don't take those drugs I'm going to be in serious pain."

"Look, I know you need 'em, so I'm going to get off your back. But from time to time, you do ask me for more than you should have."

"That's because I be trying to make a few dollars here and there. Oh, and speaking of which, I got a business proposition for you."

"What is it now?"

"I got a homeboy that will pay top dollar for twenty to twenty-five Vicodin pills."

"Jillian, are you freaking crazy?! There's no way in hell that I'm going to be able to get that many pills at one time."

"He's paying four hundred dollars. But I'm gonna have to get my cut off the top, which would be a hundred."

I sighed. "Jillian, I'm not doing it."

"Come on, Misty, stop being paranoid. You can do it," Jillian whined.

"Do you want me to lose my job?"

"Of course not. But you're acting like you've never taken drugs from your job before."

"Look, I'm not doing it. Case closed."

"Just think about it." Jillian pressed the issue, but I ignored her.

I changed the subject. "Is Grandma home?"

"She's in the laundry room folding clothes."

"Did she say she was cooking dinner?"

"Yeah, she's got a pot roast in the oven."

"Save some for me," I told Jillian.

"You know I will."

I changed the subject again. "You still talking to Edmund?"

"I just got off the phone with his frugal ass!"

I chuckled. "What has he refused to pay for now?"

"I asked him to order me a pizza online and he told me that he ain't have any money."

"Doesn't he own and operate a janitorial business?"

"Yep."

"Then he shouldn't be broke," I said. "Look, just leave that fool alone. You give him too much pussy for him to not feed you."

"I know, right!" she agreed. But I read her like a book because as soon as we got off the phone with one another, I knew she'd call that selfish-ass nigga and act like her stomach wasn't growling.

She and I talked for another ten minutes or so about her finding another job instead of sitting on her ass all day, crying about how much pain she's in. It seemed like my grandmother let her ride with that lame-ass excuse, but I knew better. My grandmother knew exactly what was going on, but looked the other way because she enjoyed Jillian's company and she didn't want to be alone in that big house. Jillian had a free ride anyway you looked at it.

"Don't forget to put some of that pot roast aside," I reminded her.

"I won't," she said, and right before I hung up, I heard her add, "Don't forget my meds either."

My only response to that was a head shake.

2

WHAT AN EYE OPENER

I headed back over to the pharmacy after I finished eating my lunch. When I walked through the front door there were two people waiting for their prescriptions, but Sanjay was nowhere around.

"Has anyone been helped?" I inquired as I circled around the customers to get behind the counter.

"No. We've been standing here for about five minutes," an elderly man said.

"He's right." Another white man spoke up. "I even peeped around the counter to see if anyone was there," he continued.

"Well, don't worry. I'll help you two gentlemen," I assured them as I walked around the counter.

I took both men's prescriptions and then I logged them into our system. Immediately after I did that, I searched the storage room where we kept our drugs and medical devices. I thought I might find Sanjay in there, but the room was empty. Alarmed, I walked to the bathroom and knocked on the door.

"Sanjay, are you in there?" I asked. But he didn't answer. So I knocked on the door again. "Sanjay, are you in there?" I repeated, and when I didn't get an answer, I grabbed ahold of the doorknob and twisted it lightly, opening the door calmly. It was plain to see that Sanjay wasn't in there.

The only other place I figured Sanjay could be was in the back of the building. So I closed the bathroom door and headed in that direction. The back door was slightly ajar, so I pushed it open.

"Sanjay, there you are," I said after I laid eyes on him shoving boxes in the trunk of his brother Amir's car. I could tell that he wasn't expecting to see me. He looked very nervous. While Amir continued to maneuver boxes that obviously came from the pharmacy, Sanjay walked toward me.

"Did you need something?" he asked me in a weird kind of way. The way he said it sounded like a mafia boss asking an innocent bystander who witnessed a murder, did he see something?

I was taken aback and I really didn't know what to say. But then it hit me. "We have two customers in the pharmacy who said they've been waiting for over ten minutes for someone to help them." I twisted the truth a little.

"Take care of them," Sanjay insisted.

"I already have," I lied.

"So, what's the problem?"

"There's no problem. I just wanted to make sure that you were still around."

"Well, I'm here," he said.

"Okay, well, I'll go back in and take care of everything while you're out here . . ." I said, and then I turned around and left him standing at the back door. I heard it close behind me as I headed back inside to the waiting customers.

"Sorry about that," I said. "The pharmacist is in the back of the building signing for some deliveries from the UPS driver." It seemed like a solid excuse.

"He may not want to do that the next time around, because instead of me and this other fella waiting around, it might be some young kids robbing you guys of all of your prescription drugs," the younger man said.

"I agree," the other man said.

Seriously? These two watched too much TV. "I will definitely make mention of that as soon as he gets back in here," I assured them.

Since Sanjay had basically given me the green light to process these gentlemen's prescriptions, I ran straight over to the cabinet where the Percocet pills were stored. I knew I had a small window of opportunity to get these pills for Jillian so we could make a few extra dollars. Immediately after I grabbed the pill bottle I heard Sanjay open and close the back door of the pharmacy. My heart started racing while I struggled to open the plastic bottle. But to no avail, it didn't open for some crazy-ass reason. I've never had a problem opening and closing a pill bottle.

"I'm so sorry, you guys," I heard Sanjay say. So I knew he was standing behind the counter near the cash register. Frozen like ice, I stood there not knowing whether to put the bottle of Percocet back in the supply cabinet or stick it in my pocket. I heard Sanjay walking in my direction, so I nearly panicked.

"Misty, who are you working on first?" he called out to me.

Feeling like I was about to have an anxiety attack, I shoved the bottle of Percocet into my pants pocket.

"Hey, there you go," he said as soon as he saw me. "What are they waiting on?" he continued as he stood in front of me.

"Mr. Lewis is refilling Trexall. And Mr. Williams is getting another refill of Metformin," I told him while I placed my right hand over my pants pocket to prevent Sanjay from seeing the bulge.

"Get the Metformin and I'll get the Trexall," he instructed me.

"I'm on it," I said and walked away from him. I swear, I couldn't tell you how scared I was when Sanjay walked up on me. I would've shit in my pants if he saw me with that bottle of Percocet in my hands. I couldn't lie and say that I had it because I was refilling one of those guys' prescriptions. No, that wouldn't have made any sense. I needed a cover, so I wasn't going to take any more pills unless I was filling a prescription for the same drug. Other than that, I was gonna chill.

A few hours later, Sanjay said, "You can leave now."

I looked at my watch. "Are you sure? I mean, we'll be closed in fifteen minutes." I needed to delay leaving cause I needed a chance to put the bottle of Percocet back.

"Don't worry. I've got everything covered. There's a storm coming our way, so get home safely," he insisted.

I sighed heavily. "Okay," I replied reluctantly. I mean, what other choice did I have? He was my boss, so I wouldn't dare tell him that I had just pocketed a brand-new bottle of Percocet from the storage cabinet and now I wanted to put the bottle back. If I did, I'd be asking this man to fire me on the spot.

"Don't forget to drive carefully," he reminded me.

"I will," I assured him as I grabbed my jacket and purse.

Sick to my stomach, I dreaded leaving the store. Why couldn't I be more careful? If I hadn't listened to Jillian, I wouldn't have this fucking big-ass pill bottle in my pocket. I could see it now: After Sanjay goes through the inventory in the morning, he's going to look me in the face and ask me where the missing Percocet bottle is. And I'm going to have to tell him the truth because who else could've moved it? I was the only employee there. Or, let's say that I did deny it, all he would have to do is look through his security camera. Now it wouldn't show me actually taking the meds because of the angle, but it might show the bulge of the bottle in my pants. Damn! I'd really fucked up now.

3

UNFRIENDLY VISITORS

My stomach had a ton of knots churning all at once. The bottle contained three hundred and fifty pills with a seal on it that had never been broken. Knowing the amount of pills I had on me was giving me an anxiety attack. After I got into my car, I sat there motionless. I thought of breaking into the pharmacy after Sanjay left, but then I decided against it because of the high-tech security system he had installed inside and around the building. I was fucked. Up the creek with no paddle is what my grandmother always said.

Twenty minutes passed, and I found myself still sitting in my car, which was parked across the street from the pharmacy. My body wouldn't move. I couldn't get up the gumption to put the car key into the ignition. So, while I sat there in the same spot, I noticed Amir pulling up to the pharmacy. But this time, he wasn't alone. I saw two guys with him. One was in the passenger seat while the other one sat behind the driver's seat. I watched them closely as Amir drove down the alleyway of the building, and immediately after he parked his car, he and the guy in the back seat got out of the car together. They closed the car doors, and my heart took a nosedive into the pit of my stomach when I saw the guy from the back seat aim a gun at Amir's back. "What the fuck?!" I muttered. But only I could hear me.

Not being able to answer my own question, I sat there in disbelief while I watched the guy from the passenger side follow Amir and the other guy to the back door of the pharmacy. "Damn! Something is really about to go down," I said to myself, at the same time trying to figure out why some guy would jam the barrel of a gun into Amir's back. What kind of business did they have going on?

Curiosity really got the best of me because without giving it too much thought, I got out of my car and crept back across the street. The sun was setting, so I took advantage of the natural lighting outside since it was light in some places and dim in others. The lighting at the front entryway of the pharmacy was dim, so I tiptoed toward it. The moment I came within four feet of the building, I looked through the glass window and saw Sanjay being shoved around behind the counter. I could also see him explaining something to those guys Amir brought with him. Amir was nowhere in sight, so I wondered where he could be.

While I watched Sanjay being pushed around, I also saw him handing the two guys boxes of prescription drugs. I couldn't read the labels, but I knew that whatever the drug was, those guys wanted it.

I stood there for a few minutes, and when I thought that I had seen enough, I scurried back across the street, got into my car, and left. En route to my grandmother's house, I called Jillian's cell phone. She answered on the second ring. "You gotta be calling me with some good news," she said.

"Girl, you ain't gonna believe me when I tell you what I just saw," I replied.

"What happened?" she asked.

"Are you still at Grandma's house?"

"Yeah."

"Good. Stay right there. I'll see you in ten minutes," I told her and then disconnected our call.

Four seconds after I placed my cell phone inside the cup holder, it started ringing again. Bothered by the sound of it, I snatched it out of the cup holder and answered it. "Hello!" I roared.

"Hey, what's wrong with you?" the male voice asked. The voice belonged to my ex-boyfriend Terrell Mason. Terrell used to be the love of my life. He was the hottest nigga in the city. Tall, dark, and handsome was what everyone called him. I guess that shit went to his head because he turned into this arrogant and unapologetic nigga overnight. I put up with it because he was paying for me to go to school to get my pharmaceutical license, with money from that party-promoting business he owned. But that all fell apart when he started cheating on me with bitches that were bold enough to come and knock on my front door looking for him at all times of the night. The last straw for me was when he got one of those bitches pregnant. I gave him his walking papers immediately after the chick showed me her ultrasound. She even had Terrell's dumb ass recorded at one of her doctor's appointments after they were told what the sex would be. I watched him from her camera phone as he held her hand throughout the ultrasound screening. I swear, my heart ached for months after that revelation. She hasn't had her baby yet, but I know her delivery date is right around the corner.

"I'm irritated about something right now, so I'm really not in the mood to talk," I told him.

"Does it have something to do with me?"

"No, Terrell. Not everything I've got going on in my life has something to do with you," I pointed out.

"Can I see you later?"

"No."

"Well, when can I come over?"

"Now is not a good time," I told him.

"You keep brushing me off like I'm some random-ass nigga that's trying to holla at you."

"Look, Terrell, I don't have time for this right now. I'm gonna have to call you back later."

"You've been saying you're gonna call me back all week. And you still haven't done it."

"That's because I've got more pressing issues to deal with. Call your baby mama," I spat. This nigga was getting on my last fucking nerve. He wasn't relevant to my life at that moment. He'd had his time with me until he cheated. I'd moved on.

He deliberately ignored my suggestion to call his baby mama and instead asked, "You seeing another man?"

"What?! What are you talking about?" I roared. Having another man in my life was the furthest thing from my mind.

"Tell me the truth," Terrell insisted.

"Look, I gotta go," I replied, and then I pressed the End button. And immediately after I ended his call, I sifted through my settings and blocked Terrell's phone number so he wouldn't call me back. I was over him and his cheating ass.

I knew I told Jillian that I'd see her in ten minutes, but I ended up getting there in less than six minutes. Jillian was on the front porch of our grandmother's house when I pulled up alongside of the curb. I didn't have the chance to park my car good enough before Jillian made a beeline toward me.

"Misty, you got my ears itching," she commented after she got into my car. Jillian was an impatient person. She never liked to wait for anything.

"I think my boss is working for some mafia type guys."

"Why you say that?"

"Because right before I left the pharmacy, I saw his brother Amir pulling up with two other guys in his car. And when they got out of the car, one of the guys put a gun up to Amir's back and pushed him into the back of the store while the other guy followed them. And then after they went through the back door, I peeped through the windows in the front part of the store and saw Sanjay being pushed around. I even saw him give those two guys boxes of prescription medication too."

"Yo, I can't believe that you're working for the mafia!" Jillian said with excitement.

I nudged her chest. "That's not funny."

"Yes, it is." She continued to chuckle.

"What if he's not? And what if those guys were robbing him?"

"You can call it a robbery all you want. But I believe that he's into some illegal shit," Jillian continued, and then she said, "Speaking of illegal, were you able to get me a few pills?"

"Is that all you care about?" I was getting more disgusted by the second.

"Whatcha want me to dwell on, that shit that happened back at your job?"

"Could you at least act like you're concerned?" I replied sarcastically, and simultaneously pulled the bottle of pills from my pants pocket and threw them at her.

Her eyes lit up like a Christmas tree. "You stole a whole fucking bottle of this shit?!"

I tried to cover her mouth with my hands while I looked around to see if anyone was watching us. Jillian mushed my hands back toward me. "Quit it. No one can hear me. It's a fucking ghost town around here. Most of Grandmother's neighbors and friends are in an old folks' home or dead," Jillian said dismissively as she ripped open the bottle of pills.

I slapped her on the thigh. "You really have no filter," I complained while I watched her poke her finger in the pill bottle.

"I can't believe that I am holding this huge bottle of fucking Percocets. Can you even imagine how much money we're gonna make from them?"

"We're not selling all of those pills."

"Yes the hell we are," Jillian protested, and then she opened the car door and stepped out.

"Jillian, I'm not playing with you," I yelled as she slammed the car door. That didn't stop me from talking. I climbed out of the car behind her. "Hand 'em over, Jillian," I yelled again, shutting my car door.

Jillian totally ignored me and made her way into the house. As soon as I stepped inside, I heard my grandmother's voice. "Where is Misty? I thought you said that she was outside." Her voice was coming from the den, which was in the back of the house and a straight shot from the front door.

"She's coming now," Jillian told her.

"Hey, Nana," I spoke as soon as I entered the den. I walked over and kissed her on the cheek. My grandmother had my heart. She was the matriarch of the family and holding the Torrey name down.

She looked at me from head to toe while Jillian took a seat on the sofa across the room. Jillian pulled out her phone and started texting someone.

"How's work?" my nana asked me as I sat down on the sofa next to Jillian.

"Work's fine," I replied, simultaneously reaching for the pill bottle between her legs. Jillian used her left hand to push my right hand back.

"What is that you're trying to get from her?"

"My bottle of vitamins," I lied while still trying to get it from Jillian.

"That's an awfully big bottle. Why do you need so many?" my nana continued.

"That's the way it comes," I lied once more.

"I'll be right back," Jillian announced to my grandmother and me, and then she hopped up from the sofa and raced down the hallway.

I wanted to get up and run behind her, but I didn't want Nana to think something serious was going on.

"So, I hear that your mother is dating a new guy," Nana stated. My grandmother was a cute old lady. She kind of reminded me of the actress Cicely Tyson. She was the nicest person in the world. The kind of woman that would take in a dozen homeless people and feed them. She'd talk about how good the Lord was to her too. You can't get her to cook you some food without hearing about the Lord Jesus Christ. Those two went hand in hand.

"If that's what you want to call it," I replied nonchalantly. My mother's name was Kathreen Heiress and she was a fairly decent-looking woman. Back in the day everyone called her Mrs. Diana Ross. She had the whole look. But after the relationship with my dad failed, she started drinking heavily and dated anyone that would give her the time of day. Her favorite pastime was daily trips to the ABC liquor store. My grandmother has tried to help her plenty of times by offering to send her to an alcohol treatment center, but my mother wouldn't hear of it.

"Have you seen him?"

"A couple of days ago when I went by there to get my mail."

"What's his name?"

"Carl."

"What does he look like?" Her questions kept coming. I forgot to mention that even though she's very generous, she's also nosy.

"He's tall and slim. Looks like he played basketball in high school."

"Does he look like one of those city slicksters from the streets? You know that's all your mama deals with," my grandmother commented.

"Maybe back in the day. He had on a uniform from a bread company downtown. So, he's probably one of their delivery drivers," I told her. But in all honesty, my mother's new boyfriend doesn't work for no one's bread shop. I just told my grandmother something so she would leave me alone about that man. I really couldn't care less. I had more pressing matters at hand and it sure wasn't that nigga my mother was fucking.

"Does he drink like she does?"

"I don't know, Grandma."

"Well, for her sake I hope he doesn't. Can't have two alcoholics running around in the family. It'll make us look bad."

"But he's not a part of our family," I pointed out.

"He will be once she marries him."

"Who said that they're gonna get married?"

"I know your mother better than you do. The moment a man shows interest in her, she's going to fly down to the justice of the peace to marry him. See, your mama has a fear of being alone. She's been like that since she was a child. I thought she'd grow out of it. But unfortunately, she didn't."

"Let's not cancel her out. She still has time," I said in defense of my mother. But on the other hand, my grandmother was right. My mother always had to have someone in her life. She was a very needy person. And old habits definitely die hard.

She changed the subject. "How is your boss treating you down at the pharmacy?"

"He's treating me good. I don't have any complaints," I lied. But I was about to shit in my pants from the mere thought of this guy. I was starting to contemplate whether

I should go back to work tomorrow. For all I knew, those guys could've robbed him and killed him. I didn't want to see his dead body on the floor in a pool of his own blood. I wouldn't ever recover from that. Now, I'd seen a few niggas on the block get their asses kicked, you know, get a couple of bruises here or there and that was it. I guess I was going to have to play this thing out by ear. I really needed to find a new job before I left this one.

I sat there in the den with my grandmother, and boy, could this lady talk. She asked me every question under the damn sun. "Did you know that fella that got arrested for selling all those drugs from his mother's house in Norfolk?" she started off.

"Grandma, there's a lot of people in Norfolk that's selling drugs," I responded casually. I mean, the statistics are being recorded every day.

"I'm sure you're right. But this fella had set up a meth lab inside of his mother's garage. They took his mother to jail too. But I heard this morning that the cops let her go after realizing that she had no knowledge of what he was doing."

"Nah, I didn't hear about that," I told her. I wasn't really interested in the family affairs of that guy and his mother. I had bigger fish to fry, and my cousin Jillian was one of them.

"Want something to eat? I've got a pot roast on, but in the meantime I've cooked up a batch of salmon croquettes. And I got a pot of turnip greens too."

"I'm really not hungry right now, but I'll get a plate to go," I said, as I looked in the direction of the door that led out of the den. "Where did that granddaughter of yours go to?"

"It sounds like she went upstairs to her bedroom," she guessed.

I stood up from the sofa. "Let me see what she's doing," I insisted.

"How long do you plan on being here?" my grandmother wanted to know.

"Maybe another fifteen to twenty minutes," I replied as I exited the den.

"Come and give me a kiss before you leave."

"I will," I assured her, and then I disappeared.

I headed up the flight of stairs that led to Jillian's bedroom, but she wasn't there. So I called her name. Got no answer though. I looked in the bathroom that was a few feet away from her bedroom and she wasn't there either. So I headed back downstairs.

"Did you see her?" my grandmother yelled from the den.

"No."

"Check the front porch. She's always hanging out there."

"Thanks," I said and walked toward the front door.

Immediately after I opened the front door, I saw Jillian sitting in the passenger side of a beat-up, smoky-gray, two-door Honda Accord. Irritated my Jillian's lack of respect for my wishes concerning the bottle of Percocet, I walked off the front porch and stormed toward the car. As soon as I got within a few feet of the vehicle, Jillian opened the passenger-side door and proceeded to get out.

"Where's the bottle of Percocet?" I wanted to know. I gave her a hard stare.

"She gave it to me," a guy said, as he leaned over into the passenger seat so that I could get a glimpse of him.

"And who are you?"

"Tedo, and I sure appreciate it."

I took my attention off the guy and looked at Jillian head-on. "Why the fuck did you do that?" I screamed. I was fucking livid.

"Stop yelling. You're embarrassing me," she snapped under her breath while she tried to close the passenger-side door.

"No, fuck that! Give me back that bottle," I demanded,

looking at Tedo while I prevented Jillian from closing the car door.

"Listen, I don't know what the fuck y'all got going on, but I ain't doing shit. So, get the fuck away from my car before you make me do something really ugly."

Shocked by this guy's words, I realized that this Tedo was no pushover and that he meant business. So I released my grip on the door so that Jillian could shut it. The moment she did, he sped off down the block. I instantly turned my focus toward Jillian.

"Can you tell me what the fuck just happened?" I hissed. I swear, I was about to lose my fucking mind. My heart was racing at the thought that I'd have to find a way to cover up that missing bottle.

"I just made you and me a shitload of money." Jillian opened her hand, revealing a wad of bills.

"I don't care about that fucking money. Do you know I'm gonna get fired for stealing all of those pills? Sanjay may even call the cops on me too," I tried to explain.

Jillian grabbed my right hand and opened it. "Take this twenty-five hundred and tell me how it feels in the palm of your hand."

"It doesn't feel like anything, Jillian. And it ain't gonna mean shit once Sanjay calls the cops on me," I expressed. I was so mad with Jillian that I wanted to smack the shit out of her.

"If what you told me really happened at the pharmacy tonight, Sanjay ain't gonna notice that the bottle of Percocet is missing," Jillian tried assuring me.

I stood there for a moment and then I said, "You better be right."

Jillian tried to embrace me, but I pushed her back. "No, don't touch me," I whispered.

"Oh no, you're gonna let me hug you," she said. I protested again as she bear-hugged me and said, "Now, come back in the house so you can get some of Grandma's food."

On my way back into my grandmother's house, I asked Jillian exactly how much that guy paid for that whole bottle. "He gave me $3200 for 330 pills, so I gave you $2,500 and I kept $750."

"What happened to the other twenty pills?"

"I kept 'em," Jillian replied, giving me a look like I'd just asked her a rhetorical question. I nudged her in the back, making her stumble as she walked over the grass in our grandmother's front yard.

"I bet you did," I commented.

Back inside the house, I got me a plate of food so I could eat it later, and then I said my goodbyes. I'd had a rough day and I figured the only way I'd be able to settle my nerves was to go home, take a nice, long, hot shower and get in my own bed so I could catch me a few z's.

Unfortunately for me, that didn't happen. I tossed and turned the entire night thinking about what Sanjay was going to say to me when I walked back into the pharmacy in the morning.

4

WHAT NOW?

I dragged myself out of bed the next morning, not wanting to go to work. I picked up my cell phone to call in sick, but I was too afraid to hear Sanjay's voice, so I put my cell phone back down on the nightstand and got up to go to the bathroom. It didn't take me long to take a piss, wash my hands, and brush my teeth. I was in and out of my bathroom in less than three minutes. Instead of going back into my bedroom, I strolled into the kitchen to fix myself a hot pot of green tea. Upon filling up my favorite Wendy Williams Wonder Woman coffee mug with water from a half-empty spring water bottle I left on the counter the night before, I placed it into the microwave to get it piping hot.

One minute later the microwave sounded off, and I grabbed my mug and dropped a tea bag in it. I used the spoon I grabbed from the silverware drawer while the mug was in the microwave, to push the tea bag to the bottom of the mug. All the herbs filled the mug up with faint green color. Moments later, I put the mug up to my mouth, blew on the tea a few times, and took a sip. The tea was hot but it was tasty. With my mug of green tea in hand, I walked out of the kitchen and headed back into my bedroom.

I placed my tea mug down on the nightstand next to my cell phone and then I grabbed the remote control and powered up the TV. It was 6:17 in the morning, so I knew that all I was going to watch was the local news. I gave in to the fact that I had no other choice. I lay back against one of my huge pillow cushions and cradled my tea mug in my hands until it got too hot, and I'd put it back on the nightstand.

I watched everything from the local news, traffic, and weather reports. It was all foreign to me 'cause I'm usually asleep or in my car during these broadcasts. What they had to say really didn't affect my day. Three minutes into my teatime I heard my doorbell ring. Irritated that some-one would stop by my house this time of the morning, I hopped out of my bed and headed for the front door. Nor-mally, I'd yell and ask who was at the door, but situations and circumstances in my life had changed, so I had to stay on my toes. Speaking of toes, I crept to my front door and peered through the peephole and realized that it was Ter-rell's worrisome ass standing on my porch. I let out a loud sigh. "What do you want?" I yelled through the door.

"Let me in and I'll tell you."

"I'm not letting you inside my apartment. So, go back to where you came from," I yelled back through the door. How dare he come to my house this time of the morning? He lost those privileges when he cheated on me. He needed to go and fuck himself.

"Misty, I am not leaving here until you talk to me." He stood his ground.

"You're talking to me right now."

"You know what I mean."

"Listen, Terrell, say what you gotta say and leave, be-cause I'm not letting you inside of my apartment."

"Well, will you at least come outside so we can talk face-to-face?"

"What is there to talk about? We're no longer together. So leave," I yelled. He was getting on my freaking nerves. I was two seconds from calling the cops on him.

"Misty, just give me one minute," he pleaded.

"No, Terrell, I'm not opening my door, so go away before I call the police," I said with finality, and then I walked away from the front door.

Boom! The front door flew open and hit the wall behind it. The cool air from outside engulfed me as Terrell walked into my home. Startled by what had just happened, I stood there in disbelief. All the years I'd known, I'd never known him to act like this. "Are you out of your fucking mind? Who's gonna pay for that?" I yelled at him as he walked by me.

Instead of answering my question, he raced down the hallway toward my bedroom. I turned around and followed him. "Where the fuck is that nigga?" he roared as he entered my bedroom.

"What fucking nigga?! There's no one here," I screamed.

Terrell didn't believe me because he kept searching. He went from looking through my closets, to looking underneath my bed, and he looked behind my shower curtains. He didn't stop there, because as soon as he left my bathroom he looked in both of my hall closets and then my kitchen closet. I stood there, livid, watching this idiot invade my space. "Are you done?" I hissed. I wanted to spit in his fucking face.

"This wouldn't have happened if you'd just opened the door when I asked you," he said as he walked toward me.

"Get the fuck out of my house!" I huffed. But he didn't move. He stood toe to toe with me while I looked him in the eyes.

"You know this is all your fault, huh?" he said, panting like he had run a mile up the block.

"Oh, so you're gonna blame it on me? Are you out of your damn mind? I caused this shit?" I spat as I pointed to the front door.

"Oh, that's nothing. I'll do it every time I come over here if you don't open the door," he threatened me.

"Terrell, just get out!" I roared while pointing at the entryway of my apartment.

"Yeah, okay, I'll leave. But I'm warning you that if you bring another nigga in here, I'm gonna kill 'im. You understand?" he warned me, and then he reached in his pants pocket, took out a couple hundred bills, and threw them at my feet like I was a fucking stripper in a nightclub.

He didn't utter a word as he exited my apartment. I stood there in utter disbelief because he had never acted out like this. He used to be this charismatic guy. He was a cheater to his heart, but he never went to his level of violence unless it was toward another guy. But never to a woman.

After I gathered my thoughts I closed the front door, even though I couldn't lock it. I called a locksmith to work some magic on my door. As badly as I wanted to take a shower and get ready for work, I couldn't because I was too afraid to leave my front door unattended. I had a total of one hour if I wanted to get to work on time. And when I realized that I wouldn't make it, I called Sanjay's cell phone number, even though I dreaded it.

My heart started racing as I sat on the living room sofa and held the phone upright in front of my face after I placed the call on speakerphone. I was literally shaking in my boots while I waited for him to answer the call. After the third ring he finally answered. "Morning, Misty, it's you?" he said.

I listened intently to the sound of his voice. I listened for distress or anxiety, but the tone in which he spoke didn't sound like he was experiencing either. This was a relief to me.

"Morning, what can I do for you?" he wondered aloud.

"I had an accident here at my apartment, so I was wondering if I could come in at nine o'clock instead of eight."

"I'm so glad you called," he started off, "I was gonna call you and tell you that you don't have to come in today. As a matter of fact, I'll give you the day off with pay," he concluded.

Shocked by his gesture, but at the same time happy, I said, "Oh thanks."

"Well then, I guess I'll see you tomorrow," he continued.

"See you tomorrow," I replied and then I ended the call. I placed my cell phone on the coffee table in front of me and wondered what was really going on down at the pharmacy. Sanjay had never told me to take a day off with pay unless I put the request in for myself. And to top it off, he didn't even mention anything about the missing bottle of Percocet. Something wasn't right. And whatever it was, I knew it had something to do with those guys that were smacking him and his brother around yesterday.

5

SOMETHING ISN'T ADDING UP

The second after I got Sanjay off the phone I called Jillian. "Hello," she answered groggily.

"Get up. We need to talk."

"What time is it?" she asked.

"It's time to get up," I insisted.

"Okay. Hold your horses and calm down," she huffed.

"I'm calm. Now listen to me, because I'm only gonna say this once."

"Well, say it," Jillian spat after she yawned once more.

"I just got off the phone with my boss to tell him that I was gonna be running late this morning and he told me that he was going to call me and tell me to stay home and pay me for the day."

"Okay, and what's wrong with that?"

"Jillian, he's never told me to take off and that he's gonna pay me too."

"Maybe he's turned over a new leaf."

"No, I think he's trying to hide something."

"Like what?"

"Do you know that he didn't even question me about the missing bottle of Percocet?"

"Isn't that a good thing?" Jillian replied sarcastically.

"Of course, it's a good thing. But you know that I don't like to be in the dark about things going on around me."

"Just take a chill pill. You'll feel better," Jillian joked.

"It's not funny, Jillian. There could be some major shit going down there at the pharmacy and I could get caught up in the crossfire."

"Stop being all paranoid. You say it yourself that he always sends you home or on lunch when someone stops by to see him."

"Yeah, I know, but—" I started, but Jillian cut me off.

"But nothing, I think you're overthinking this too much. Just enjoy your day off with pay and take care of some things that you've been neglecting to do."

"Speaking of neglecting, do you know that Terrell stopped by my apartment about ten minutes ago and kicked in my front door because I wouldn't open it?"

"Are you freaking kidding me right now?"

"No, I am not. I'm sitting here on the edge of my sofa waiting for the damn locksmith to come by and fix the door."

"What's his deal?"

I sighed heavily. "He thought I had another guy in here. So he searched all my closets and underneath my bed. And when he saw that I hadn't, he throws a couple of one-hundred-dollar bills at me and threatens to kill something if he catches a guy in here."

"What? Aren't you two broken up because of all the bitches he's cheated on you with?"

"That's exactly my point."

"So, when has he started throwing his weight around like he's gangsta or something?"

"I don't know. I asked him that same question."

"Well, be careful either way."

I let out another long sigh. "I will," I assured her.

She and I talked until the locksmith guy showed up. Before we hung up with one another, she planted a seed in my mind and said, "I know this may be too soon, but when you go back to work and happen to stumble over another bottle of those stress relievers, let me know because I've got another buyer for em."

"See, I'm not messing with you. You're trying to get me fired."

"Girl, please, your boss ain't thinking about that bottle because if he was, he would've said something. And besides, I know you could use another twenty-five-hundred-dollar payday."

"Bye, Jillian," I said, and then I ended the call.

6

BACK ON THE J.O.B.

The locksmith showed up, fixed my door, and even added a dead bolt above the other locks, so I should be good just in case Terrell gets the idea to kick in my front door again. Speaking of which, I still couldn't get over the fact that Terrell did that. Was he insane or what? Was I going to have to keep my guard up? Or be forced to take out a restraining order because I refused to live in fear? No way. I won't let that happen.

"Thank you for helping me out with this," I said to the locksmith as I paid him with the money Terrell gave me.

"That's what I am here for," he said and then he handed me his business card.

I smiled and let him out of my apartment. I thanked him once again, closed the door, and locked it.

I finally got my mind right after everything that went down this morning. It seemed one thing happened after the next and it was nonstop. I was just glad that now I could climb in my bed and watch a TV show or two without any interruptions from my boss and the other people in my life. I'd had more than enough of them for one day.

* * *

I tried to watch a few television shows and take a nap, but I couldn't. I couldn't get my mind off my boss, Sanjay. The incident that happened yesterday after I clocked out from work and the fact that he didn't mention anything about the bottle of Percocet I took had my mind running in circles. Was he really genuine when he told me to take the day off with pay? Or was he trying to hide something from me? Whatever the situation was, I hoped it didn't affect me negatively.

Not having anything to do, I got undressed and got into the shower. The entire time I was in the shower, I couldn't take my mind off everything that was going on around me. The drama with Terrell, having to deal with the fact that my mother was a fucking alcoholic, my cousin was a prescription junkie, and the man I work for allows guys to come into his place of business and smack him around. I knew I needed to make some changes concerning everything going on around me, I just needed to figure out what to do.

I decided that the only way I'd be able to get my mind off of everything, is to go out and spend some of that $2,500 I got from Jillian the day before. Who knows, I may splurge a little bit on a Louis Vuitton tote bag. I've been wanting one for a few months now. And now I could say that I could afford it.

After I got out of the shower, I got dressed in a pink Puma sweatshirt with the sweatpants to match. Then I slipped on my favorite white Puma sneakers. And since my hair was braided up in the big, poetic braids, I didn't have to do my hair, so I looked in the mirror in my bedroom to make sure none of my hair was out of place, and when I saw that everything was good, I grabbed my handbag and car keys from my dresser and headed out the front door. The cool air hit my face and it felt good too. My day started off rocky, but who knows, things might turn around for the good.

I drove a 2015 Nissan Maxima, and it wasn't anything fancy, but it was mine and I loved it. When Terrell and I were together, he tried on several occasions to buy me a few nice cars, but I always turned him down. I remember one time he tried to buy me a Mercedes-Benz, and it was nice too, but I told him no thanks. I'm good with what I already have.

As I drove away from my apartment I thought about what store I was going to go into. Where I live we didn't have a lot of high-end stores, so I called Jillian and asked if she wanted to ride with me to Richmond. When she said yes, I drove by my grandmother's house, picked her up, and then we hopped on Highway 64.

While we were driving, Jillian kept getting one phone call after the other from street hustlers wanting to get their hands on a few bottles of Percocet and Vicodin. With every phone call she got she would look at me and try to give me the guilt trip. I told her butt to leave me alone because I was not taking another bottle of pills from the pharmacy.

"Misty, we could make a whole lot of money."

"Don't you think I already know that?"

"Well, you act like you don't."

"Listen, I'm not trying to go to jail behind you and whoever you were talking to on the phone. I'm trying to stay out here on the streets. A prison uniform will not look good on me at all."

"Stop being dramatic. You know you got this weak set-up at your job and you won't even take advantage of it."

"Call it what you want. But I'm not taking another pill bottle out of the place."

"Yeah, whatever."

As soon as we arrived at the mall in Richmond, we headed straight into the Saks Fifth Avenue store. I'd been here once or twice before, so I knew where the handbags were. I walked over to the handbag department and saw the bag I wanted from ten feet away. "There it is," I said aloud as I walked toward the signature Louis Vuitton bag with a pink design on the inside.

Jillian followed me. "Yes, I love it," she agreed.

Fortunately for me there was a salesperson in the department, so she helped me retrieve the bag from the shelf. "How much is it?" I asked the Caucasian woman.

"Fifteen hundred dollars. That's not including tax," she told me.

"Okay, great, I want to get it," I said while I was taking money from my purse.

"Misty, that bag is really nice," she pointed out. "Now just imagine, if you get down with the program you could buy at least two or three of them a month and put a few dollars towards your high-ass student loans. You know them bills out of control," she continued.

I sighed. She had a point. "You're going to find a way to get me to change my mind, aren't you?" I questioned her.

"I just want to see you shine. And what better way to do it than to pull in some coins?"

"Ma'am, how much do I owe you?" I asked the woman, refusing to entertain what Jillian had just said.

"The total is $1,630.21."

I pulled out $1,700 and handed it to the woman so I could purchase my bag. While I waited for the change, I stood there proudly because it felt good to treat myself to something as nice as this without worrying about a man taking it back from me. I can honestly say that I really feel good about myself.

Immediately after the saleswoman handed me my bag and the change, Jillian and I decided to have lunch. So we went to a nearby restaurant, sat down and had something to eat. It was an American cuisine type of restaurant. Their signature meals on the menu were all American cheeseburgers. I ordered a bacon cheeseburger with fries and Jillian had a regular cheeseburger and an order of onion rings. She even topped it off with a strawberry milkshake. I am lactose intolerant, so I got a Sprite and it was good.

While we sat there and ate, my cell phone started ringing. I pulled it from my purse and looked at the caller ID. I started not to answer the call when I noticed it was my mother. It takes so much of my energy to deal with her. "Who's calling you?" Jillian asked me while I held the phone in my hand.

"My mother."

"Answer it," Jillian said as if it was an easy task.

"Why don't you answer it?" I said and pushed the phone in her direction.

She took it and before she answered the call I instructed her to tell my mother that I was busy doing something and that I would call her back. Jillian agreed. And when the call went to the fourth ring, Jillian answered. "Hello," she said and then she put the call on speaker so I could hear every word of the conversation.

"Who is this?" my mother asked.

"Aunt Kathy, it's me, Jillian."

"Where is Misty?"

"She's in the grocery store picking up some stuff and I'm sitting in the car waiting for her to come back out," Jillian lied.

"What store are you guys at?" my mother wanted to know.

"Walmart," Jillian lied again.

"Well, go in there and tell her to buy me a twelve-pack of Coronas and bring them by here," my mother instructed Jillian.

"Aunt Kathy, we're not at a Walmart in your area."

"Then where the hell are you?"

"We're in Richmond."

"Why the hell are you in Richmond?"

"Because I needed to get a new birth certificate." Jillian's lies continued. I mean, she was pulling one lie after the next out of her bag.

"Well, tell her to call me when she comes out of the store," my mother said.

"All right," Jillian said and then she disconnected the call.

"At one point I thought you was about to fold on me," I commented while Jillian cracked a smile.

"I wasn't expecting for her to ask me all those questions," Jillian explained.

"You know how my mother is. She's so freaking nosy. And she always wants money or for me to bring her a case of beer. I'm so tired of her bullshit!"

"Hopefully one day it'll get better."

"Girl, please, she's going to be like that until she dies," I stated and then I started digging back into my plate of food.

Not too long after we finished our food, Jillian and I got in my car and headed back to our city. Normally driving from Richmond to the Tidewater area, it would take an hour and a half, but for some reason I got us back to the area in one hour.

"Coming in?" Jillian asked me after I pulled up to our grandmother's house.

"No, I'm kind of tired. So I'm gonna go home. But I'll probably come back over here tomorrow."

"A'ight, well call me if you need me," Jillian told me.

"All right," I said, not knowing what she meant by that because I don't remember the last thing she did for me. She was more likely to call me because she might need something. As a matter of fact, that's what she should've said. After I blew my car horn at her, I drove off.

When I drove away from my grandmother's house, my first thought was to go home. But five minutes into the drive, I thought about Sanjay and how his day was going.

I also thought about if he noticed the bottle was gone, but didn't know how to question me about it. Not knowing what was going on around me was a mind game I don't like playing. So instead of going home, I made a detour and headed toward the pharmacy.

The moment I pulled up curbside on the opposite side of the street, I could see his car parked on the side of the building, but I wasn't able to see if he had any customers in the store. While my stomach muscles did somersaults, I sat there a moment and wondered what I was going to say to him. Because I knew he was going to ask me what I was doing there, especially on my day off. The only explanation I could conjure up was that I was in the neighborhood and decided to stop by. I wasn't sure if he was going to believe me, but I wouldn't know if I didn't try.

I took a deep breath, turned the ignition off, and got out of my car. With each step that I walked toward the pharmacy, my heart rate increased. I began to give myself a pep talk. "Come on, Misty, you can do it. Just take a deep breath, smile and act normal. You'll be fine," I continued to say while I put one foot in front of the other.

As I approached the glass front door, it opened and out came an elderly black woman that I recognized. Her name was Mrs. Landry. When she saw me, her eyes lit up. "Hi, darling, how are you?" she asked as she embraced me.

"I'm great. How are you?"

"I'm doing okay. But I hate that I have to go down the street to the other pharmacy to get my prescription filled."

"Why you can't get it here?" I asked her. This was a cause for concern for me.

"Well, my doctor is putting me on a higher dosage of my pain meds, but y'all don't have it. Sanjay said that you guys ran out of it. So now I've gotta get in my car and get it from somewhere else." The lady sounded irritated.

"I'm so sorry that we're putting you out of your way," I apologized.

"It's okay, baby, it ain't your fault. Your boss needs to stay stocked up with the medicine the people need. We don't wanna be running all over town for it."

"I'll make sure this doesn't happen the next time," I tried to reassure her.

"You have a nice day."

"You too, Mrs. Landry."

Mrs. Landry was a regular customer here at the pharmacy. According to Sanjay, she's been coming here to have her prescriptions filled for the past four years. So to lose her business would really hurt the store.

While she headed toward her car, I opened the door of the pharmacy and entered. There was one other customer waiting for their meds, so I spoke and then I walked around the counter. Sanjay was typing something in the computer when I greeted him. He smiled at me and I knew then that he wasn't aware of the missing pill bottle. If he was, he wouldn't have smiled at me when he laid eyes on me.

"I told you to take the day off," he said while he continued to type on the computer keyboard. The angle he was sitting, I immediately noticed a fresh bruise underneath the right side of his eye.

"I was in the neighborhood so I decided to stop by and see how you were doing. What happened to your eye?" I said as I took a seat in front of the consultation booth.

"Oh nothing. One of those boxes fell down from the shelf up there when I walked by it," he replied as he pointed toward the self near his workstation.

"A box left a scar like that?" I pressured him. I wanted him to be honest with me and let me know if this was a one-time occurrence. Because I was on the other side of the door and watched those guys push him and this brother around.

"I thought the same thing when I got up this morning and saw how bad it looked. I put some of that aloe cream we have on it, so it should go away in the next few days," he explained. "So what did you have to do in the neighborhood?" He changed the subject.

"I had to pick up dry cleaning from down the street."

"How long are you gonna be here?"

"What? Here in the area? Or the store?"

"In the area."

"Oh, maybe another five minutes," I told him as I watched his body movement. I knew he meant to say the store, but didn't have the gumption to say it because he didn't want to sound weird.

"How is your mother?" he asked. And what's so crazy about it is that he never asks me how my mother's doing. He knows that we have a rocky relationship and that I barely talk to her, so what was the reason behind the question?

"She's doing okay," I finally replied.

"What about your grandmother? How is she?"

"She's doing okay too," I answered.

"Tell them both I said hi," he continued. Now it took every fiber within me not to question Sanjay about all of these weird questions about my family. I even wanted to ask him why he was interested in them. I'd worked for Sanjay for some time now, and he'd never asked this many questions about me and mine. Was he crying out for help, but didn't know how to ask?

My interest in figuring this all out ended when Sanjay handed the gentleman his prescription and, in so many words, asked me if I would walk him out. I swear I was dumbfounded. I was even more shocked that he just indirectly asked me to leave the store while the elderly man was right in front of us.

"Am I coming to work at my regularly scheduled time tomorrow?" I asked him as I made my way around the counter.

"Yes, come in at your regularly scheduled time," he confirmed.

"Okay. See you then," I replied and then I left.

I sat in my car, feeling really troubled. Every move and sound Sanjay made a few minutes ago made me so uneasy. This, combined with those dudes that I saw bullying him, made me feel like I needed to find myself a new pharmacy tech job at another pharmacy.

7

THE AHA MOMENT

Looking back at the size of Sanjay's bruise had me convinced that he was in deep with some dangerous guys. Guys I wanted to stay clear of. I had too much drama going on in my life now as it was. So, adding another level of bullshit wasn't how I wanted to live my life. I mean, I just got rid of Terrell.

Moments after I got back into my car, I called Jillian. Thankfully she answered quickly. "What's up, Cousin?" she asked me cheerfully.

"Yo, you ain't gonna believe me when I tell you this shit," I said and then I fell silent.

"What happened?"

"I just went to the pharmacy to see what was going on and to see if Sanjay finally noticed that I took the bottle of Percocet, and guess what I saw?"

"What?"

"This nigga had a big-ass cut and bruise around his right eye."

"You bullshitting!"

"No, I am not."

"Did you ask him about it?"

"Yeah."

"And what did he say?"

"He said a fucking box fell down on him from one of the shelves near his workstation."

"Damn! That's fucked up!"

"Tell me about it. I swear, I ain't gonna be able to work around there in that type of environment. I mean, what if one of those guys hits me?"

"Come on now, you know he's not gonna let that happen to you."

"What the fuck is he going to do? Tell em to stop? He can't even defend himself."

"Just calm down."

"Fuck that! I'm gonna look for another job," I said with finality.

"And go where? You can't leave there. You're sitting on a fucking goldmine at that place."

"Look, Jillian, I told you I'm not taking another fucking pill from that place," I spat.

"Will you be quiet long enough for me to finish my thought?"

"If it has anything to do with opioids then I don't want to talk about it," I expressed. I needed her to understand that I was a nervous wreck when I took the first bottle. I couldn't rest in my own bed the entire night thinking about the fact that if Sanjay realized that it was gone, then I could be fired and hauled off to jail.

"Okay. No problem." Jillian finally waved her white flag. "So, when are you going to start looking for another job?"

"I'm gonna go online tonight to put in a few applications. And who knows, I may get a hit," I said optimistically.

"Are you going to give your boss two weeks' notice?"

"I haven't thought about it. I don't know. I guess I'll figure that part out when I cross that bridge."

"Look, just take your time and don't do anything hasty," Jillian advised me.

"Believe me, I won't," I told her. "Where's Nana?" I changed the subject.

"She's in the den watching *Two and a Half Men*."

"She still watches that show? I mean, didn't they fire Charlie Sheen?"

"Yeah, but she doesn't care. You know, she watches the same thing every day."

"Did Nana cook dinner?"

"She made a pot of chicken and dumplings."

"Oh damn! I love her chicken and dumplings. Save me a bowl of it and I'll stop by in the morning to pick it up so I can have it for lunch," I instructed her.

"A'ight," she said. "Oh yeah, did you ever get your mother's beer and take it to her?"

"Fuck no! And I'm not. If she dies one day of alcohol poisoning it won't be because of me."

Jillian laughed. "You so damn funny!"

"I wasn't intending it to be. And on that note, I'm gonna get off this phone and tend to my own mess."

"I love you, Cuz," Jillian said to me.

"I love you too," I replied sarcastically, but she knew I meant it.

8

FAMILY DRAMA

I didn't realize how tired I was until I walked into my apartment, threw my things onto the floor, and flopped down on the sofa. Wanting to rest for a few minutes turned into an hour-long nap. I knew that if my cell phone hadn't rung, I'd probably still be asleep. I wiped my eyes with the palm of my right hand so I could focus on where my cell phone was. After sifting around in my purse, I finally located it down in the bottom of it.

I didn't bother to look at the caller ID. I was more interested in stopping the phone from ringing because it was driving me crazy. "Hello," I said after I placed the phone to my ear and laid my head against one of the cushions on my sofa.

"What happened to you bringing me a case of beer?" my mother griped through the phone.

"Ma, I never told you I was going to bring you beer."

"Jillian told me that she was going to tell you to pick me up a case of Coronas."

Now, I'd heard the whole conversation between my mother and Jillian, so why was my mother lying? This addiction of hers was fucking up her mind. "Mom, aren't you tired of drinking?"

"Are you my sponsor?"

"No."

"Well then, stop questioning me about my drinking and carry your ass to the store," she spat.

I let out a long sigh. "A'ight, I'm leaving my apartment now," I told her.

"Good. And bring me a bag of tortilla chips and a jar of salsa too," she added.

"Okay," I replied and then I ended the call.

I swear I didn't feel like going anywhere. All I wanted to do was lie around my apartment and catch up on the reality shows I'd recorded over the last few weeks. Sorry to say that that wasn't going to happen today.

Instead of stopping by a grocery store, I stopped off at a convenience store in the hood not too far from my mother's place to get her a case of beer. I parked my car three parking spaces from the front door of the store because it was the only spot left. So, after I got out of the car and locked the door, I hurried inside the store, got a six pack of Coronas, paid for it, and then I left out of there. When I got back into my car and drove away, I realized that I didn't get the salsa and chips my mother asked me to bring her. I knew she was going to be upset when I walked into her house without them, so I turned my car around and headed back to the store. I was in and out of there in less than three minutes.

I finally made it to my mother's house twenty minutes later. When I pulled into the driveway, I noticed that her new boyfriend's car was there. "Where is your man?" I didn't hesitate to ask her after she opened up her front door and let me into her house.

"He's in the room asleep. Why?" she replied sarcastically.

"Why is he asleep this time of the day?" I pressed the issue while I followed her down the hallway toward the kitchen.

"Because his job just changed his shift to nights. So, he sleeps during the day."

"Oh, so that's why you didn't ask him to make that beer run for you?"

"Who do you think you're talking to?" my mother said as she pulled one of the beer bottles from the case.

"Look, Mama, I didn't come over here to argue with you about your man and God knows what else. All I want you to do is to consider stop drinking. It's taking your youth from you."

My mother took the top off a beer and took a seat at one of the chairs at the kitchen table. She crossed her legs and then she took a sip of the beer. After she swallowed it, she gave me a crooked smile and said, "What are you, my sponsor?"

I stood there with my back pressed against the countertop and watched the smug look on her face. "Why do you always shoot me down every time I tell you something that would help you?"

"So, you think you're helping me?"

"Of course."

"Well, you're not. I'm a grown woman. And I'm your mother. I know more shit than you'll ever know. Now, I appreciate you for thinking that you're looking out for me, but I got this. I've been taking care of myself longer than you'll ever know," she said and then she took another sip of her beer.

"Look, Mama, I'm not gonna go back and forth with you about your drinking. Do what you wanna do. I'm over it." I turned to walk out of the kitchen.

"You always wanna run off when it gets hot in the kitchen," she yelled.

I turned around and stopped at the entryway. "Mama, stop with all the drama. If you can't see that I want the best for you then I don't know what else to do."

"You know my brother has always been my mama's favorite child," she said.

"What are you talking about?"

My mother took another sip from the beer bottle and placed it on the kitchen table. "From as long as I can remember, I couldn't do anything right in my mother's eyes. It didn't matter if I came home with honor roll, she'd always find a way to give my brother the shine. And I hated her for that. She always favored my brother over me, which is why she's got Jillian living over there in that big house she's got. He couldn't do no wrong. But when I met your father and dated him for a year, I jumped at the chance when he asked me to marry him. That man treated me so good. He loved me like no one else in this entire world. So, when he got sick with that colon cancer and passed away, I was devastated. When he died, a huge piece of my heart died with him. Do you think I really wanna be an alcoholic? Do you think I wanna sit around here all day and do nothing? I want my old life back. I wanna go out and take long walks on the beach and smell the fresh air. Or perhaps go on a few vacations a year. But I can't because my heart won't let me. Dealing with the loss of your father, and you and I not spending time together like we used to, has taken a massive toll on me." She sobbed.

"Mama, you and I not spending time with each other and hanging out like we used to is your fault. Right after Dad died, I came here every day to get you out of the house, but you wouldn't budge. You wouldn't get out of bed. And you wouldn't even talk to me sometimes. So, I just stopped trying," I explained.

"That was because I couldn't stop thinking about your father." She continued to cry.

That's when I walked over and embraced her. I tried to hug her like I wasn't going to let her go. I think I stood there and hugged her for the next three minutes without letting her go. And when she felt like she had cried enough, she released my embrace and started wiping her tears from her face. I wiped a few of her tears away too with the back of my hand.

After we stood in the kitchen for a while we decided to go into the living room. We took a seat next to each other on the sectional she had placed directly in front of the television. I thought she would want to sit down and watch TV for a while, but she didn't. She started a dialogue about my father once again. "I remember the good times me and your father used to have," she said after she took a swallow of the beer she'd carried with her from the kitchen.

I sat there and looked at my mother while she talked about the good times her and my father had. But then, once again I saw the hurt in her eyes. This was my first time ever hearing her tell me her true feelings about my grandmother and my dad. My mother was dealing with some serious shit. And now that I knew the reason why my grandmother and her didn't get along, it shed a lot of light on their beef of twenty-plus years. I sure would hate to be in her shoes right now because she really needed some help.

For the first time in years, I could honestly say how much I felt sorry for her. I didn't know if I'd be able to help mend her and my grandmother's relationship. Maybe after I spoke to my grandmother, she'd be a willing participant to bridge the gap in her and my mother's relationship. If she wasn't, my mother might never stop drinking.

"Mama, I won't ever judge you again. I just wanna see you win. That's all," I told her, and then turned around and left.

My heart felt so heavy. I felt sorry for her and all that shit she'd been holding on to all her life. How had she done it this long? I would've checked myself into a psychiatric hospital by now. I knew she didn't see herself as a source of strength, but in my eyes, she was a strong-ass lady. The next time I saw her, I was going to remind myself to tell her that too.

9

MOVING ON

Ithought about my mother the entire drive back to my apartment. At one point I wanted to get my grandmother on the phone and talk to her about the conversation I had just had with my mother, but I figured that it wouldn't be an effective way to get my mother's point across. My grandmother would talk all over top of me. The only way I'd be able to get her to really listen to me would be to talk to her face-to-face. And I planned on doing that tomorrow after I got off work.

Mentally tired because of the visit I had with my mother, I got out of my car and made my way up the sidewalk to my apartment building. Out of the left side of my peripheral vision I saw movement. Startled, I turned around and saw Terrell walking toward me. My heart rate sped up and I wondered how this meeting was going to end. I stopped in my tracks and turned around to face him. "What do you want now, Terrell?"

He smiled wickedly. "I just stopped by to see you."

"You stopped by yesterday," I replied sarcastically. He of all people knew that I don't want him around me.

"So, you don't wanna see me?"

"Terrell, what is wrong with you? I can't do this with you anymore. We aren't ever getting back together, so this popping up to my apartment anytime you want to has got to stop," I told him.

"Where did you just come from?" he asked me, not acknowledging what I had just said.

"Why?" I said in an irritated manner.

He stepped closer to me. Fear ripped my heart open. "Whatcha just came from seeing another nigga? So, you're cheating on me?"

As badly as I wanted to tell this motherfucker to get lost, I thought about the possibility that he could embarrass me out here where all my neighbors could see. I was not up for that kind of drama, so I played his game. "No, I wasn't. I just came from seeing my mom," I told him.

"She still drinking her life away?"

"Drinking is all she knows."

"What a waste of life," he commented cynically.

"Not everybody can live the same way you live, Terrell."

"Come on, let's go inside your apartment," he insisted and grabbed me by the hand.

I snatched my hand back from his. "Terrell, please go home. I've got a lot of stuff on my mind right now, so I'm not in the mood to entertain." I let him down easy.

He reached for my hand and snatched it back. "Don't ever snatch your hands from me again," he hissed.

"Can you please stop it and leave?" I pleaded with him.

"Why do I have to leave? Whatcha don't wanna spend any time with me?"

"Terrell, stop it. You're embarrassing me," I said quietly while I saw a few of my neighbors peering out their windows at me.

"Do you think I give a fuck about your people seeing us? They can kiss my ass!" he said into my ear.

"If you don't stop, they may call the cops. And you of all people don't like the cops," I warned him.

"You know that I don't give a fuck around the po-po. Let 'em call them." Terrell tested me.

"I guess if I get your baby mama on the phone and tell her how you're harassing me, I know she's not gonna be happy about that."

"Call her. I don't care," he replied, and that's when I knew that he really didn't care. I also knew that I needed to change my tactics if I wanted to get rid of this asshole because threatening him wasn't working.

"Okay look, why don't you leave and come back later," I suggested, trying to defuse the situation.

"Why do I've gotta come back when I'm here now?"

"Because I'm tired. I've been out all day dealing with my family's issues, so I just need to get some rest. After that, we can do whatever."

"Nah, I don't feel like going anywhere. I'm here now."

Tired of going back and forth with this fucking jerk-off, I took a long look at him and said, "Why are you acting like this? I didn't cheat on you, you cheated on me with over a dozen bitches! And if that's not enough, you come here and attack me like I'm the one that fucked around on you. Who did who wrong? You! So why are you here harassing me? You've never acted this way before. I've never ever seen this side of you. What, are you on drugs?" I snatched my hand back from him.

"Fuck nah, I ain't on no drugs. I just want you back."

"But that's not gonna happen, Terrell. I've given you too many chances. I'm over that whole relationship. So, move on," I said, trying to let him down easy.

Terrell looked straight into my eyes and chuckled loudly. "So, you think it's gonna be that easy? You think I'm gonna let another nigga come in and take my place? My mama warned me about you."

"What have I ever done to your mother?" I asked him. I'd only met Mrs. Faye a couple of times and each time was good. So, what the fuck was he talking about? If anything, my mother warned me about his disrespectful and cheating ass.

He ignored me and stormed off back in the direction of his car. "I'll be back," he yelled and then he disappeared into the night.

10

WHEN I SAY NO!

I don't know why I was a bit rattled after I woke up this morning to get dressed and head off to work, but I was. I mean, it wasn't like I'd be walking into the unknown. I saw Sanjay and spoke with him when I walked into the pharmacy yesterday. So why was I plagued with all of this anxiety? Whatever was burdening my shoulders, I hoped that it could be sorted before it engulfed me.

When I pulled up to the pharmacy and parked my car, I noticed that Sanjay hadn't made it here. This wasn't unusual for him, so I let myself into the pharmacy and tried to disable the alarm, but it was already off. I thought that was weird, but didn't look too much into it because this has happened before. After I powered on the lights in the store, I logged onto our computer system to see how many orders we had to fill this morning. While I was doing that, I got this nagging feeling to check out our medication supply. The Vicodin and the Percocet supply was my focus.

Upon entering the supply closet, I noticed that there were a few cases of diabetes meds, blood pressure meds, arthritis meds, and dementia meds to name a few, but there were no Vicodin or Percocet boxes in sight. I was flabbergasted. "What the fuck is going on?" I whispered to my-self.

The thought that Sanjay cleared out this closet had me baffled. I mean, what was he going to do if and when someone came in to get their prescriptions filled with those drugs and we didn't have them? Now I see why our regular customer Mrs. Landry was sent to the other pharmacy down the block. We were really out of the fucking drugs that really count around here.

Not knowing how to process what my eyes were taking in, I backed out of the supply closet and continued to log in today's prescription orders.

Sanjay walked into the pharmacy through the back door about thirty minutes later. He smiled as he greeted me. "It's a beautiful day out, huh?" he said cheerfully.

"Yes, I thought the same thing," I lied, trying not to address the elephant in the room.

"Do we have a lot of orders to fill this morning?" he wondered aloud as he hung up his jacket and placed his briefcase on the floor next to the wall.

"Yes, we have a few," I told him.

"Has the UPS driver made his rounds?" he questioned once more.

Without taking my attention from the computer screen, I told him no. Seconds later, I heard him walking over to the supply closet. After he opened it, he went inside and moved a few boxes around. A couple of minutes later, he called my name. "Misty, get in here right now," he demanded frantically.

"What is it?" I replied after I met him in the closet.

"Did you move any of the narcotics meds out of here?" He got straight to the point as he pointed to every inch of the closet.

"No. I haven't. When I looked in here after I let myself into the pharmacy, I noticed that they were gone, but I thought you did it."

"No. When I left here last night we had a huge supply of medicine. Get on the phone and call the cops. I think we've been robbed," he concluded.

"Oh wow! This is scary," I commented while I watched Sanjay go through the motions. One part of me wanted to believe that we really did get robbed. But since he'd been acting really weird lately, it had me questioning the validity of his robbery story. Now, if we really did get robbed, that of course would have me spooked and worried for my safety, but then what if he was lying? What if he got rid of those drugs in exchange for a large payoff and wanted to cover his ass just in case one of the pharmaceutical companies decided that they wanted to blow the whistle on his ass? Either way, this business of his was a scam, so I wanted out now, more than ever. I was going to start looking for another job.

"What are we going to do in the meantime?" I questioned.

"Once the cops get here we're gonna put in a robbery report and once that happens, we get the report number for our pharmaceutical company so they can give us a clearance number. After that happens, we'll be clear to order more meds," he explained.

I couldn't lie, this crooked-ass negro thought I was stupid as hell. He knew damn well that he sold all of those fucking drugs that were in that closet last night. See, I got all this shit figured out. He didn't come to work before me this morning, because he needed an alibi. A witness. He needed me to fall into his trap. Make it look like he didn't have anything to do with it. But should I tell 'em the fucking alarm wasn't set last night? Should I throw Sanjay underneath the bus? He thinks he's so fucking slick. But I had a trick for him. I really gotta find me another job now. I refused to get mixed up in his bullshit! Not now. Not ever.

Sanjay got on the phone and called 911. After he gave the dispatcher what they needed to call a cop out to our address, he and I waited patiently for their arrival. As we waited, Sanjay started making small talk and giving me directions as to what to say when the cops started taking my written statement. I wasn't a dumb chick. In fact, I was street smart. No one could get over me for nothing in the world. I guess being raised in the ghetto really worked out for me in a good way.

"Think you got everything I just told you?" he wanted to know. I could see the spooky shit overtaking Sanjay again. I hated that he got like this. He didn't make me feel safe in this store at all. I needed to get away from this man, before I get caught up in the mix.

The cops finally showed up like thirty minutes later. Both cops were black. One of them was cute as fuck. Boy, do I love men in uniform. "Good morning, gentlemen," Sanjay greeted them after they walked into the pharmacy. He shook their hands as they approached the counter.

The officer that I found attractive stood there while the other cop spoke. "My name is Officer Cooper and this is my partner, Officer Flowers. We will be working the investigation," he stated.

"Thank you. I appreciate you officers for coming by," Sanjay said while Officer Cooper reached for a mini notepad from the pocket of his shirt.

"So, what was taken?" Cooper asked, looking at us both as he prepared to take notes.

"Come around the counter and I'll show you," Sanjay insisted. While Officer Cooper followed Sanjay to the supply closet, I continued to process the prescription orders. I could feel the eyes of Officer Flowers piercing through my body. I knew he was looking at me so I looked up from the computer screen.

"What's your name?" he asked me as our eyes connected.

"Misty," I said lightly.

"How long have you worked here, Misty?"

"Not long. A few months."

"When did you guys notice that you had been burglarized?"

"I didn't notice it until Sanjay went into the supply closet and brought it to my attention," I replied, but I was nervous as fuck. Sanjay should be out here answering these questions, not me. What if Sanjay said something different to the other police officer? We'd be like a pair of liars.

"When was that?"

"A little over an hour ago."

"Is there an alarm system in here?"

"Yes,"

"Was it activated?"

"I got here before Sanjay did. And when I let myself in, I noticed that the alarm system had been disarmed. So, I figured that either the robber disabled the system when he broke in here and didn't turn it back on before he left, or Sanjay forgot to turn it on altogether," I explained.

"What did I forget?" I heard Sanjay say behind me.

"We're talking about the alarm system," I told him.

"What about it?" Sanjay pressed the issue as he walked over and stood next to me. The other cop walked back to the other side of the counter and stood next to his partner.

"I was just telling Officer Flowers that when I came in this morning the alarm wasn't on. So, whoever broke in either didn't turn the alarm back on or the alarm wasn't on in the first place."

"Oh, the alarm was on. I made sure myself." Sanjay got a little defensive. I could tell that he wasn't at all happy about the answer I gave to the cop.

"How did you make sure?" Officer Cooper asked.

"Let's just say that I never forget not to turn it on before I lock up the place," Sanjay assured them.

"With the alarm system, you have to have a security cam, so where is that?" Officer Cooper asked.

"Yes, I do have one of those. But it hasn't been working for some time now," Sanjay explained. But he was lying. That camera runs every day. So, why not hand it over to the cops so they can do this robbery investigation more efficiently? Well, now I knew exactly what was going on. And what blew my mind was that Sanjay was trying to hide it.

"Has this store ever been robbed before?" Officer Flowers asked.

"No sir, it hasn't, which is why I'm so shocked that it happened now. This is a very respectful neighborhood," Sanjay told him.

"Have you noticed any seedy-looking characters hanging around in here or around the building?"

"Well, I haven't," Sanjay answered first.

Both cops looked at me next. "No, I haven't either," I told them.

"So, let me get this straight. You had five boxes of Lorcet stolen from you, along with seven cases of Vicodin, ten boxes of Percocet, and three boxes of Lortab?"

"Yes," Sanjay answered.

"Would you tell me the street value for those missing items?" Officer Cooper pressed on.

"I can't say off the top of my head, but I figure that it could be in the neighborhood upwards of a half million."

"Wow! That's a lot of money, and for you to know the value of it is astounding," Officer Cooper said.

"Yes, it is," Officer Flowers agreed.

Sanjay gave off a cheap little smile. "I guess it's because I've been in the business for so long," Sanjay explained.

"Well, do us a favor and do not touch anything else in here. I'm going to my squad car and get a fingerprint test kit. My partner is going to stay here with you guys."

"Okay. Sounds great," Sanjay said. But I knew he was a nervous fucking wreck. I swear, if I had the gumption to throw Sanjay under the bus, I would. He knows that I know he's lying to these cops. First with the story that someone broke in here and robbed the place, then to setting the alarm before he locked up the pharmacy last night. But the big kicker is when he told them that our camera system wasn't working and it hadn't worked for a while. That was straight bullshit! There was no doubt in my mind that that motherfucker set up this whole scheme. And the fact that he was trying to pull me in made me angry. I didn't sign up for this shit when I first took this job. All I wanted to do was make a paycheck and that's it.

It took the cops less than twenty minutes to pull the fingerprints from the supply closet, the back door of the pharmacy, and the front as well. Before they left, Officer Flowers handed me his card, so I took it and shoved it in my pants pocket. But what was so bizarre was that after they left, Sanjay asked me to hand it to him. Right after I handed it to him, he put the card in his white jacket and continued on as if the police hadn't been there.

I couldn't stand there and act like everything was hunkydory, so I turned around from the computer and said, "Why did you lie to them about the security camera? It works perfectly fine."

"Don't question me like I work for you."

"Look, Sanjay, I don't wanna get in an argument with you. I just wanted to know why you told them that the security camera didn't work. I mean, what if they find out that it is working?"

"You just let me handle that," he said coldheartedly.

Instead of feeding further into his bullshit, I turned my attention back to the computer monitor. I was regretting that I even brought that fact up.

"Regardless of what you think of me right now, I want you to know that I know your hands are dirty too."

I turned back around and faced him. He stood there three feet away from me with his arms folded. "That security camera system that we have in here caught you stealing from our supply closet every chance you got. You'd steal a few pills here and there. But just recently you walked off with a brand-new bottle of Percocet. So, before you start asking me questions about my involvement with my business, make sure you have enough room to talk."

Fear engulfed me. I swear if I could pull out a pair of wings and fly out of here, I'd do it. The tension between Sanjay and me had suddenly become so thick I wouldn't be able to cut it with a knife. I wanted to say something to rid myself of the guilt I was feeling, but I couldn't. This fucking guy had me backed up in a corner. "So, we really didn't have a robbery, huh?" I finally managed to say.

"I don't have to answer that," he said, gritting his teeth.

I got up the gumption to ask, "Well, can you tell me why those guys that put a gun into your brother's back also smacked you around in this store after I left?"

"What I do and who I do it with is none of your concern. Now if anything that we're talking about goes out beyond these walls, you will pay for it," he warned me.

"Wait a minute, are you threatening me?"

"You can call it what you may. And let me leave you with this: If you ever rat me out to the cops, you're going down with me."

"Yeah, whatever!" I responded after feeling a surge of anxiety. I had to play the tough role with this asshole, even though my head had started spinning in circles and the knots in my stomach started churning like a freaking food blender. I mean, did he just say that if he went down, I was going with him? The amount of drugs he pushed out of here was kingpin status compared to mine. I only made a couple of grand. He was probably making hundreds of thousands.

I wanted to say more to this idiot, but I left well enough alone. After having this conversation with him, I knew where I stood. And I knew that he was playing a very dangerous game. The fact that he was spying on me and watching me take drugs from out of here showed me that he was a heartless coward. I was sure that when he saw me stealing, he got excited about it. I felt like I was in the whole crab-in-the-bucket scenario. It was time for me to map out my exit plan. If he thought he was going to bring me down with him, he had another think coming.

11

TRYING TO FIGURE THINGS OUT

The time for me to go to lunch seemed like it would never get here. When the clock hit twelve, I hauled butt out the front door. And as soon as I got into my car, I pulled out my cell phone and called Jillian.

"What's up, Cuz?" she answered.

"You are not going to believe this shit."

"What's wrong? What happened?"

"Girl, my fucking boss staged a huge robbery at the pharmacy so he could sell the drugs to his connect. The cops came and took a report and they swabbed for finger-prints too."

"Yo, that's some bold shit to do."

"But that's not all. He told the cops that our security cameras weren't working. So, after the cops left, I asked him why he lied to the cops about the cameras not work-ing, and he looked at me and told me not to question him. He also told me that he knew I've been taking drugs from the supply closet, and that if I ever go to the cops and men-tion anything about the robbery, he wasn't going down by himself."

"What the fuck does he mean by that?"

"He basically said that if I snitched him out, he was going to let the cops know that I've stolen from the pharmacy too."

"Oh, that's fucked up!"

"Tell me about it," I agreed.

"So, where is he now?"

"He's inside the store. I'm sitting outside in my car."

"So, what are you going to do?" Jillian wanted to know.

"I don't know, Cuz. I do know that I gotta find myself another job. I won't be able to survive in this place but for another week or so."

"Did you tell him that you're gonna leave?"

"Fuck no! I ain't telling that piece of shit nothing, especially after telling me that if I ratted him out, he was going to bring me down too. Ratting niggas out is what a lot of women do."

"So, what are you going to do now?"

I let out a long sigh. "I don't know, Jillian. I just feel so violated. I always have other people's back, but they never have mine. I liked working at the pharmacy until Sanjay started dealing with these shady-ass guys. I would do anything he asked me to do. So, to have him come at me with that bullshit earlier was not called for." I began to cry.

"Misty, please don't cry. Everything is going to be all right."

"I know it is, it's just that it's hard to go through these motions. And speaking of motions, Terrell is starting to stalk me. He came by my apartment yesterday talking about how we're not broken up and that if he finds out that I'm seeing someone else, he's gonna go off on me and the guy. I swear I am so over that fucking guy. He's been a thorn in my side for the last couple of months. I wish I could just pack my shit up and disappear."

"Why don't you tell him what's going on with your boss? If he's acting like this because he suspects you have another boyfriend, I'm sure he'll take care of that problem."

"Are you crazy? What if someone gets hurt?"

"Just tell Terrell to scare him."

"Nah, I don't like the sound of that. I'm just gonna quit and find me somewhere else to work."

"What time you get off today?"

"At four, why?"

"Stop by."

"A'ight," I said.

"Keep your head up. Today is almost over."

"Okay, I will," I assured her and then I ended our call.

When my hour was up for my lunch break, I headed back into the pharmacy. There were a couple of regular customers waiting around to get their prescriptions, so I clocked back in and went to work. I thought Sanjay and I would have another heated conversation, but we didn't. He kept it professional for the rest of the day, acting like nothing ever happened. That eased my nerves a bit, but my eyes were still wide open.

12

ELIMINATING PROBLEMS

I raced over to my grandmother's house the minute I put my car in gear. I was so relieved to not be inside that pharmacy right now. A huge chunk of anxiety fell off my shoulders two miles into the drive. It felt liberating.

When I arrived at my grandmother's house, I found her in the den, in her favorite chair.

"Hi, baby," she greeted me right at first glance. I leaned down and gave her a kiss on her cheek.

"Where's Jillian?" I asked her while taking a seat on the sofa on the other side of the room.

"I don't know where she went to. She just told me she'd be back and left the house. Call her on her cell phone."

"No, I'll just wait until she comes back."

"So, how's work?" my grandmother asked.

"It was hectic."

"What happened?"

"It's nothing that I can't handle," I said, brushing off the subject.

"Now don't let that man down at that pharmacy steal your joy," she warned me.

"I'm not, Grandma."

"Have you talked to your mother today?"

"No. But I stopped by her house yesterday and talked to her for a few minutes."

"Was her new boyfriend there?"

"Yeah, but she said he was asleep."

"Was she drinking?"

"Yeah, she was."

"You know if she doesn't stop all that drinking, she's gonna end up dead."

"I know," I started off saying. "I asked her if she'd go to rehab, but she said that she doesn't have a drinking problem."

"She's out of her damn mind," my grandmother commented sarcastically.

"You wanna know what else she told me?"

"Yes, let me hear it."

"She says that one of the reasons she drinks the way she does is because you never loved her as child growing up. She said that you showed favoritism to Jillian's dad. So, when she got older and met my dad, he gave her a love that she never experienced before. But what devastated her the most was when my dad passed away, it killed her inside because the only person that ever loved her was dead."

"That's a bunch of baloney," my grandma protested. "She knows daggone well that she was loved. If I didn't love her, I would've gave her up to be adopted or sent her butt off to boarding school. She needs to quit it with that lame excuse. She's drinking because she ain't living her life right."

"When she was telling me how she felt, I couldn't help but feel sorry for her."

"Don't let her feed you with that crap. She's a grown woman trying to find excuses why she's drinking her life away."

"I think she's crying out for help."

"Help for what?"

"She sounded like she wants to build a relationship with you."

"I tried for years to bond with your mother, but that's not what she wanted. She'd rather go off on her own, doing what she wants to do."

"Would you be open to sitting down and talking with her?" I wanted to know. From where I was sitting, my mother and my grandmother were some strong-willed and stubborn people. My grandmother saw their relationship one way while my mother saw it another way.

"What is there to talk about?"

"Maybe y'all can clear the air about everything that went on in the past," I suggested.

"Trust me, it'll be a disaster because your mother is not going to take responsibility for her actions."

I tried to reason with my grandmother. "But what if she does?"

"Baby, just leave it alone. Your mother is on another planet, so I refuse to sit around and listen to her lies."

"Would you be willing to try to talk to her, if I can convince her to sit with you?"

"Listen, sweetie, I love what you're trying to do. But I'm in a good place in my life. I don't feed into drama and I don't get into other folks' business. Just let me sit in my peaceful house and watch my TV shows."

I let out a long sigh. "All right, Grandma, you win."

"It's not about winning, baby. It's about keeping your sanity," she told me.

I looked down at my watch and realized that my grandmother and I had been talking for almost twenty minutes and Jillian hadn't come back to the house. I started to call her on her cell phone, but I decided against it when the idea popped up that I needed to be online looking for another job.

While I sifted through the internet on my job search, I ran across a couple of posts on the local jobs-search websites. Two posts stuck out among the rest, so I sat there on my grandmother's sofa and applied to both jobs. Once I had completed the applications, I put my cell phone in my handbag and told my grandmother that I was going to head home.

"Well, come over here and give me some sugar before you leave," she insisted.

After I kissed her on the cheek, I told her I loved her and for her to tell Jillian that I stopped by. "I sure will, baby," she said and then I made my exit.

13

MAKING A CHANGE

Not too long after I got home, got comfortable and lay down, Jillian decided that she wanted to call and talk to me. "Don't be calling me now," I said to her while I snuggled my head into one of my bed pillows.

"Don't be mad at me. I had to make a run with one of my homeboys."

"Come on, Jillian, you knew I was coming. And you also know what I'm going through, so I really needed to talk to you."

"I'm sorry, Cuz. I'm here now," Jillian apologized and then she said, "Grandma told me you stayed here for a while."

"Yeah, I did. I went online and put in a few applications to other pharmacies in the area."

"Wait, slow your roll. You can't leave just yet."

"Girl, please, I'm getting out of there as soon as I get the chance."

"Wait, check it out. I told the guy that bought the whole bottle of Percocet what happened to you earlier, and he said that if your boss rats you out, he'll take care of him."

"Tell 'im I'm good. I don't want that motherfucker causing any more emotional turmoil."

"Well, since you're leaving there and going to work somewhere else, why don't you rob his ass real good this time? Instead of taking one giant bottle, fill a box up with a bunch of shit he got stashed in that closet you were talking about earlier."

"You know what? That's exactly what I'm going to do. Rob his ass blind and see if he calls the cops again. I mean, what is he going to do, tell them I robbed him? Fuck no! He knows that I could back his ass into a corner just like he did me. So, let's do it." I gave Jillian the green light.

"So, when are you trying to do this? Cause, we can do it anytime. You don't have to give him two weeks' notice."

"I know. But if we do it, we gotta do it later because right now, we don't have shit in there. Whoever he had rob the place took all the good medicine. So let me find out when we get our next shipment and then we'll go from there."

"A'ight, well just let me know when."

"I will," I told her.

"Grandma, told me what your mama said," Jillian pointed out.

"Yeah, but you know Grandma wasn't trying to hear me tell her anything my mama had to say."

"I just wish they would bury all that unnecessary bullshit and let's make our family whole again."

"I wish we could do it too." I agreed.

"Have you heard from Terrell again?" Jillian changed the subject.

"Nah, and I'm glad too. He's been acting really weird since I broke up with him."

"He misses that good pussy!" Jillian said and chuckled.

"Stop, Jillian, it's not funny. That guy needs some fucking help. Maybe take a trip to see Dr. Phil."

"He's just now realizing that he let a good thing go. That's all."

"So, you're telling me it's okay for him to come by my apartment and stalk me?"

"No, silly. I'm just trying to make light of the situation. You know I don't like him and you know that I'm glad you're not with him anymore. So loosen up."

"I wish it was that easy. Speaking of which, I'm gonna lay my butt down. Today was exhausting."

"A'ight. Well, hit me up tomorrow. And call me if your boss messes with you."

"I will," I assured her and then I ended the call.

14

I COULDN'T BELIEVE IT

I don't know how, but I was able to get a good night's rest. I got up, took a shower, got dressed, and then I fixed myself a bowl of instant oatmeal. I sat down in my living room and watched a little bit of TV while I ate my food. Five minutes into eating, my cell phone rang. I told myself that it couldn't be anyone but Sanjay. The sounds of the ring made me dread answering it until I looked at the caller ID and saw that the call was coming from someone else. "Hello," I said.

"Hi, may I speak with Misty Heiress?" a woman asked. The sound of her voice lifted a weight from my shoulders.

"This is she," I replied.

"Hi, Misty, my name is Priscilla Binsley and I'm calling from High Health Pharmacy.

"Hi."

"I'm calling you because you just applied for a position at our pharmacy so I was wondering if we could get you to come in for an interview?"

"Wow! That was fast."

The lady chuckled. "We don't waste anything around

here," she told me. "So, let me ask you, would you be able to come in tomorrow for an interview?"

"Absolutely."

"Can you come in around twelve o'clock?"

"Can we make it two?"

"Yes, that's fine. But do you know where we're located?"

"Yes, ma'am, I do."

"Okay. So, I guess that settles it. And when you get here, just ask for me."

"I sure will. Thank you so much," I said graciously. She had no idea how happy she just made me. The thought of leaving that fucking place and going over to that new job felt liberating. Some people would tell me not to get excited because I hadn't gotten the job yet. And I would tell them to take their negative asses away from me, because I was getting that job by any means necessary.

I can't lie. I used to love working for Sanjay. He really looked out for me in the beginning. He used to give me bonus checks. Gave me time off with pay. Let me go home early. He was a very generous man. But now that he was in cahoots with those other Middle Eastern guys, I don't even know who he is anymore. I'm determined, now more than ever, that I'm not going to let him steal my joy. When I went to work, I was gonna act like nothing ever transpired between us, because I knew that after tomorrow, I was going to be out of there, and there was nothing he could do about it.

15

TIME TO START PLOTTING ON YOUR ASS

I tried to call my cousin Jillian on my way to work to give her the good news, but the tramp didn't answer her phone. She always did that to me. I started to call my grandmother to see if Jillian was anywhere around her, but I decided against it. I figured she'd notice that I called her and she'd call me back.

When I pulled up outside the pharmacy, I parked in my normal spot and while I was heading into the pharmacy, I noticed that Sanjay's car wasn't parked in his usual place. I did, however, see his brother's car and I wasn't at all happy about that. His brother was a sneaky asshole. He never said more than four words to me every time we were in the same vicinity. I hoped he wouldn't be around too long, because I couldn't deal with his negative energy for long.

Shockingly, I noticed that we didn't have any customers this morning. There were always at least two or three people waiting by the time I came in to work. I didn't see Sanjay either. Normally he'd be standing behind the computer, processing prescription orders or ordering quantities of medicine so that we can restock our inventory. I did, however, see his brother. Surprisingly, he was standing behind the computer wearing Sanjay's white medical jacket. This seemed pretty odd to me. His brother has never, ever stood behind the counter, acting like his brother. "Good morning." I started the conversation.

"Good morning," he replied in his Middle Eastern accent.

"Where is Sanjay?" I wanted to know.

"He had to leave town."

"When did he leave town? I just saw him yesterday and he didn't tell me anything about leaving."

"We had a family emergency."

"When will he be back?"

"He will be back tomorrow."

I wanted to question him further about how his explanation didn't add up. If Sanjay left for his native country, it would take him well over twenty-four hours to fly there and come back, so did his brother think that I was an idiot? I may not have a doctor's degree, but I have common sense, and something is telling me that something is wrong with this picture. I did have one more question for him though. "When did Sanjay leave?"

"He left last night," his brother replied. But I knew that was bullshit. Sanjay was hanging out around here somewhere. He could be in hiding too. Or maybe in jail because of the prescription-drug heist that he initiated. I wished I had that business card that the cop gave me. I would have called him immediately if I'd had it, because something wasn't right, and I would figure it out.

After I hung up my handbag and jacket, I jumped on my computer and logged in so I could process all our new prescription orders. In my peripheral vision, I saw Amir watching me. This made me feel really uncomfortable so I turned around and said, "Do you need me to help you with something?"

"Oh no, I'm fine," he said, and then turned his attention back to his computer screen.

"Can I ask what you're doing?"

"My brother told me to order more prescription drugs because you guys don't have any."

"Yeah, I know," I started off and then I said, "Did he tell you about the robbery?" I asked this to put him on the spot.

"Yes, he told me. That's why I am here to send out new orders."

"Do you know how to do that?"

"Yes. He showed me how to do it a long time ago. I did it before you started working here."

"Oh really?"

"Yes, I used to work here before you came. And when I left here to start another business my brother hired you."

"Oh, wow, I didn't know that."

"Yes, this is part of my store too. I'm his partner."

"So, what other businesses do you have?" I continued to question him because this was the only time I'd been able to get him to say more than four words. This conversation was quite interesting.

"I own a gas station."

"Really?!"

"Yeah. My wife works there sometimes."

"Is that a good business to get into?"

"It's okay. It pays the bills."

"That's all that counts, right?" I commented because in reality I couldn't care less about him, his family, or how he pays his bills. He's an asshole and I didn't want no parts of him, his brother, or the other men that smacked them both around recently. These were some shady individuals, so the faster I got out of there, the better I would be.

I cut my conversation off with Amir immediately after

one of our regular customers came through the door. After I took the prescription from the customer, I started processing it. I carried on a little small talk with the customer so I wouldn't have to say anything else to Amir. My plan went well, because once I was done processing the first order, another customer came walking in. The steady traffic went on all day, and boy was I happy about it. When I look back at it, Amir and I really didn't talk for the rest of the day. And by the time my shift was over, I didn't waste any time leaving. When I turned around to tell Amir that I was about to leave for the day, he was on his cell phone. And he was talking quietly, so I couldn't tell if he was talking to Sanjay or his wife or anyone else, for that matter. "It's about that time for me to leave," I whispered to him, trying not to interrupt his phone conversation.

He turned around in my direction, muffled his phone and said, "Okay, have a nice day."

"Are you gonna be here tomorrow?" I asked him.

"Yes, I will be here tomorrow."

"Do you know what time Sanjay is coming back?"

"It will be tomorrow night."

"Okay, well, I guess I'll see you tomorrow."

"Okay," he said, and then he carried on with his phone conversation.

Instead of going straight home, I went through the Panera Bread drive-through to order myself a sandwich and a bowl of soup, and then I headed to my grandmother's house. Unfortunately, when I got there my cousin Jillian wasn't there. Once again, I came over to see her and she wasn't there. I knew she was with one of her seedy-ass prescription-drug-peddling friends and they were getting high, because that's her MO. I wished she would just straighten her life out, because there is more to life than getting high off prescription drugs all day, every day. Speaking of my mother going for rehab, Jillian needed to go to one herself. I'm gonna remind her of that the next time I see her so she doesn't end up an addict like my mother.

My grandmother was sitting in her normal spot and watching the news channel when I walked into the den to greet her. I gave her a kiss on the cheek and asked her how she was doing.

"What is that you have in the bag?" she inquired.

"Soup and a sandwich that I got from this place called Panera Bread."

"Oh yeah, heard about that place," my grandmother told me.

"So how are you, Grandma?" I asked while I placed my food on the coffee table in front of me.

"My arthritis hurts me from time to time. And my sugar levels have gone up some, but other than that I feel great."

"What kind of arthritis medicine are you taking?"

"That mess you bought me like a month ago."

"Oh yeah, I know which one you're taking. It's not helping you?"

"Sometimes it does and sometimes it don't."

"I'm gonna have to take a look at that and see if I can find you something stronger. I don't want you sitting around here hurting while I have access to those meds."

"Don't be doing anything illegal, girl," my grandmother warned me.

"Come on, Grandma, you know I am not into that mess."

"You better not be, because I will put you over my knees and give you a good beating myself."

I chuckled and said, "Boy, do I remember those beatings you used to give me."

She cracked a smile and said, "I used to do Jillian the same way."

"Yeah, we were terrible back in the day, huh?"

"Yes, you were. But you're doing good now and that's

all that matters." My grandmother changed the subject and said, "Spoke to your mama today?"

"No, I haven't. But I'm gonna call her before I go to bed tonight."

"When you talk to her, tell I said hello."

I smiled at my grandmother's gesture. But before I could make a comment, my cousin Jillian walked into the house and came straight to the den where my grandmother and I were sitting. She smiled when she saw me. "Hey, favorite cousin!" she said as she walked toward me.

"Don't be saying, "*Hey, cousin* to me because you don't be treating me right," I told her, and then I took a bite of my sandwich.

Jillian sat next to me and gave me the biggest smile she could muster up. "You know I love you, right? I love both of y'all. And I would hurt somebody if they tried to hurt y'all," she said while she flickered her eyelids. She leaned her head back against the sofa and then she closed her eyes.

"Have you given her any pills lately? Because she's acting like she's high," my grandmother questioned me. I could tell that she was not a happy camper.

Jillian leaned forward, opened her eyes, and started smiling once again. "You know, Grandma, she hasn't given me anything. And I'm not high either. I'm just tired."

"Jillian, don't lie to me. I know what high looks like and you, young lady, are high," my grandmother replied. She knew what she was talking about. Jillian was looking a little woozy. My grandmother knew that I worked at a pharmacy so I could be the only person giving her the drugs. I was becoming more and livid with her by the second. I hit her on her thigh and said, "Will you please tell Grandma that I don't give you any prescription drugs?"

"I don't need her to tell me anything. I know what's going on. I hear her talking to you on the phone all the time about bringing her a few pills here and there," my grandmother spat.

"Grandma, it's not that serious," Jillian protested, as her words began to slur.

"Jillian, just be quiet," I interjected, because all she was doing was making the situation worse. My grandmother was not a naïve lady. All the stuff my mother and uncle put her through these past years had made her a very smart woman. She could see bullshit from two miles away.

"She sure better be quiet," my grandmother agreed.

"I'm not trying to argue with y'all. I'm going to my room," Jillian said and then she got up from the sofa.

"Misty, follow her to her bedroom before she falls and hurts herself."

"Okay, Grandma." I got up from the sofa.

I followed Jillian to the bedroom and made sure that she got on her bed safely. I fussed at her about coming into the house all drugged up, but I knew she didn't understand what I was saying. So I covered her with a blanket and then I exited her bedroom.

I dreaded going back downstairs because I knew my grandmother was gonna fuss at me because of Jillian's prescription drug habit. But there was no way around it, so I put on a brave face and walked back into the den.

"I'm gonna need you to stop givin' her those drugs."

"Grandma, I'm not giving her any prescription drugs," I lied, even though I knew my grandmother didn't believe me. I even gave her the most sincere facial expression I could. It didn't work though.

"Let me tell you something," she started off. "I hear almost every conversation you and your cousin have. She puts you on speakerphone when you two call each other, so I know what goes on."

Blindsided by my grandmother's confession, I sat there like a dog with my tail between my legs. I really didn't know what else to say. She caught me red-handed. So how could I talk myself out of this? Nothing I said was going to change her mind, so I sat there and listened to her chastise me.

"I'm telling you right now that if you don't stop giving her those prescription drugs, I am going to stop you from coming over here. Do you understand me?"

"Yes, Grandma, I understand."

After my grandmother gave me a piece of her mind, I realized that I had lost my appetite and could not eat the rest of my food. She and I exchanged a few more words and then I kissed her and told her that I would come by in a couple of days to see her. She said okay and then I made my exit.

I reflected back on the conversation I had my grandmother concerning my cousin Jillian. She was right. I shouldn't be giving Jillian anything, because it would make her life worse than it already was. Jillian was not going to be happy about it, but she would be all right in the end.

16

SOMETHING SMELLS LIKE A RAT

The following morning, I still felt kind of bad that I'd let my grandmother down by giving my cousin Jillian prescription drugs. My grandmother meant everything to me. So, when I saw the hurt in her face, I knew I was doing something wrong. Now I had to get back in her good graces. I didn't care how I was going to do it, all I knew was that it would get done.

On my way to work, I got a call from Jillian, but I refused to answer it. She threw me underneath the bus last night, coming in the house high, so I was going to put her on ice for now. If I felt good about talking to her later, then I would.

Being forewarned that Sanjay wasn't going to be at work today, made me wonder how my day was going to go. I really disliked his brother, but working with him yesterday was not as bad as I'd thought it would be. I wanted to do my work and end the day on a nice note. I hoped today went the same way, because if it didn't, I'd walk out of there without even looking back. My sanity was more important than working in a toxic environment. I have only one life, and I will live it to the best of my ability.

I heard Amir shuffling around in the supply room the moment I walked into the pharmacy. I saw a few boxes stacked up on the floor outside the closet. I knew they must be the new shipment of prescription drugs to replace the ones that Sanjay told the cops were taken in that fake robbery he conjured up. So, while I was sneaking around and kneeling down to get a peek at the labels on the boxes, Amir caught me in action.

"What are you doing?" he asked immediately after he opened the supply closet door.

"I was just checking the inventory," I replied and stood back up.

"No need to worry about the inventory. Just get on your computer and process the online prescription orders," he hissed. I could tell that he was irritated by my being there and the fact that I was looking around.

"As you wish," I replied sarcastically. I wanted to tell him to go to hell, but I wasn't about to let him know that he just got underneath my skin. That would be too much control for him to have.

So, as instructed, I logged onto my computer and started processing the online prescription orders. I watched Amir in my peripheral vision. When he wasn't in the supply closet shuffling through the boxes, I saw him rearranging them and I even saw him packing a lot of small boxes into the other big boxes outside of the supply closet, which was odd because Sanjay never did that. When we got our shipments, I'd check the barcodes into the system and then I'd put those boxes where they needed to be in the supply closet. What Amir was doing was a sign that he didn't intend to keep that shipment in the store. I would bet money that those drugs didn't stay here. I didn't know who he was packing that stuff up for and taking it to, but I knew it wasn't the customers that frequent this place. These drugs were going to someone very important. But at this point, I didn't care.

While in the middle of helping a customer, my cell phone started vibrating. So I told the customer to give me a moment. Thankfully Amir was still in the supply closet, so I was able to answer the caller in privacy. "Hello," I said quietly.

"Hi, this is Priscilla. Am I speaking to Misty?"

"Yes, you are," I said cheerfully because I knew in the next hour and a half I would be having an interview with her, and before I walked out of there she was gonna give me the job.

"Hello there, I hope I am not calling you at a bad time."

"Absolutely not," I replied.

"Well, I'm calling you because something came up and I won't be able to interview today. But if you can come tomorrow, I would greatly appreciate it."

Disappointed by the sudden change of plans, I sighed heavily and said, "I was looking forward to meeting you today."

"I know. I was looking forward to meeting you as well. But don't worry about it, we will get a chance to meet each other tomorrow. Okay?"

"Okay," I said and then I pressed the End button.

"You are not supposed to be on a personal phone call while you're on the clock," Sanjay's brother said, coming from out of nowhere, as though I didn't even know he had been in the supply closet. He's one sneaky-ass coward. I wished I could bitch-slap him right now. That would definitely take some of this pressure off my ass. One more day before I could get out of this hellhole. And when that day did arrive, I was gonna tell Sanjay and his brother to kiss my ass.

"Yeah, whatever," I commented and then I turned my back to him and got back to work.

When three o'clock rolled around, it surprised me when Amir told me that he was closing the store for the rest of the day. That was music to my ears, because normally the store didn't close until seven PM. So he was giving me four hours off. I definitely didn't see that coming. And I didn't question it. I quickly grabbed my handbag, my jacket, my car keys, and then I headed out of there.

17

THE INTERVIEW

The following morning, I dragged myself out of bed, got dressed, and headed to work. On my way there, I decided to call Jillian. She had tried calling me over a dozen times last night, but I was so upset with her after she made a fool of herself in front of our grandmother the night before, I didn't want to hear her voice. Today was different, though. I had time to think about it. Not only that, you can't talk to people when you're still upset about something. But I'm good today.

"I see you're finally calling me back," she commented right after she answered my call.

"Oh hush. What are you doing?" I replied.

"I'm in my bedroom lying down on my bed trying to figure out what I'm gonna do today."

"You need to be looking for a job."

"Don't worry about me. I'm good over here."

"Well, I'm not good. You caused Grandma to fuss at me about you being high the other night. She is really upset with me right now."

"Don't worry about her. She'll be all right."

"Yeah, that's what you say. But before I left the house

the other night, she said she'll cut me off if she finds out that I gave you more prescription drugs. And speaking of which, why do you put me on speakerphone when I call you? She said she hears all of our conversations."

"No, she doesn't. She just said that so you can fall into her trap. And the crazy part about it is that you believed her."

"Look, Jillian, I'm not trying to hear anything you're saying right now. Grandma told me to stop giving you drugs and that's what I'm gonna do."

"I wish you would," she dared me in a playful manner.

"I can show you better than I can tell you," I told her, and then I changed the subject by saying, "I got a job interview today."

"Where?"

"At this pharmacy not too far from the one I work at now."

"Look, I know you're ready to get out of there, but remember we gotta hit your job before you leave, so let's not be hasty."

"Girl, I know what we planned to do. So calm down," I told her.

"So, how's your boss treating you?"

"He hasn't been there. His brother has been filling in for him for the past two days."

"What, is he sick or something? I mean, you guys do have enough drugs around there for him not to get sick."

"You're absolutely right about that," I agreed. "But I was told that he's out of the country."

"Wow! So, when does he come back?"

"I was told last night."

"Is that where you're on your way to?"

"Yep."

"Well, keep your head up and don't let that asshole get underneath your skin."

"Trust me, I won't. Oh, and speaking of which, while I was at work yesterday, UPS dropped off a ton of prescription drugs and instead of Sanjay's brother stocking them in the supply closet, he packed the smaller boxes into a bigger box and left them on the floor, outside of the closet. So, when I asked him about what he was doing, he got sarcastic with me and in so many words he told me that I needed to get to work and not worry what the fuck he was doing."

"He cursed at you?"

"No, he didn't. But the way he said it, he might as well have."

"What do you think he did with those boxes of pills?"

"He took them out of the pharmacy."

"Wow! You're really working with some big-time drug dealers," Jillian said, and then she burst into laughter.

"Shut up! It's not funny."

"Yes, it is. I know one thing, if I was working there, I would be stealing all kinds of drugs from there. I mean, I would have it going on. And the awesome part about it is that they wouldn't be able to call the cops on me because they're doing the same shit I would be doing. Everybody in that pharmacy would be getting paid big bucks. Speaking of which, how much money do you think they're making off all those fucking jobs?"

"I heard Sanjay tell the cop the other day that the street value of the drugs that were 'stolen' the other day was over a half million dollars."

"Are you fucking kidding me?!" Jillian yelled through the phone with excitement.

"Will you stop? You're hurting my damn ear."

"To hell with your ear. We need to get our plan in motion. Shit, I would love to have a piece of that half-million-dollar pie. Do you know what I could do with half a million dollars?"

"I'm sure you're going to tell me."

"You got-damn right," she said and then she paused. "First, I would get me a Mercedes Benz truck. I'd go shopping and get a whole new wardrobe. And then I'd get me a diamond necklace and earrings like the rappers be wearing."

"Sounds like you'll blow through that money in one week."

"No, I wouldn't. I'd still have a lot of money left to play with."

"Yeah, okay," I said nonchalantly because I knew she'd throw that money down the drain in a matter of five, six days. It's good to fantasize about places you'd go and how much you'd spend. That's all a part of dreaming.

"You know what, Misty? We need to set the bar high when we make the move on your job. Because real shit, if your boss robbed his own store and got away with a half million dollars' worth of drugs, I know we can do it too."

"Are you out of your fucking mind? I wouldn't dare let you take that much."

"Then how much do you think we should take?"

"I'm thinking like, fifty thousand. You know, something that'll give us a nice cushion to sit on."

"Hell nah! We should at least take one hundred grand. That way, the guys who are running in there could get a nice chunk of the pie too. Because on some real shit, I'm not trying to split up fifty grand worth of drugs. If we're gonna do this, we gotta go out with a bang," Jillian reasoned.

"Oh, I don't know about that. But I'll consider it."

"Yeah, you better because you deserve this."

Jillian and I talked up to the moment I arrived at the pharmacy. I told her I'd call her again after I had my interview with the lady at the other pharmacy. After she told me that she loved me, we ended the call.

When I got out of my car, I noticed that Sanjay's car wasn't anywhere in sight. But his brother's car was. Knots in my stomach formed at that instant. I swear, I wanted to get back in my car and leave. "Don't do it, Misty. Don't let this guy win. Go in there and show him that you don't fear him. Let him know that you can stand your ground no matter what kind of environment. Show him where you're from," I said, giving myself a pep talk as I strolled toward the building.

After I entered the store I saw Amir standing behind the counter looking down at the computer that Sanjay normally worked from. I was shocked when he looked up from the monitor and said good morning. I greeted him back and then I went straight into question mode. "Where is Sanjay? I thought you said that he was going to be here today," I pointed out.

"He's still out of the country because we had a family situation and he has to take care of it."

"Aren't you his blood brother?"

"Yes,"

"Well, then why aren't you there too?"

He got defensive. "Because I'm supposed to be here."

"Do you know when he'll be back?"

"In a couple of days. Now stop asking me questions and get to work," he instructed me. Right off the rip, I've pissed him off. I know today is going to be one rocking day.

As instructed, I got to work, processing the online prescription orders. But when I started processing a customer's prescription order for Lormat, I noticed in the system that we were out of it. Now this puzzled me, because I remember seeing a case of it, stacked on other boxes that were on the floor near the supply closet. In my head, I knew Sanjay's brother packed them up and took them out of the store, but I felt like I needed to put his ass on front street and ask him where they were. So, I got up the gumption and asked him why the system hadn't been updated. "Can you tell me if we're out of Lormat? Because I don't see them in the system."

"If it's not in there then we don't have it," he said coldly.

"Well, that's strange because I saw a whole box on the floor yesterday while you were in the supply closet," I pointed out while I searched his face for guilt.

"That box was empty."

"Are you sure? Because I saw a UPS tracking ticket on it, like it had just come in with yesterday's bulk order."

"Look, the box was empty. And if we don't have that brand in the system, then give the customer the generic brand," he hissed. He was getting upset with me.

"We don't have any more of the generic brand either."

"Well, write it down and I'll order some later."

"Do we have any Percocet, because I don't see that in the system either," I said, pressing the issue.

"If it is not in the system then we don't have it."

"That's strange, because I saw three boxes of that yesterday too."

"Those boxes were empty too," he insisted.

"Did Sanjay tell you what was stolen in the robbery?"

"Yes, he did."

"Well, it seems like we can't keep the most potent prescription drugs in here," I commented and waited for him to say something.

"My brother told me about the drugs you stole from here. And if it were up to me, you would've been fired. So, don't question me anymore about the supply of drugs we have. If it's not in the system, then we don't have it," he barked.

I don't know why I was surprised that Sanjay told him about the bottle of pills I took. I guess hearing it coming out of his mouth was the shocking part. My first thought was to tell him to go to hell, but I decided against it because I had an overall goal here. And once that was completed, then I could make my exit.

18

DAMN! DAMN! DAMN!

This interview couldn't have come at a better time. I told Amir that I was going on my lunch break and left without hearing him say okay. The pharmacy where I applied for a job online was like three miles away from where I was already working, which wouldn't affect my driving time.

My adrenaline was pumping mighty fast because I knew that when Priscilla got to meet me she would find out that I was going to be an asset to that business, that when I left that place I was going to have the job.

After I parked my car, I took one last look at my face just to make sure my makeup wasn't flawed, I played with my hair a little bit, and then I said to myself, "Misty, go get that job, girl."

Armed with intelligence, willingness to make my life better, and wanting to be prosperous, I held my head high and strolled into the pharmacy. I was greeted by one of the store clerks, and then I was escorted to the back of the store. Surprisingly, Priscilla wasn't there. The guy that ended up interviewing me told me she was out today because of a family emergency.

I was bummed out that I didn't get to meet her, but it didn't matter because my interview went very well and the gentleman offered me the job and told me I could start working for them as soon as seven days from now. I accepted the offer, shook his hand, and told him thank you while I was leaving.

The moment the fresh air from outside hit my face, I inhaled it and then I exhaled. "You did good, Misty," I told myself after I popped my collar.

But then out of nowhere two white men approached me. I knew they were plainclothes cops after I looked at them from head to toe. I was standing outside near my car when they approached me.

"Hi, Misty, my name is Special Agent Sims and this is Agent Montclair. And we are investigating Sanjay Malik," the agent said.

As if I'd been hit by a ton of bricks, my legs buckled and I almost fell down on the ground. Both agents saw me about to lose my balance. They grabbed ahold of my arm. "Are you all right?" Sims asked me as he held on to me gently.

"Yes, I'm fine. Thank you."

"Can we talk for a minute?" the same agent said.

"That depends on what you want to talk about," I said as I leaned up against my car.

"Well, first of all, we are here to talk to you because we're investigating your boss."

"Yes, I know that already. What does that have to do with me?"

"We know you've been working for him for a few months now. So, we know you've seen some things while working there."

"Listen, you guys, yes I've been working there for a few months, but I don't know how I can help you. I mean, it seems like you're doing good by yourself. Especially after telling me that you know how long I've been working there."

"Misty, your boss is running an illegal prescription drug enterprise. So, we're building a case against him and his brother so we can make the arrests and shut them down."

"Look, I know nothing about that," I quickly lied.

"Misty, cut it out. We know you've seen a lot of things, so were asking for your help."

"But I can't help you," I protested. I did not want to be implicated in anything Sanjay had going on.

"Do you know that we can book you on charges too?"

"What charges? I haven't done anything wrong," I spat.

"We know you've been taking prescription drugs behind Sanjay's back. We also know that he told you that he knew you did it too."

Hearing these DEA agents tell me that they knew I stole drugs from the pharmacy and that they wanted me to rat Sanjay out so they could arrest him, formed over a dozen knots in my stomach. Those knots in my stomach tossed and turned with every word these guys uttered. *Please tell me that this is a dream.*

"What exactly do you want me to do?"

"We want you to wear a wire and a hidden camera. So we can record everything that goes on in there."

"So, what exactly are you trying to catch on camera?" I wanted to know.

"We want you to engage in conversations with your boss and his brother about the drugs they are selling. And we want you to record them taking boxes out of there and stashing them in the trunk of their cars."

"And how long do you want me to do that?"

"For as long as we need you to."

"Well, this is not gonna happen because I just got a new job. And I start working there next week," I explained to them.

"You're gonna have to call them and tell them that you cannot take the job."

"I'm not doing that. Do you know how bad that would look for me? I don't want to work with Sanjay and his brother anymore after this week. I'm ready to get out of there. That place stresses me out," I started complaining. "Do you know that Sanjay and his brother both got smacked around with guns at the store a few days ago? That shit scared me to death. You want me to still work in that environment? What if those guys come back and pistol-whip me too? Are you gonna run in there and save me? Fuck no! You didn't save them, so I know you wouldn't run into the pharmacy and save me," I continued while my heart rate exploded.

"Those guys that smacked Sanjay and his brother around are part of a mafia in the District of Columbia."

"Wait, did you just say mafia?"

"Yes, I did."

"So, you want me to help you bring down Sanjay and his brother and possibly those two guys that are in a mafia? Are you out of your fucking mind?" I roared. These two idiots standing in front of me had some nerve asking me to help them bring down my boss, his brother, and possibly some guys from a mafia in DC. Those badge-wearing motherfuckers sounded like they were on drugs. I refused to help them with their case.

"It's either help us with our investigation or we will charge you with stealing the bottle of Percocet and you'll serve three to five years in federal prison."

I panicked at their accusation. I didn't know what kind of evidence they had on me, and I didn't want to find out. "Tell me you are kidding? You will charge me with prescription drug theft because I don't want to help you?"

"Yes, that's exactly right. We lock up those who commit crimes. And you committed a crime when you stole the prescription drugs."

"So why didn't you arrest me then? Why wait until right now? Because you know this is bullshit!"

"Listen, Misty, we know you're upset right now because we're throwing all of this on you at one time. So here, take my card and give me a call by tomorrow. At that time, I'm gonna need to know where you stand in this investigation. If you decide that you aren't going to help us, then clean out your house, because we're going to bring charges against you," he said and then he walked away.

I watched both DEA agents as they walked toward their black Yukon SUV. I wanted to scream in the air as loud as I could, but I knew it wouldn't help me in this situation. I had to admit that I fucked up my life over some damn prescription drugs. So, what was I gonna do now?

When I went back to work, I found Amir helping one of our regular customers. He didn't say hi to me when I came back into the pharmacy and I didn't care. The customer said hi though. After I greeted him, I put my things away and went back to work. What's so crazy is that those knots I had in my stomach wouldn't go anywhere. They stayed in the pit of my stomach and continued to toss and turn. I felt like walking away from this place and never looking back, but I knew I couldn't do it. Those DEA agents had me by the balls. And there was nothing I could do about it, and that hurt my soul.

Amir let me off two hours early today. And boy, did I need it. I hopped in my car and I sped off in the direction of my grandmother's house. I knew she was still mad at me about me giving Jillian the prescription drugs, but I didn't care about her feelings today. I had something majorly going on in my life and I needed someone to talk to. Jillian was the first person that came to mind.

I called her while I was driving in her direction and she told me she was home, so I was happy about that. Instead of going to my grandmother's house, I asked Jillian to come outside and get in my car so we could talk without my grandmother eavesdropping. I couldn't risk her hearing anything I had going on with Sanjay, his brother, and the DEA agents.

"What's going on? And why you looking like that?" Jillian said immediately after she got inside my car.

"You're not gonna believe this," I started off.

"What happened?"

"When I was leaving from my interview today, two DEA agents approached me while I was walking to my car."

"What the fuck did they say?" Jillian asked me. She looked spooked, like I was about to tell her that they're investigating her or something.

"They told me that they are investigating Sanjay and his brother for dealing illegal prescription drugs."

"Oh my God! Are you serious right now?"

"Of course I am, stupid."

"What else did they say?"

"They said that they need my help to arrest them and that if I don't do it, they're gonna charge me and put me away."

"They can't do that!" my cousin spat.

"Yes, they can, Jillian. They said they know about the big bottle of Percocet that I stole from there last week. So, if I don't cooperate and help them, they're gonna lock me up too."

"Oh my God, Cousin. I can't believe that this shit is happening."

"Me either."

"So, what are you gonna do?"

"I don't want to do anything. I just want all of this shit to be over with."

"I wish it were that simple."

"Me too."

"Tell me exactly what they want you to do." Jillian pressed the issue.

"They want me to wear wire and a small camera and

record everything that goes on behind the counter," I started explaining. "They want me to have a dialogue with Sanjay and his brother about the drugs. But that's not gonna happen. They don't like having conversations with me."

"Did you tell them that?"

"Yes, I did. They told me to try anyway."

"Do they know what they want you to do is very dangerous?"

"Of course, they do. They don't care. They just want to get an arrest by any means necessary."

"Did they say anything about me or my homeboy that copped the bottle of Percocet from us?"

"Nah! His name didn't come up. Their only concern is arresting Sanjay, his brother, and whoever else they deal with. Speaking of which, remember when I told you that I saw two guys smacking Sanjay in the head and put a gun in his brother's back?"

"Yeah, what about it?"

"The DEA agent told me that those guys are part of a mafia from DC."

Jillian's eyes doubled in size. "Get the fuck out of here! They told you that?"

"Yeah, they did."

"I don't know, Misty, I don't feel good about this."

"Neither do I."

Jillian turned around in her seat and looked forward. I saw her quietly staring through my windshield. I knew my cousin like the back of my hand, so when she did this I knew she was in complete thought mode.

"What are you thinking about?" I didn't hesitate to ask her.

"Did the agent tell you when they wanted you to start wearing the wire?"

"No. But he did tell me that I need to give him an answer tomorrow."

"An answer about what?"

"If I was gonna help them or not."

"You know we are going to have to plan the heist to a tee. We can't mess up for nothing in the world."

"What do you mean, we can't mess up? You're still trying to rob the store even after I told you that the DEA agents are investigating them?"

"Yeah, why not?"

"Because we can get in a lot more trouble. The DEA is closely monitoring that business."

"Look, what you're saying is right, but we can't walk away from this. If anything, knowing that the DEA is watching your boss only helps us more. We could've went in that place and robbed it, not even knowing that the DEA was investigating it. With you working with them, you're gonna know exactly where they are and how long they're going to be there. It's a blessing that they approached you. Do you know how catastrophic it would've been if we were robbin' the place and they were watching us the whole time? They could've arrested us on the spot and we would've been in jail right along with your boss and his brother. See how that works?"

"God has nothing to do with this. This is all your doing," I reminded her.

"Has your boss come back from out of town yet?" Jillian asked me.

"No. His brother says that he's still out of the country on family business."

"Did he say how long he was going to be out of the country?"

"Not really. I was in the middle of filling a prescription order for one of our customers and noticed that we didn't have a few meds in stock or in the system, so I started questioning him about certain drugs. He come up with different reasons why we didn't have them. So, I told him that I saw the boxes of meds on the floor near the closet.

And he says that those were empty boxes. I went even further and told him that those weren't empty boxes because they had new UPS tracking tickets on them. And when I said that, he got a little upset with me and told me to mind my business. I did get a chance to tell him to reorder more, because if he doesn't then we won't be able to fill our customers' prescriptions."

"What did he say?"

"Nothing but *okay*."

"Do you really believe that drugs were in those boxes?"

"Fuck yeah! I do. I know what new order boxes look like when the UPS driver drops them off. I've been cracking those boxes open and filling up the supply closet with them ever since I started working there."

"Think he's gonna order more drugs?"

"He has no choice. So, if he puts in the reorder today, we'd get more by tomorrow or the day after."

"We need to figure out when would be the right time to run up in there."

"Is that all you're thinking about? Shit, I just got approached by a law enforcement officer about helping him bust my boss, and all you wanna talk about is how you're gonna get your piece of the pie," I argued.

Jillian began to aggravate my nerves with her bullshit-ass speak about how much she loves me and that when either one of us gets into a situation, we're in it together.

"You know I'm always talking shit. And I may even sound selfish sometimes. But you know I will always have your back. You're like my sister. Niggas in the street already think you're my sister, so that's how it's gonna stay. You hear me?!" she said, and then she leaned over and kissed me on the cheek. "What time are you calling that agent?"

"Probably in the morning, why?"

"Because I wanna be with you when you do. I wanna

hear how they're gonna execute their investigation. See how they plan to orchestrate this shit! Remember, you and I are in this shit together."

"Please don't tell your homeboy about this whole DEA thing," I begged her.

"No worries. I won't. Now let me get out of here. Gotta make some runs. So, I'll call you later," Jillian said and then she got out of my car.

By the time I got home, I was too mentally tired to do anything, so I took off my clothes and shoes and took a long, hot bath. My cell phone rang over four different times, but I ignored it. I needed a bath and I wasn't going to let anyone interrupt me.

19

I JUST WANT TO BE LEFT ALONE

The moment after I got out of my warm bath and went to my bedroom, I slid on my bathrobe and grabbed my cell phone from my dresser. Next to my cell phone was the DEA agent's business card. I placed it next to my phone because he would be the first call I made in the morning.

Immediately after I picked up my cell phone I looked at the caller ID I saw that my mother called me once, Terrell called me twice from a different number, and I don't know who was the other caller because their phone number was blocked.

I sat on the edge of my bed, contemplating on whether or not I should call my mother back. She drained me a lot of the time when she and I engaged in a serious conversation. And what I don't particularly like is when she tries to act like the victim all the time. That mess just eats away at me. As a matter of fact, it chips away the layers of love for her I'm still trying to hold on to. She doesn't make it easy for me. So I asked God for patience to deal with her on a daily basis.

After getting up the gumption to dial her cell phone number back, a private call appeared on my caller ID. I took a deep breath and spoke in a whisper-like tone, "Hello," I said, not sure who to expect on the line.

"Don't be trying to act like you're asleep," Terrell replied in a humorous fashion, and then he chuckled.

"I wasn't asleep but I am lying down."

"Who's there with you?"

"Nobody."

"Well, get up and open your front door."

"Do what?" I spat.

"I'm standing outside your front door, so come and open it."

"Terrell, why are you standing outside my apartment?" I asked him. The thought of him standing outside of my front door irritated the hell out of me.

"Because I wanna see you."

"Terrell, I'm already in the bed."

"That's even better."

"Come on now, Terrell, let me get some rest and I'll call you in the morning." I tried to reason with him.

"Misty, I am not leaving until I see you."

I so badly wanted to tell him to go fuck himself. But I knew he'd fly off the handle if I did, so I stood up from my bed, told him to give me a minute, and disconnected our call. I tossed my bathrobe into my clothes closet and grabbed a set of pajamas and a pair of panties from my dresser drawer, slipped them on and then I headed to the front door. As soon as I opened it he gave me a huge-ass smile. I'm sure he thought that he looked handsome, but I thought he looked really creepy.

"Are you gonna let me in?" He didn't waste any time.

"Before I let you in, I want you to know that you're not spending the night. Do you understand?"

"Yeah, I'm cool with that."

I stepped to the side of the door and gave him enough space to walk by me. "Whatcha cook today? It smells good in here."

"Cut it out, Terrell. You know damn well you don't smell no food in here," I told him after I closed the front door and locked it.

"I do. I'm not lying." He smiled.

I wanted to smile with him because he's a handsome-ass man. Always looked good, smelled good, and he always kept plenty of money in his pockets. The quality that initially attracted me to him was that he was very funny. I'm talking Dave Chappelle funny. We used to have a ball with one another when we first started dating a few years ago. He and I even talked about getting married, but that all went down the drain after I caught him cheating on me. I took him back a couple of times. But nothing got better. It actually felt like it got worse. Thankfully, I was able to keep my sanity after I broke it off for good.

I took a seat on the love seat the same time he sat down on the other sofa. "So, do you think you could give me another chance?" he asked me, trying to give me the most alluring facial expression he could muster up. He was looking a little bit like the actor Omari Hardwick from *Power*.

"Terrell, you know I can't go back to that life we used to have together. I was unhappy and depressed for most of the time we were a couple."

"Look, Misty, I changed, so I'll never take you through that shit anymore."

"Terrell, you've been singing this same song as long as I've been knowing you."

"Why don't you just give me a chance to show you?"

"That's not gonna happen," I said adamantly.

He slid to the edge of the sofa. "You're fucking with another nigga, huh?"

"No, I am not. Jumping into another relationship is not on the to-do list for me."

"Where is your cell phone?"

"It's in my bedroom. Why?" I asked him. But instead of answering my question, he hopped off the sofa and ran into my bedroom. I jumped up from my chair and ran down behind him. By the time I walked into my bedroom, Terrell was standing next to my dresser with DEA Agent Sims's business card. "Yo, what's up with this? You dating a DEA agent now?" he questioned me.

"No, I am not, stupid," I replied and snatched the card from his hand.

"Well, if you ain't dating that dude, then what are you doing with his card?"

I sighed heavily. "It's complicated," I told him.

"Stuff ain't complicated until you make it that way. Now tell me why you got that dude's business card?"

I hesitated for a second and then I said, "If I tell you why I have that agent's number, you gotta promise me that you won't tell anyone."

"Yeah, a'ight. So, what's up?" he asked as he stood in front of me. He held on to the DEA agent's business card while he gave me his undivided attention.

"You know I work at the pharmacy, right?"

"Yeah."

"Well, when I was leaving work earlier today, two DEA agents walked up to me before I got in my car and told me that my boss and his brother are selling prescription drugs and making millions of dollars doing it."

"And what do you have to do with it?"

"They want me to talk to them and tell them if I know or see anything going on while I'm there."

"So those dudes want you to snitch?"

"Essentially, yes."

"Hell nah! Tell them dudes that you ain't no informant."

"I already told them that."

"If you told them that, then why do you have his business card?"

"He told me to take it just in case I change my mind."

"Well, call him back and tell him that you ain't doing it."

"Already did it."

"What did he say?"

"He didn't say anything. I got his voicemail, so I left him a message," I lied.

Terrell looked at me and then he shook his head as if he was appalled at my actions. After he threw the business card back on my dresser, he looked at me and said, "So your boss is really making millions selling prescription drugs?"

"That's what the DEA agent said."

"Damn! That's some good money. If I was into that game, I would surely hit them up."

"Stop, Terrell, this isn't funny. It's some serious shit going on at my job and I really don't want to work there anymore."

"Quit."

"That's what I'm trying to do. I applied for a couple of jobs in the area, so hopefully I'll get a new job soon," I told him even though I had already been on an interview today and was given the position. I figured if I told him about the job offer then he'd know that I agreed to help the DEA agent bring Sanjay and his brother down.

"Are you gonna tell your boss that the DEA agent wants to rat him out?"

"No, I am not. I'm trying to stay away from this thing as far as I can. I don't want him to know that I talked to the DEA agent and I don't want the DEA agent to know that I told him what they said. It will be in my best interest if I let the chips fall where they may."

Terrell and I talked for another thirty minutes or so after we got off the subject of the DEA agent's business card. We ended up going back into the living room. I thought that I was going to have to push him out of my apartment, but surprisingly he got a phone call and left. The person that called him sounded like a woman. After he got off the phone, I asked him about it, and he denied it, of course. I laughed at him because he just told me that he'd changed, but in reality, I didn't care who called him. My point was proved and that's all I needed.

20

I'M SO OVER THIS SHIT

I called Agent Sims the following morning and told him that I would help, but he had to guarantee that I wouldn't get charged with anything. He sounded very pleased to know that I decided to give him a helping hand. "What's your lunch schedule for today?" he asked me.

"I normally go in around eight, but today I don't have to clock in until eleven," I told him.

"Good, that'll give us two hours to work with," he said.

"What do you mean? What happens in two hours?"

"We're gonna need to come by your house and wire you up."

"I wish there was another way of doing this. I mean, why can't you put cameras on the inside of the store?"

"If we did that, then we wouldn't need you."

"How long is it going to take to plant the wire and camera on me?"

"Not long. Twenty minutes, if that."

"So, what time are you guys coming over here?"

"We can be there within the hour, so be dressed and ready to go."

"Okay," I said nonchalantly and then I hung up.

* * *

The timing couldn't have been more perfect. As soon as I got out of the shower and got dressed, both DEA agents, Montclair and Sims, and a female wire specialist arrived at my front door. She was a little Caucasian woman who resembled a little boy. I'm talking no breasts or curves at all. After they greeted me we settled in the front room of my apartment, they introduced the woman to me as Gail Horn, and she started the process of wiring me up.

"I'm gonna tell you something right now, but I don't want you to get alarmed," Agent Sims said.

"Why do I feel like I'm about to get alarmed?" I replied while the woman began to cover my waist area with a wire that was connected to a camera that looked like a small button.

Agent Sims sat on the edge of my sofa and said, "We've got reason to believe that Sanjay has either been kidnapped or is dead."

A sharp pain shot through my heart and I instantly became weak as my knees buckled. The female agent grabbed me by the arm. "Are you okay?" she asked.

"Just give me a minute," I said and pushed her away from me. I sat down on the love seat and buried my face in my hands.

"I'm sorry I had to spring this on you like that. But we just got the intel late last night. And we couldn't call you and tell you on the phone because that's not our protocol, which is why I thought it would be best if I told you in person," Agent Sims said.

I looked up from my hands. "Tell me the truth, is he dead or alive?"

"We're trying to find that out right now. We do know for a fact that he has been kidnapped, which is why he hasn't been back to the pharmacy. See, Sanjay owes a lot of money to those guys you saw beat him up. But apparently, he didn't get their money to them fast enough so they decided to kidnap him. Now that Sanjay is gone,

Amir is left with the task of coming up with the rest of the money his brother owes, which is why he's taking huge boxes of prescriptions to pay off the ransom. And we figure that if he doesn't come up with it soon, they may kill Amir or his family next."

"What's gonna happen if Sanjay's dead?"

"We're going to take action and bring the perpetrators to justice."

"If he's dead, do you know who killed him?" I spat. I was about to blow a fuse. I mean, how could these fucking idiots drop this bomb on me like this?

"We're trying to find that information out right now."

"Okay, let's just say he was kidnapped, do you have any idea who kidnapped him?"

"We're thinking it was probably those guys you saw shoving the gun in Amir's back as they pushed the store."

"I take it they're part of the mafia from DC?"

"As far as we know, yes."

"And you want me to get information from guys like that! Are you out of your fucking mind? Those guys will kill me if they find out that I am wearing a wire!"

"Misty, what you need to do right now is calm down. Sanjay may not be dead. . . ."

"Oh yeah, he may be kidnapped!" I replied sarcastically.

"Yes, exactly."

"But you're acting like being kidnapped isn't a serious matter. No matter how you look at it, those people are fucking dangerous. And I want no parts of this," I roared, and then I stood up on my feet.

"I'm sorry, but you have no choice. I mean, if you prefer to go to jail for two to five years, then by all means. But if you wanna stay out here on the streets then you've gotta do your part," he threatened me.

My eyes turned fiery red. My blood started boiling. I wanted to hawk and spit in his face. The disregard for my safety was not his concern. All he wanted me to do was wear a fucking wire so I could help him bust two Middle Eastern guys who're dealing illegal drugs. I've definitely been dealt a shitty hand of cards. "As soon as I get the information you guys need to arrest those fuckers, will you leave me alone once and for all?"

"Yes, we will."

"Come on, lady, hook this shit up so I can get out of here," I instructed her and then I held my arms up.

I stood there with my eyes closed, beating myself up as I thought about how I got myself into this bullshit. All I wanted to do was work in the pharmaceutical industry and become a pharmacist. I'd had this dream since I was a child. Helping people with pain management issues was and would always be a passion of mine. So, to be caught up in this bullshit by stealing fucking prescription pills makes me so mad with myself.

Immediately after the woman finished taping me up, she gave me a tutorial on how the wire and camera worked. "The broach is your camera, so you don't have to worry about that. It looks fashionable, so Amir won't suspect it. As far as the wire, I hid it behind the broach, so while the camera is filming, the wire will serve as the recorder."

"Is it secure? Because if it comes off while I'm standing around him, he's gonna know what's up," I pointed out.

"It's safe and secure, so don't worry yourself."

"Easy for you to say. You aren't wearing it." I sucked my teeth.

"Misty, you're gonna be fine. We're gonna be set up in a van outside the pharmacy, so we're gonna see who comes in and who goes out."

"Am I supposed to feel safe knowing that you guys are outside? It only takes a second to pull a gun out and shoot someone in the head with it. By then, it would be too late for me."

"Don't worry, you will be fine."

"Yeah! What the fuck ever. Tell me anything." I gritted my teeth.

21

MY FIRST DAY WIRED UP

Before the agents left my apartment, they gave me more instructions about how to maneuver around in the store and how to act when Amir and I exchange dialogue.

"Just act normal and you'll be fine," the woman said.

The last instruction the agent said to me was, "Don't forget to inquire about Sanjay's whereabouts."

"You know perfectly well that guy isn't gonna tell me shit. He acts like he barely wants to talk to me."

"Ask him anyway. We wanna see his body movement and facial expression when you ask him this time around."

"I'm telling you right now, if that guy touches me, I am going to go the fuck off! So, be ready to bust that damn door down."

"I told you not to worry."

"And I believe you less than I did the other times you said it."

Agents Sims and Montclair and Gail Horn walked toward the front door and I opened the door for them. Horn and Montclair walked out of my apartment slowly, giving Sims time to catch up with them. But he walked over the threshold and then he turned around. "Smile and you're gonna be fine," he said.

"Man, if you don't get the hell out of my face—" I said, and right before I closed my front door, I heard a voice so I looked over Agent Sims's shoulder and saw Terrell walking across the grass.

"Don't leave. Stay right there," I heard Terrell say. And boy was he pissed off.

"Isn't that your ex-boyfriend?" the agent asked me.

"How do you know that?" I replied.

"Believe me, I know a lot of things."

"Oh my God! What does he want?" I uttered softly.

"Don't tell him why we're here. It would blow our investigation."

"Too late, he already knows," I said quickly before Terrell could hear me.

"So, is this the DEA agent you were telling me about?" Terrell asked after he stopped directly in front of us.

"Yes." I glanced at the agent to get his reaction.

"So, you want my girlfriend to snitch on her boss, huh?" Terrell asked boldly as he poked his chest out.

"No, not exactly."

"I'm not your girlfriend, Terrell."

"Look, let's not talk about that right now," he said and then he turned his focus back on Agent Sims. "Then what do you call it? 'Cause when you get a person to help arrest somebody, that's what it's called," Terrell continued sarcastically.

"Terrell, let's not do this now. He's trying to leave."

"Not until he tells me what he wants with you. Now you already told me that he wants you to help him get your boss down at the pharmacy locked up. So, why can't he say the same thing to me?"

"Because now is not the time nor place," I reasoned and then I grabbed his arm and tugged on it.

"I guess my time is up here. Call me if you need anything," Agent Sims said.

"Nah, don't leave now! If you man enough to ask my

girl to snitch on her boss man, be man enough to tell me about it too," Terrell yelled.

"You are fucking embarrassing me. Do you think I want my neighbors to know what's going on? And are you trying to get me killed?" I snapped, and then I tried to slam my front door in his face. He blocked me from doing it and then he pushed his way into my apartment. So I stormed down the hall toward my bedroom.

When I walked into my bedroom, he blocked me from closing that door too. I had no other recourse but to go into my bathroom and lock the door. He stood on the outside of the bathroom door while I sat on the edge of the bathtub.

"Look, baby, I'm sorry if I embarrassed you. But you told me last night that you weren't going to help them. You said that you were gonna call them today and tell that dude no. So how do you think I should act when I pull up and see those motherfuckers coming out of your apartment?"

"I understand what you're saying, but that still doesn't give you the right to cause the scene that you did."

"Misty, those fucking agents don't give a damn about you. All they care about is locking niggas up and throwing away the keys," he continued.

"Terrell, don't you think I know that already?"

"You don't act like you do."

"Well, I do," I yelled through the bathroom door.

"Are you gonna help them or not?" Terrell pressed the issue.

"I have no choice." I began to sob lightly. I didn't want him to hear me.

"Yes, you do have a choice!" he yelled back through the door.

"I stole some pills from the store and they know about it. They said that if I didn't help them, I would go to jail for two to five years."

"You did what?"

"I stole some Percocet for Jillian and they found out. They're using that against me."

"Why the fuck did you do that?"

"You know she had that surgery a while ago and her doctor stopped prescribing the Vicodin. He stopped giving her pain meds altogether, so I'd take a few pills here and there so she wouldn't hurt anymore," I said, but what I told him wasn't the whole truth. I figured if I told him the real amount that I took from my job, I wouldn't stop hearing his mouth.

"How did they find out?"

"I don't know. I'm thinking they got cameras in a few places around somewhere."

"Damn, Misty, I'm so fucking mad with you right now."

"Yeah, well join the fucking club because I'm still mad at you about some shit you've done too," I said as I wiped the tears that were falling down my face.

"What did they say they want you to do?"

"Just to plant a bug near Sanjay's office and near his computer," I lied. I couldn't tell this negro that I was wearing a wire and camera. I wouldn't hear the end of it.

"When do they want you to plant it?"

"Tomorrow when I go to work," I lied once again. I couldn't tell him that I was starting my informant job today. He would want to know more specifics and he'd even ask could he see the bugging device I would plant. He was a very inquisitive man. He would question me all day if I'd allowed him.

Terrell and I talked a little bit more, but I came out of the bathroom not too long after I calmed down and pulled myself together. On our way out of my apartment, he tried to give me a hug but I pushed him back. I couldn't chance him feeling the wire taped on me. He did ask me for a kiss on the cheek and I allowed him to do it. Someone would probably look at that and think that I was going to get back with him, but that's not what that was. With all the mess that was going on around me, I needed to feel a sense of love. And that's to say I wanted Terrell to love me, I wanted to feel the touch of someone other than the hands of the white lady that just left my apartment. Feeling alone in this world isn't a nice feeling. Hopefully, after all this is over, I can take me a nice trip somewhere, to clear my head.

I was nervous as fuck when I walked into the pharmacy. I was scared shitless, especially after finding out that Sanjay was kidnapped and that he also might be dead. I couldn't believe what I'd gotten myself into.

As usual, Amir was standing by Sanjay's computer like he was working on something. My only thought was that he was either ordering more drugs or processing prescription orders. I'm sure he thought I was going to say hello to him, but I refused to do it this morning. With all the shit I knew about him and his brother, I was not the least bit concerned about getting along with him. And Amir was playing a very dangerous game with those mafia guys, so I wanted to stay as far away as I possibly could.

"There's a few prescription orders online, so fill those and then I'm gonna need you to go to the bathroom and clean it up."

"Clean up the bathroom? Sanjay has a cleaning crew that does that."

"Sanjay isn't here anymore. So you're gonna do it from now on."

"Wait a minute, did I just hear you say that Sanjay isn't gonna be here anymore?" I asked, because I wanted him to repeat himself. I even turned around toward him so that the camera and wire I was wearing could get him in full scope.

"No, I didn't, now get back to work," he instructed me in a very disrespectful way.

"Yes, you did. You just said that he wasn't going to be here anymore so it is my duty to clean up the bathroom." I pressed the issue while I became nauseous. This guy just confessed to me that Sanjay wasn't going to be here anymore. He said it out of his own mouth. And now he was trying to make it seem like I was hearing things.

"Don't question me, young lady. Get to work or this is your last day," he threatened me.

I wanted to get away from this place as fast as I could. If it were up to me, today would have been my last day. And I would have told Amir to kiss my ass.

I tried to stand there behind my computer screen and block out what Amir had just said. It made me sick to my stomach. I hated to say it, but the DEA agents were right. I figured that Amir had taken over Sanjay's debt, and if he didn't come up with the money that he owed those guys from DC, then his life would be taken next. What a scary thought.

While I stood there and pretended to work, our UPS driver walked into the store with four huge packages. He got Amir's attention instantly.

"Hello, good morning," he said to the UPS driver.

"Good morning to you, sir," the UPS driver said and then he handed Amir his digital pad to sign. Immediately after the driver left, Amir took the boxes to the supply room and then he closed the door behind him. It didn't take a rocket scientist to figure out what he was back there doing. He was going to take the bulk of the prescription drugs out of here and leave a small amount. I recorded his every move.

While Amir was in the supply closet stealing all the drugs he needed to pay the mafia, an influx of customers filed into the store. I told Amir that I needed help, but he just kept shooing me away, telling me that he was busy. One time, I knocked on the supply-room door and asked him if we had any two-milligram opioids and he told me no, yet

I had just seen a huge box of it delivered by the UPS driver. I just shook my head and worked with what I had.

I finally got the crowd down during the next hour. And I noticed that when I was not busy I was thinking about the possibility of Sanjay being dead. I couldn't get this off my mind for nothing in the world. The fact was that I might never see that man again.

22

THROWING STONES

When my lunch break finally rolled around I damn near broke my neck trying to get out of that pharmacy. "I'm leaving now," I yelled into the supply closet and then I bolted for the front door.

I could tell that the DEA agents were monitoring my every move because as soon as I got in my car and drove away from the pharmacy, a black van followed me. I drove close to a mile before the black van stopped me. Agent Sims got out of the van, walked to my car, and then he took a seat in the passenger side. "How are you feeling?" he asked me, giving me his full attention.

"What kind of question is that? Did you hear him tell me that Sanjay isn't coming back to the pharmacy?"

"Yes, we heard. We're thinking that maybe he made a mistake by saying it."

"That man did not make a mistake. He said what he meant. And I believe that I came through on my part, so you can take this camera and wire off me."

"I'm sorry, Misty, but it doesn't work like that. If we take this to our prosecutor, he won't be able to get a government indictment, based on that alone. We need more.

We need for you to get him to talk more. This is the only way we can wrap this case up and you can go on about your life."

"Are you fucking kidding me right now? You have him on tape. His words were clear," I protested.

"Okay, let's say that Sanjay is dead. We don't have anything to prove it. We need a body, so that's why you gotta go back in there and get as much information from him as you can."

"Are you hearing me right now? The fucking man doesn't like me!" I screamed. "He hates me, so why are you throwing me in the lion's den?"

"Call it what you want. But you still have a job to do," he said, and then he opened the car door. But before he got out he said, "Oh, and that stunt your boyfriend pulled this morning better never happen again. He could've compromised our investigation with his antics. And if it does, I will lock you and him up in jail cells next to each other. Now try me!" Agent Sims then got out of my car and slammed the door.

"So, is that it?" I roared, and then I started banging on my car's steering wheel. My horn sounded off a few times while I hit it. I saw the agent get back into the black van and close the sliding door. I felt so fucking stupid and used. It's like going from one bad relationship to another. I swear, I am over it.

I had no appetite whatsoever so I didn't bother to stop anywhere to get something to eat. I did, however, drive over to the self-service car wash one block up the street and call my cousin Jillian to see what she was doing. I couldn't believe that she answered her cell phone. "What's up, Cuz?" she said.

"Girl, I am so tired of everyone playing with my feelings. I am so over this shit."

"What happened?"

"I can't talk about it right now," I said because I was wearing the wire.

"Are you working today?"

"Yeah, I'm on my lunch break right now."

"Have those DEA agents been bothering you?"

"I told you I can't talk about that right now."

"Why the fuck can't you talk about it? You talked about it with me before," Jillian protested. She was really throwing me underneath the bus right now.

"Look, I'm gonna call you back because you're tripping and my mind can't deal with your mouth right now."

"You're acting like I called you," Jillian replied sarcastically.

"I called you so we could talk about something other than my job. Like, what's the weather going to be like tonight? Or what basketball team's playing tonight? Or which celebrity has cheated on their spouse?"

"When have we ever talked about that shit you just listed. If we ain't talking about your man problems, Grandma, or your mama, we ain't talking."

"I guess I made a mistake by calling you. You're probably sitting next to Edmund's tight ass."

"He's in the bathroom."

"I figured that much. I'll talk to you later," I said and then I hung up.

Jillian was right, we never talked about those things I mentioned. Drama was always the thing to talk about. That's what kept our conversations going. But I couldn't talk about those things right now. I was wired up. And if Agent Sims heard the information I'd be giving Jillian, he could become livid like he did a few minutes ago.

After I disconnected my call with Jillian, I called my mother since I didn't call her back last night. I knew she was going to give me an earful, so I braced myself.

"Hello," she said.

"Hey, Ma, how you doing?"

"I'm doing better today. But I would've appreciate it if you would've called me back last night."

"Terrell stopped by my apartment unexpectedly, so that's why I didn't call you back."

"Please don't tell me that you let that fool back into your life. You know he doesn't mean you any good," she said with disappointment.

"No, Ma, I'm not letting him back into my life."

"So, why was he there?"

"He came by to get some old mail," I lied. I couldn't tell her why Terrell was really there. Nor could I tell her what he and I talked about.

"You didn't let him spend the night, did you?"

"No, Ma. He was only there for a few minutes and then he left," I lied once again.

"Look, Misty, I hope you're not lying to me. That boy took you through some serious heartache. And it would hurt my heart if you get mixed back up with him. He doesn't deserve a woman like you. You're special, so you deserve to be with someone special. And not his ol' cheating butt," she continued.

"I know, Ma. Trust me, it's over."

"You promise?"

"Yes, Mom, I promise," I reassured her.

"Are you working today?"

"Yes, I'm on lunch break now."

"Have you talked to your grandmother today?"

"No, I haven't," I told her and I refused to tell her why. Not only would the DEA agents hear my admission of giving Jillian prescription drugs, my mother would be livid at the fact that I'd been feeding Jillian's addiction.

"You know tomorrow is my birthday?"

"Yes, I know."

"I was thinking that maybe you, myself, and my new love would go to dinner. Or I could cook and you come by here?"

"Why would you want to cook on your birthday?"

"You know I don't care about cooking. I just want to be around the people that I love."

"If you decide to cook, what will be on the menu?"

"I was thinking of making a good ol' lasagna. You know lasagna is one of my favorite foods."

"Mine too. What time do you want to do this?"

"Think eight o'clock is good? Aren't you off work by that time?"

"Yeah, I get off at six tomorrow. So that gives me time to pick up a gift for you," I replied, and then I said, "Since you're cooking, I'm gonna get your cake. So, tell me what kind you want."

"Get me a strawberry cake with buttercream frosting."

"That sounds good. I can't wait to try a piece of that," I continued. My mom and I talked for another ten minutes. I started driving back to the pharmacy near the end of our conversation. Before we hung up, she asked me to promise her once again that I wasn't going to give Terrell another chance. After I did that, she told me to have a nice day and for me to call her later.

23

WHAT ON EARTH WAS HE THINKING?

When I walked back into the pharmacy once my lunch break was over, I never expected to run into the same two mafia guys that'd had a gun shoved into Amir's back the other evening. One of the guys was sitting down in the chair Sanjay normally used. I had no idea where the other guy was until I heard the bathroom door open and close. He smiled and greeted me as he passed me by. I was as nervous as a whore in church. Seriously though, I wanted so badly to turn around and leave the pharmacy, but I knew I had a job to do. So, I walked behind the counter and logged back into the system. I could feel both men staring at me while I pretended to be working. Thankfully, the guy that came from the bathroom went directly into the supply closet while the other guy stayed to watch what I was doing. "Do you like working here?" he asked me. I wanted to ignore him, but I knew it would be rude and dangerous at the same time.

I slightly turned my head around, facing him, and said, "Yes, I do." But I was lying through my teeth. I really wanted to ask him where the hell Sanjay was. And if they killed him, where was his body? I would ask both questions while this broach and wire were recording it.

"You seem like you are quiet. Are you a quiet lady?"

"I can be."

"Please let her work. She has a lot of prescriptions to fill," Amir interjected.

"Are you trying to tell me what to do?" the guy asked Amir after he stood up on his feet. His tone was menacing.

Amir became extremely nervous. "No, it's just that we have a lot of orders and she has to do them before she leaves today," Amir explained.

"I don't care how much work she has. If I want to carry on a conversation with her, then that's what I will do," the guy informed him.

"What is your name?" the guy asked after he sat back down in the chair.

"My name is Misty," I answered, while I tapped a few keys on the computer.

"That's a nice name."

"Thank you."

"You're welcome. Would you like to know my name?"

"If you want to tell me."

"My name is Ahmad."

"That's a nice name."

"Thank you."

"You're welcome," I told him while I continued to stare at the computer monitor.

"Misty, do you have a boyfriend?"

"No, I don't."

"That's too bad, because you are a beautiful woman."

"Thank you," I replied modestly.

"Want to come work for me?"

"I'm fine working here."

"You don't even know what job I could be offering you. I could be offering you a million dollars to come work for me and you didn't even give me a chance to put the proposal on the table," he said, trying to convince me to do more than I wanted to.

"I'm sorry. It's just that I don't like jumping from one job to the next," I lied. I couldn't wait to get out of this freaking place.

"Okay, I get it. You win."

"Ahmad, leave the lady alone and come help me with these boxes," the other mafia guy instructed. And at that moment, Ahmad stood up from his seat and walked into the supply closet and helped the other guy carry some boxes out. I turned around and faced them all three times that they walked into the closet and came out with boxes. I figured this would be some nice footage for Agent Sims's and Montclair's investigation. Amir didn't have much to say. Those two guys were running the show and I wanted Sims and Montclair to see that as well.

Once they got the last box, I heard Ahmad tell Amir that they'd be back in two days to finalize everything. Yes, my wiretap recorded him saying those very words too. Let's see what the DEA agents had to say about this intel.

As I left my job, I noticed Terrell's car parked directly behind mine. The sight of him got me so irritated. "What are you doing here, Terrell?"

"I'm checking up on you."

"But I don't need you to do that."

"What kind of man would I be if I didn't check on my woman?"

"Terrell, I am not your woman," I reminded him while I stood next to the driver-side door of his car.

"Forget about all that. I saw all those Arab dudes when they left the pharmacy not too long ago."

"That was over an hour ago. You've been out here that long?"

"I ain't have nothing else to do. And besides, I just wanted to see the dudes that the DEA agents trying to arrest."

"Terrell, please don't do that anymore."

"Girl, stop overreacting."

"Look, I gotta go, I can't take this shit from you anymore. I'm over it."

"You act like this is the end of the world."

Instead of making a comment, I got in my car and drove away from that dumb-ass nigga because he had no idea the type of people Sanjay and Amir deal with. They're cut from a different cloth. And to know they were affiliated with some sort of mafia, took this mission to another level. I was gonna stay in my lane until this was all over.

24

FAMILY WILL GET YOU KILLED

En route to my grandmother's, Agent Sims called my cell phone. Before I answered it, I knew exactly why he was calling me. I was sure he heard every word Terrell uttered after I approached his car. I disliked Terrell and the man he had become, but I didn't like the law telling people where they can go and congregate. It irritated me to see Terrell parked outside the store, but legally I couldn't do anything about it. I had more important things to do than to babysit a grown-ass man. I'd let Terrell create his own demise. I wanted no parts of it.

I finally answered Agent Sims's call on the fourth ring. After I said hello, he chimed in and said, "You did a good job today."

"Really?" I questioned his sincerity. This guy never said anything nice to me.

"Yes, really. We heard some good things today. But we need just a little bit more."

"How did I know you were gonna say that?"

"Great minds think alike," he said with dry humor.

"Am I supposed to laugh?" I replied sarcastically.

"Just continue to do a good job. The quicker you can get the information we need, the quicker we can let you go."

"Haven't I heard that somewhere before?" I commented nonchalantly.

"I'm sure you have."

"Is that it?" I asked, because I was ready to get off the phone with him.

"Yeah, I guess," he said as if he was unsure. "Oh yeah, tell your boyfriend to stay away from our investigation. If we see him again hanging around the pharmacy, we will lock him up."

"Why don't you tell him? And stop saying that he's my boyfriend, because he's not."

"Boyfriend, baby, husband, partner. All of it is the same."

"Are you done?"

"Yes, I am. Oh yeah, remember you have to be very gentle when you take the wire from around your waist. There is an off button directly at the bottom of the case so you can turn down the volume. You can even shut it off."

"That's good to know. Talk to you later," I said, and disconnected our call. "Fucking moron!" I uttered.

I pulled up to my grandmother's house, and Jillian's car was nowhere in sight. This woman stayed on the go. She had the energy of ten football players. And I can't tell you where she gets it from, because the pills I give her are downers. So how is it that she's always on the move? She may need her doctor to reevaluate her.

After I pulled up alongside the curb in front of my grandmother's house, I called Jillian's cell number. "Hello," she said with loud music playing in the background.

"Girl, turn that music down," I demanded. There was no way she was going to hear me talk over all that loud music.

She turned the music down a few notches and said, "I was getting ready to call you."

"Where are you?"

"I'm on my way to your house."

"Well, I'm here at Grandma's house. So, turn the car around and come back here."

"Okay."

It only took me eight minutes to get to my apartment from my grandmother's house. It was late in the evening. The sun had already set. And the air felt marvelous. The only thing I was missing was peace of mind. Anxiety had consumed me. I felt like I had no say-so about what went on in my life. I had Terrell stalking me and trying to bully his way back into my life. My mother was an alcoholic and in denial about it. She and my grandmother had the worst relationship ever. My cousin was a prescription drug junkie. And last but not least, I worked for men that were indebted to a notorious mafia. But what's worse, I was being forced to work for the DEA so they could bring those guys down. I never thought that I would ever be an informant. I'd seen documentaries on television where people got killed for snitching on big-time drug dealers. How did I get here?

I noticed Jillian was on her cell phone when I pulled up to my apartment building. Immediately after I got out of my car, I motioned her to come to my apartment after she finished her call, because that's where I was going to be. She joined me a couple of minutes later.

"Whatcha got in here to eat? I'm starving," she told me as she sifted through the things in my refrigerator.

I stood near my counter and started going through the mail I picked up on my way to my apartment.

"I got some leftover spaghetti in there and the other half of the Subway sandwich I was eating yesterday."

"I don't want no spaghetti. But I'll eat this other half of Subway sandwich," she said as she retrieved the sandwich from the refrigerator. "What's in it?" she asked while she was sniffing it.

"It's a cold-cut sandwich, Jillian."

"When did you get it again?"

"Yesterday. Love, you don't have to eat it. I'll eat it later."

"Oh no, I'm good," she said and sank her teeth into the sandwich.

"I'm so sick of bills."

"Aren't we all?" she commented between chews.

"The only bill you have is for your cell phone," I replied sarcastically after I dropped the cable bill down on the counter and turned around to face her.

"What is that thing on your shirt? Is that a broach?"

"Oh yeah, I need to take this off," I said and then I removed the camera from my shirt. After I laid the camera down on the countertop, I lifted my shirt so I could pull the tape and the wires from my waist. When Jillian saw this, her eyes grew wide.

"Is that a fucking wire?" she whispered as if someone else was in the apartment.

I placed my finger over my mouth, giving her a signal to be quiet. So she stood there in silence and watched me as I gently pulled the tape and wires away from my body. After I had the case in my hand, I turned the switch off and then I placed it down on the countertop.

"Can I talk now?" she whispered as she walked slowly toward me.

"Yeah." And then I smiled.

"Did the DEA agent give you that to wear to work?"

"Yeah."

"How did it feel to tape that to your body like that?"

"It was uncomfortable. Plus, I felt self-conscious while I was around Sanjay's brother today."

"It isn't bulky. I didn't even know you had it on you until you lifted up your shirt."

"That's good to know, because I was a nervous wreck

when I walked back into the pharmacy after my lunch break and saw those same two guys were hanging around the supply closet."

"Oh my God! Did they say something to you?"

"Yeah, one of the guys did."

"What did he say?" Jillian pressed me for more information. She had become intrigued.

"The guy that sparked up a conversation with me was named Ahmad." I told her about the conversation.

"You're kidding, right?"

"No, I'm not."

"And what did Amir do?"

"He didn't do shit! That guy shut him down."

"Damn!" Jillian said and then she changed the direction of the conversation. "Where was Sanjay when all of this was going on?"

"If I tell you, you gotta promise that you will not tell anyone else. This information cannot leave this kitchen," I instructed her.

"I promise. What is it?"

"The DEA agent said that Sanjay owed those men a lot of money. Unfortunately for Sanjay, he couldn't pay them fast enough so they kidnapped him. Now the pressure is on Amir's back, so if he doesn't deliver what's owed to those guys, he's going to come up missing too."

"Yo, this is some Italian mob-boss type of shit here."

"Call it what you want. But let me tell you what Amir said when I asked him about Sanjay."

"Go head."

"Okay. So, when I went to work this morning, I asked Amir when was Sanjay coming back to work? And he slipped up and said that Sanjay wasn't ever coming back. When he said that, his words hit me like a ton of bricks."

"Are you fucking serious right now?"

"Yes, I am. So check it out."

"What?"

"When I asked him to repeat himself, he wouldn't do it. He tried to act like he didn't say what he said."

"Do you think you heard him wrong?"

"Fuck no! I can hear really good. I caught him off guard and he tried to clean it up, but he couldn't."

"So, what are you gonna do?"

"I'm not gonna do anything. I'm gonna work at that pharmacy for the next couple of days and then I'm out of there."

"But wait, you said you was going to let us hit it up before you resign."

"Look, it's gonna be nearly impossible for you to get drugs, because every time the shipment comes in the front door, Amir and those other guys are taking it out the back door."

"Well, let's rob the UPS guy."

"Are you stupid? You're really trying to go to jail, fucking with a UPS truck."

"Well, we can rob the guys coming out the back door."

"Who is we?"

"I'm talking about my homeboys."

"If your boys are trying to rob the pharmacy, they're gonna have to do it in two days."

"What happens in two days?"

"That's when the next shipment comes in."

"What time?"

"It always comes in the morning. That's when our UPS guy delivers to us."

"We can't rob it in the morning time, unless we are already in the store when they get there. We can act like we're waiting on a prescription."

"Yeah, I think that plan works better," I began to say, and then I looked Jillian in the eyes and said, "You are not gonna be anywhere around the store, right?"

"I'll be in the getaway car," she said and cracked a smile.

"Jillian, no you are not. So, stop it. This is not a laughing manner. Not only are we trying to take a huge shipment of drugs from the pharmacy, we are also robbing the men that my boss owes a huge amount of money to. And let's not forget, if I don't turn off my camera and the wiretap, all of it will be recorded while the DEA is outside waiting around in their black van," I explained to her.

"Oh shit! I forgot about the camera and wire."

"Don't worry, I'll tell the agent that I'm gonna switch it off every time I go to the bathroom."

"Perfect excuse," Jillian said with excitement.

"How much you think we can take out of there?" Jillian pressed the issue. She was more concerned about the value of the prescriptions drugs than the possibility that someone could get hurt if the mafia guys refused to give up the drugs.

"All I know is that the take away from the shipment could be anywhere between two hundred and fifty thousand to half a million dollars."

Jillian's eyes grew bigger. "I can't wait to get my hands on those pills," she said as she rubbed both of her hands together.

"I'm stuck on the money part of it."

"Me too," Jillian agreed.

Jillian and I retreated to the living room so we could talk more. But I was doing the most talking. After I told her about Terrell's shenanigans, I told her that my mom wanted me to come by her house and eat dinner with her for her birthday.

"Who's doing the cooking?"

"She said she wanted to."

"On her birthday?"

"Yeah, that's what I said."

"Is her boyfriend going to be there too?"

"I'm sure he is."

"How do you feel about him?"

"I don't feel anything. He's there to make her happy.

Not me. You know she told me that Grandma didn't love her the way she loved your dad?"

"Yeah, I heard about it."

"What was your reaction when you heard it?"

"I'm like you, that's not my battle. So, I don't have any feelings either way you look at it. But let me ask you a question."

"Go ahead. I'm listening."

"Do you think your mother likes me?"

"I'm sure she does."

"I don't think so. I think that when she sees me, she sees my dad, and she can't get past it."

"Hmmm, I never thought about it that way. I can ask her the next time I talk to her."

"No bother," she said, while her cell phone started ringing. She looked down at the caller ID and said, "Wait, give me a minute, this is my homeboy."

I sat there on the sofa and watched Jillian as she brought her homeboy up to speed about the upcoming robbery.

"When you talk to those guys later on, I don't want you telling my name. It's bad enough that they know that I work there," I instructed her.

"Why are you acting so paranoid? No one is going to rat you out. We are going to handle everything perfectly," she tried to assure me. But I wasn't buying it. When Jillian was high, she talked like a fucking know-it-all. She had all the answers. She needed to be reminded that what we're about to do would be dangerous. This was not a game. There was no turning back once we rolled the dice. I just hoped she was ready. More importantly, I hoped those guys were ready too. There was a lot of money and drugs involved, so someone could lose their life. And that some-one wouldn't be me.

25

ONE LIE AFTER THE NEXT

Immediately after Jillian left my apartment, I hopped in the shower, bathed really quickly, and then I called it a night. I thought I was going to get me some rest tonight, but it didn't happen. Like all of those other times, I tossed and turned the entire night. It seemed like everything crossed my mind at one time. It felt like it was all jumbled up and couldn't be fixed. I couldn't tell if I was coming or going. What a mess my life had become.

In no time, I was back at work at the pharmacy. Amir had called the pharmacy and said that he had a family emergency, so he wasn't coming in today. Not only did he make my day with that public service announcement, I felt a huge relief lifted from my gut.

But this change of plans did not sit well with Agent Sims. In fact, he was livid when I called his cell phone and told him what Amir said. While I was talking to him, I watched the van he was in, parked across the street, drive off. I didn't ask him where he was going because I didn't care. But in the back of my mind, I knew Amir not being here today alarmed him. It wouldn't surprise me if he and the other agents were heading over to Amir's home.

My day wasn't all that productive since we didn't have a lot of opioids to give out to customers who really needed them, but I made the best of it.

As my lunchtime approached, I realized I couldn't head out for my break because I was manning the store by myself. So I picked up my cell phone and called Jillian to see if she could bring me something to eat.

"Hey, where you at?" I asked her after she answered her phone.

"Me and Edmund are at the store picking up some flour for Grandma."

"Think you could stop off the Taco Bell and pick me up a couple of supreme tacos?"

"What's wrong with your car?"

"Nothing. I'm at work by myself today. And I can't leave. So, are you gonna do it or what?"

"Yeah, I can do that."

"Bring me a Sprite too."

"A'ight, I gotcha," she assured me.

"Who was that on the phone?" I looked up, and sure enough, that rude question came from Terrell. Shocked by his sudden appearance, I looked at him like, *what are you doing here?*

"I came to see how my future wife is doing," he said, smiling from ear to ear.

Before giving this fool my attention, I said to Jillian, "Thanks. See you soon." Then I gave Terrell an evil glare. "First of all, I could never be your future wife. And you couldn't care less about how I am doing. Because if you did, we would never have broken up. Now, tell me the real reason why you're here."

"I came to see if I could holla at your boss right quick."

"Holla at my boss for what?" I wanted to know. His presence was irritating the crap out of me.

"I want to see if he and I can do a business deal before your peoples lock him up," he continued as he leaned over the counter.

"Are you out of your fucking mind?"

"No. I'm good. But I think you are," he said sarcastically.

"Get out right now!" I roared.

"Oh, you're scared that your boss may hear me?"

"He's not here, Mr. Fucking Know It All!" My pitch got louder.

"Where is he? On lunch break?" Terrell guessed as he looked down at his watch.

"Get out right now!" I screamed.

"What seems to be the problem?" a male voice boomed from the front of the store.

Terrell and I turned our focus toward the front entrance of the pharmacy. I gasped for air when I saw Ahmad, one of the mafia guys, walking toward us. I swear, if I had magical powers I would instantly disappear.

"Who are you?" Terrell asked Ahmad.

"No, my friend, the question is, who are you?" Ahmad said confidently as he approached us. I wanted so badly to tell Terrell to shut up, but my mouth wouldn't move. I looked at Terrell's body movement and what he was going to do next. See, Terrell has a huge ego, so having me there with him wasn't going to make the situation better. I knew that he was going to tell this guy to leave, or insult him like he's beneath him. And not for nothing, Ahmad wasn't going to have it.

"Hey look, we're not gonna play his game. Me and my fiancée is trying to have a conversation, so if you trying to buy something then you need to leave," Terrell replied sarcastically.

"Misty, I thought you said you didn't have a boyfriend," Ahmad asked me, right after he took his last step. We were face-to-face.

"I don't have a boyfriend. He is my ex-boyfriend though."

"Oh, so now you want to disrespect me in front of this nigga!" Terrell's voice became louder.

"Terrell, will you please leave?" I warned him. He had absolutely no idea what this man was capable of doing. Unfortunately for him, he didn't listen.

"I'm not going anywhere. I'm trying to get this nigga out of here and you want me to leave?" Terrell boomed.

"That's what she said," Ahmad told him.

Terrell chuckled while he looked at me and Ahmad. "Oh, so I get it. You must be related to the motherfucker that owns this store. And now you're trying to flex your muscles," Terrell said.

"Correction, I own this store," Ahmad told him with finality.

Terrell looked at me, puzzled. "Oh, so you're the new owner? Because you were not the owner when she first started working here a few months ago."

"I don't care who was the owner a few months ago. I am the owner now, and that's all that matters. Now get the hell out of the store before I force you out of here," Ahmad said, and then he pulled up his shirt, revealing a huge-ass gun in the waist of his jeans.

Terrell chuckled once again. "Oh, so you think you're gangsta, huh? Show that shit to the feds because they're watching your ass, nigga!" Terrell hissed.

"What did you just say?" Ahmad asked him.

"He didn't say anything," I interjected and grabbed Terrell by his arm. I couldn't afford to let Terrell repeat himself because things would get really ugly. Not only would he be jeopardizing my life, he could mess up the DEA's whole investigation.

"No. Don't push him. Leave him alone," Ahmad instructed.

Shaking on the inside like a leaf dangling from a tree, fear engulfed me as I stood there next to Terrell. Ahmad took another step toward him. "Repeat what you just said," Ahmad demanded.

Terrell looked at me first before he opened his mouth. I gave him a look of caution and fear, hoping that he'd take heed because there was nothing else I could say. The ball was now in his court. "I said, don't be showing me your gun because it ain't that serious. I'd rather do business with you more than anything," Terrell finally answered.

Boy, what he just said didn't sound like anything he said before, but hopefully it worked. Ahmad stood there quietly, looking as if Terrell was lying to him.

"So, can we do business?" Terrell continued, trying to deflect what he really said.

"What kind of business are you talking about?" Ahmad asked him, even though he looked as though he was still mulling over what Terrell actually said to him.

"Misty told me you sell Xanax and Vicodin for dirt cheap. I could move a lot of that shit for you and make you a killing," Terrell uttered enthusiastically, as if he was giving Ahmad the pitch of the day.

"Misty, you told him that I could sell him some Vicodins dirt cheap?" Ahmad looked at me with intimidation.

"No, I didn't. I told him no such thing," I replied, giving Terrell the most disgusted look I could muster up.

"Why you lying, Misty? You did tell me that shit," Terrell protested.

Fire was brewing up inside of me. I couldn't believe I was standing here with Terrell while he was telling Ahmad this bullshit. For one, Ahmad is not the one who was selling the drugs, it was Sanjay and Amir. And two, they were not actually selling the drugs, they were paying a debt to Ahmad, which was why Ahmad said that he owned the pharmacy. Every prescription drug of value coming through that pharmacy belonged to Ahmad and whoever else Ahmad worked for. It was as simple as that. So, to be standing here with this dumb-ass nigga while he was digging a deep-ass hole for us, my blood was boiling. "Listen, Ahmad, the only thing I told him was that Sanjay was giving me a few pills here and there so I could make some extra cash. That's it," I finally said, hoping this lie would work, considering Sanjay wasn't here to refute what I just said.

"Oh, so why didn't you just say that?" Ahmad said as he cracked a smile.

Terrell smiled too. Then he gave Ahmad a handshake. To see them both defuse the situation was a huge sigh of relief. "Hey listen, give me your number and I will call you," Ahmad instructed him.

Giddy like a kid in the candy store, Terrell started calling out his cell phone number so Ahmad could program it into his phone. "Terrell, I'll give him your number," I said. I just wanted Terrell to leave. He had already caused enough drama. And giving Ahmad his number would be a disaster if they ever talked on their own, away from me.

"A'ight, cool," Terrell agreed.

"I'll call you later after I get off work today," I told him, even though I was lying. I was saying everything he wanted to hear so that he would leave.

"Don't forget to give him my number," Terrell reminded me as he headed toward the front door of the pharmacy.

"I won't," I lied once again.

After Terrell finally exited the pharmacy, it felt like there was still an elephant in the room. In my mind, I didn't think Ahmad believed what Terrell said when he asked him to repeat himself. I also believed that he might put me on the spot and force me to tell him the truth. But guess what? I couldn't do that. Not when there were other people involved, like the DEA. I was pissed off at myself that I let Terrell in on the secret. He was a loose fucking cannon and he might have done damage to an already fucked-up situation.

"That was an interesting conversation, huh?" he started off.

I didn't know if I should say yeah, or no. This felt like a trick question. "That depends on what you call interesting," I finally said.

"Let's just say, things could've gone wrong if I hadn't contained myself."

"I'm glad you did," I replied, and then I turned the direction of the conversation. "So, what brings you here today? Amir isn't coming in."

"I came to see you."

"For what?" I asked him. He was creeping me out with his words. More fear and anxiety started brewing in the pit of my stomach.

"So I could ask you out."

"What do you mean by that?" I wanted to know. Here I was wearing a fucking wire and a broach for a camera so that I could get information for the DEA, and he wanted to take me out. He wanted to be in my company? Not only that, I knew that he was a killer. Well, if he hadn't killed anyone, then I knew that he was capable of doing it. At least, that's what the DEA assumed because of Sanjay's disappearance.

"I want to take you to dinner."

"No. You don't wanna do that," I informed him. I mean, was this guy really serious? Take me out to dinner? Was he playing some type of game with me?

"Why not? You're a beautiful woman and I want to get to know you," he explained.

Taken aback by his offer, I caught a lump in my throat. My mind started turning in all kinds of directions and I couldn't put complete thoughts together. I'm sure I looked shell-shocked. "Listen, Ahmad, I appreciate you asking me out, but I'm not your type. And besides, aren't you married?" I said with hopes of turning this thing around toward him.

"No, I am not married."

"Well, men like you don't date American women."

He cracked another smile. "What do you mean, men like me?"

"I'm talking about your culture. You engage with women from your own country because you guys share the same beliefs. I mean, don't you guys marry women that are submissive? Because I am not submissive."

He smiled again. "You're so cute."

"No, I'm not cute. I'm average. And I'm not fun to be around too," I told him. I was trying to say anything that would turn him off. I couldn't be in this guy's presence for a long period of time and especially in an intimate setting like a restaurant.

He chuckled, this time showing all of his teeth. And I have to admit that this guy was so fucking handsome. It was like I didn't see the killer or mafia type. I saw this handsome man with power and money. Power and money could make a bum look like 50 Cent. But of course, this didn't mean that I gave him a pass. I needed to stay focused on the task at hand so I could walk away from this thing alive, and go on my merry way.

"I won't accept no for an answer. Now, give me your phone number and I will call you later," he demanded.

"Look, Ahmad, please listen to me when I tell you that I am not fun to be around. Plus, I take care of my grandmother when I'm not at work. She has a nurse taking care of her while I'm at work, and then I go to her house right after I leave here," I lied. I needed a concrete explanation, and telling him that I take care of my elderly grandmother should do the trick.

"Okay, why don't I pick up dinner and bring it to your grandmother's house? We can all eat together," he insisted. This guy wasn't giving up.

"Ahmad, everything that you're saying is flattering. But I can't allow you to do it. My grandmother is very sickly.

And we have to have her in a closed environment so she won't contract any outside diseases."

"Why do I take it that you're giving me a lot of excuses?"

I paused before I answered him because I really didn't know what to say. I couldn't tell him the truth, so what could I tell him that would make sense? I needed something that was plausible. "Can I ask you a question?" I said, finding a way to take me out of the hot seat.

"Sure," he replied.

"Where are you from?"

"India," he said quickly.

"How long have you been in America?"

"About ten years."

"How old are you, if you don't mind me asking."

"I'm thirty-one years old."

"Do you have any children?"

"No, I don't. But one day I'm sure I will."

"Is Sanjay ever coming back to work?" I asked him. And I swear, I had no knowledge that I would form my lips to ask that question. I don't know where it came from. And after I realized that I said it, Ahmad's facial expression changed. He looked at me suspiciously.

"Why did you ask me that?"

Once again, a mountain of fear fell down upon me and I couldn't think of anything to say. My mind went completely blank.

"Did Amir tell you anything?" Ahmad said.

"No, he didn't," I finally was able to say as the heat in my body started consuming me.

"He had to have said something to you for you to ask me that question. Now, tell me what he told you." Ahmad pressed the issue.

I stood there quietly and looked away from Ahmad. I looked toward the front door and tried calculating how long it would take me to make a run for it. But then when

I really thought about making that escape, what was going to happen to my jacket, handbag, and my car keys? I wasn't going to be able to get away without them. So, I reassessed my position.

"Misty, I don't have all day. Tell me what Amir told you." Ahmad wouldn't let up.

"Okay, he said that Sanjay wasn't ever coming back here to work."

"Is that it?"

"Kind of, sort of."

"What do you mean by that?"

"You see how nasty he is to me. He acted as if it's you and that other guy's fault that Sanjay isn't coming back to work," I said, trying to pull my lie together. I figured that if I blamed this whole thing on Amir, I could get information for the DEA and I could also pull Amir into the hot seat too. I mean, it's not like he doesn't deserve it. He's an evil-ass dude. He's rude to me for no reason, so why not start some drama for him?

"Did he say anything else to you about Sanjay?" Ahmad pressed me.

"No, not that I can remember."

"Well, I'll tell you what, the next time he says something to you about anything dealing with Sanjay or this pharmacy, you let me know."

"I will," I assured him.

He changed the subject. "So, let's talk about this dinner date again."

"I'll tell you what, if you give me a couple of days, I'll let you know when and where I would like to go," I said. I figured by then the DEA would have all of their asses arrested and I wouldn't have to really go on this date.

Ahmad continued talking to me until an elderly customer came walking through the front door. "I see you gotta get to work," he said.

"Yes, I do."

"Well, give me your number and I'll call you tomorrow."

Giving him my number wasn't how I wanted this conversation to end, so I told him to give me his. Thankfully, he didn't give me any problems and called the numbers out to me. After I wrote it down with the paper and pen I had on the counter, he smiled and told me to have a nice day.

Seeing him walk out that front door was liberating. I mean, there was no other way to describe it. That guy was a fucking drug-dealing killer. Now why would I want to be in his company? And if he knew what was going on behind the scenes, I'm sure he would kill me on the spot. This guy literally walked around with a fucking pistol in the waist of his pants. And the fact that he showed Terrell that he'd use it on him, was even more scary. Ahmad was nothing to play with. I just hoped that this investigation ended quickly before anyone else got hurt. Or even worse, got killed.

26

SO MELODRAMATIC

Only two customers walked into the pharmacy after Ahmad left. This gave me some time to make two necessary phone calls. The first call I made was to Agent Sims, who was probably still out looking for Sanjay instead of monitoring my wire from the van. Didn't want any of the cameras inside the store to document my conversation, so I went outside in front of the pharmacy. "Agent Sims, Ahmad just left the pharmacy."

"Wait, when did he come there?"

"About forty-five minutes ago. He came here and started flirting with me. Telling me that he wants to take me out on a date."

"Wait . . . he did what?" Agent Sims said as if he was trying to wrap his head around what I just said.

"He came here over an hour ago and asked me if he could take me to dinner," I repeated.

"And you have this on tape?"

"Of course, I do. I'm wearing it, aren't I?"

"So, what did you say?"

"I told him that it wouldn't be a good idea."

"Did he ask you why?"

"Yes, and I told him that I wasn't his type, and that I have to take care of my grandmother when I leave work every day."

"And what did he say?"

"He wasn't hearing anything I told him."

"And when, again, did this happen?"

"Over an hour ago."

"Listen, I'll tell you what, I'm gonna send Gail by there to get the wire and broach from you so we can go over the footage."

"When will you do that?"

"Within the hour. You're gonna be required to meet her outside the store."

"I already know that. I'm standing outside now, talking to you on the phone."

"Good girl," he commented. Before we disconnected our call he said, "Keep your head up. This footage may be your ticket out of this mess."

"Yeah, you say that now, and tomorrow it will be something else."

After Gail and Agent Sims showed up to grab the camera and the wire device, everything in the pharmacy returned to normal. The rest of the day at the pharmacy went by kind of quickly. Before I locked up the place, I took inventory in the supply closet and there was not a narcotic in sight. Ahmad and his partner had cleaned the place out. Now I couldn't say how much Sanjay and Amir owed them, but it had to be in the millions.

27

NAILING DOWN THE PLAN

Jillian and that guy Tedo were sitting in his car outside of our grandmother's house when I pulled up curbside. I told her that I didn't want to deal with this dude face-to-face and didn't want him to know my name, but it seemed like everything I said to her went in one ear and out the other.

She motioned for me to get in his car with them, so I did. Jillian opened the floor and started the dialogue. "Misty, Tedo got his homeboy Rick to help him get the shipment once it comes in."

"How are y'all gonna get it from the two guys that are coming there to get it themselves?" I wondered aloud. I wanted to hear details.

"Jillian told me about the situation of your boss owing them Arab dudes all that dough and that's why they're taking the prescription drugs in place of it, so I was thinking that we could wait for them to come out the back door and stick them up there before they can get it in their car."

"There's a camera in the back of the store so you're gonna have to be careful. I would hate for them to see you. The plan would go up in smoke."

"Tell me how you think we should do it," Tedo wanted to know.

"I was thinking that one of y'all could come through the front door and the other two wait for the shipment to arrive at the back door."

"What time?"

"Well, the shipment comes in the morning. So, Amir and his people got it set up to where they show up either while I'm at lunch or later in the evening. So I'll tell you what, when the shipment comes in, I'll call Jillian so she can give y'all the cue."

"What kind of burners do those dudes carry?" Tedo asked me.

"I think it's a nine-millimeter Glock."

His questions continued. "Are they big guys or what?"

"Nope. They're your average size guys. So they don't mind pulling out their weaponry," I warned him.

"Do they carry any money on them? I mean, cause if we got some money too, this would be a sweet heist." He grinned like he was devising a master plan.

"Look, I can't answer all of that. Just do like I said. Send one guy through the front and have the other two waiting in the back."

"A'ight. Will do. But let me ask you," he said and then he fell silent.

"What?"

"How big is the area behind the store? Will this car fit back there?"

"Yes, it will. But I don't think you should park back there. What you should do is have the two guys in back waiting, like I said before, and when the guys come out the back door, you take the drugs and take off with their car. It can't get no simpler than that," I replied sarcastically because this nigga was getting on my freaking nerves. *Just sit back and listen sometimes and then maybe you'll learn something.*

"Two days from now, right?" He needed reassurance.

"Yes, two days from now. Not tomorrow, but the day after that."

"Sounds like a plan," he commented.

I let out a long sigh. "I gotta get out of here," I said aloud, and then I exited Tedo's car.

"Wait, you're getting ready to leave?" Jillian asked me.

"Yeah, I need to get home. I'm tired," I told her and closed the back door.

"I'm coming, so wait," she said. She told Tedo she'd call him later and crawled out of his car. We stood there on the lawn in front of our grandmother's house. "We're gonna have to figure out a way to get that shipment without the DEA seeing us."

"So *now* you're finally worried about the DEA. I told you, this whole situation is tricky. I can't do anything about where they'll be, but I can make sure they don't hear us by taking off the wire when Tedo and his boys get there."

"What's up with Terrell? And what made him come up to your job today? Is he off his fucking rocker?"

"I don't know what the fuck is going on with him. First, he starts stalking me since I told him that our relationship was finally over. Then he burst into my crib asking me if someone is hiding in one of the rooms in my apartment, and then he comes up to my job like he's the man and he runs shit. Do you know that he almost slipped up and told that guy Ahmad that the feds are watching him?"

"No way!" Jillian said, her eyes growing.

"Yes way," I started off. "I swear, I thought Ahmad was going to shoot us both in the head. Thank God, I came up with a plausible rebuttal."

"How did you get Terrell to leave?"

"I don't remember. All I know is that immediately after he left, Ahmad gave me the side eye like I was holding back information. I don't know how I was able to walk out of that place alive today."

"So, he really wants to take you out to dinner?"

"I don't know if it's a fucking setup or what."

"So, what do you think it is?" Jillian wanted to know.

"I don't know. Because if he wanted to get me alone and kill me, then he could've done that in the pharmacy or followed me to my apartment and did it there."

"I think he wants to fuck you. I mean, look at you. You're pretty, you got a fat ass, and you smell good."

"Oh, shut up, Jillian!" I said, cracking a smile.

"It's true," she continued.

"Well, I—" I began to say, but then my cell phone started ringing. I pulled it from my handbag and looked directly at the caller ID.

"I betcha it's Terrell." Jillian guessed.

"No, it's the fucking DEA agent." I pressed the Answer button. "Hello," I continued.

"Misty, we need to see you," Agent Sims said.

"When?"

"Now. Where are you?"

"I'm at my grandmother's house."

"How long will it take to get to your apartment?"

"Fifteen minutes."

"Well, I will see you then," he said, and then my cell phone went radio silent.

"I gotta go," I told Jillian and turned around toward my car.

"What do they want now?"

"I don't know."

"So you're gonna leave without seeing Nana?"

"Don't tell her I was here."

"But I already told her that you were coming."

"Well, tell her that something came up."

"You always make shit difficult."

"No, you do. So, I'll call you later," I assured her and then I got into my car and left.

When I arrived at my apartment I noticed that the black van that the agents travel around in was parked at the far side of the lot. Once they saw me parking my car, they got out of the van and walked toward my apartment building. I didn't wait for them to catch up with me because they knew where I lived and I didn't want any of my neighbors seeing me with them. The neighbors that live within a few yards from me, I didn't care about. But the rest of my neighbors were off-limits.

"We've got a lot to talk about," Agent Sims said as soon as he and Agent Montclair entered my apartment and closed the door.

"I'm sure we do," I responded sarcastically, because I knew these guys were getting ready to start talking out of their asses.

After they took seats on my couch, Agent Sims started off by saying, "We're gonna need you to take him up on the date offer."

"Are you fucking crazy? I'm not going out with that lunatic. Did you see how he pulled up and showed his gun to Terrell? Terrell would've gotten his head blown off if I hadn't defused that situation," I roared while I stood up in the middle of my living room.

"Well, if you wanna know my opinion, I think he should've gotten his head blown off. He walks around with his head held high like he's the king. He talks to people like he doesn't have any respect for them, so I say let the chips fall where they may," Agent Sims replied.

"I agree with Sims," Agent Montclair stated.

Agent Sims continued. "He shouldn't have been there in the first place. Do you know that he almost blew our whole investigation by running his mouth? In so many words, he told Ahmad that the feds are watching him."

"Yeah, he did," Agent Montclair agreed.

"Oh, so because Terrell almost blew this investigation, you're sending me into the lion's den with Ahmad?" I was fucking livid. But I was disgusted more than anything that these agents thought so little of me. This case was their number-one priority, regardless of whoever died. Fucking pieces of shit!

"Calm down, Misty! We are not throwing you in the lion's den. We will be with you every step of the way," Agent Montclair said.

"That's bullshit and you know it!" I spat. My insides were boiling as I started pacing my living room floor.

"Misty, if you want us to wrap this investigation up quicker, all you have to do is agree to go out on this date and we'll take it from there," Agent Sims chimed in.

"You know that that's a lie from the pits of hell!" I told him while I continued to walk back and forth from one end of my living room to the other. My living room wasn't that big, so I was turning around more frequently than I would do if I were at my grandmother's house.

"Can you stop moving and listen to us?" Agent Sims asked.

"For what? So you can continue to lie to me? And when am I supposed to go on this freaking dinner date?"

"We were hoping that you'd do it tomorrow night."

"I can't. My mother's birthday is tomorrow and she's cooking dinner."

"What about going out with him on a lunch date?"

"I don't know, you guys. This could be dangerous."

"Look, Misty, if you go out on the date with Ahmad, then you don't have to do anything else for us," Agent Sims stated.

"What's the catch?" I asked him after I stopped in my tracks.

"You're gonna have to get him to talk about where Sanjay is and other key players in his operation," Agent Sims explained.

"Are you out of your mind? I'm not asking him that bullshit! He'll suspect that I was wired and then he'll rip my fucking clothes off and see that I'm setting him up. And then without hesitation, he's going to take my life just like that. Boom! Bullet to my skull."

"Okay, I'll tell you what, if you could plant a couple of bugs in his car, that would do it for us."

"And put them where?"

"Underneath your seat."

"But you said two. Where am I supposed to put the other one?"

"In the back seat."

"And that's it?"

"Yes. If you can do that, then we're good."

"Why don't I believe you?"

"That's because your ex-boyfriend has rattled your brain," Agent Sims commented and then he chuckled. "Speaking of ex-boyfriend, I think you should let him do business with Ahmad."

"Is that a joke? Am I supposed to laugh?" I replied sarcastically.

Agent Montclair laughed.

"Okay, now I see you two got jokes. But I'm not in the mood to laugh, so if we're done here, y'all can go on and leave," I encouraged them.

They both stood up. "I thought we were becoming friends," Agent Sims commented.

"Please don't insult me," I replied nonchalantly while I showed them the door.

"Montclair, give her the wires and camera for work, and the other two bugs for Ahmad's car," Agent Sims instructed.

"Everything is in that black bag on her coffee table," Montclair pointed out.

I looked back at the coffee table while I was escorting them to the front door.

"Let us know when the date is set," Sims said.

"Yeah, I will," I told them. "Fucking idiots!" I mumbled under my breath after I slammed my front door.

28

IT WAS AN ACCIDENT

I knew it was too good to be true when Terrell walked out of the pharmacy earlier today, acting like everything was all good after Ahmad crushed his ego when he showed him his gun. Terrell had a lot of pride, so I knew I was going to hear his shit sooner than later.

He started calling me like his mind was going bad after Agents Sims and Montclair left my apartment. I finally answered his call after the tenth time. "Terrell, what do you want?" I asked him.

"Don't pretend like you're sleeping," he said.

"Who said I was asleep?"

"Whatcha doing?"

"I'm in my bed. Why?"

"Because I just pulled up to your apartment. So open the door."

"Terrell, I'm not in the mood for your shit tonight. I had a long day and all I wanna do is go to sleep."

"Well, it's too late. I'm here now. Open the door," he instructed.

"Terrell, I am not getting out of my bed to open the door. Now please go home."

"Girl, if you don't open that door I am gonna cause a scene out here," he warned me.

"Well, go right on ahead and do it. My neighbors will call the cops on your ass so quick."

"Misty, stop playing with me and open your front door."

"For the last time, I am not getting out of my bed."

"If you don't get out of that bed and open this front door, I'm gon' go up to your job tomorrow and tell one of those Arab niggas that the feds are watching them."

"Terrell, are you fucking crazy?! Do you know what those guys would do to me?" I screamed through the phone. It felt like my whole life was about to run into a brick wall.

"I don't give a fuck about that. Open the motherfucking door."

"Get away from my house. You ain't shit!" I continued to scream.

BOOM! BOOM! BOOM! "You hear me knocking at the door, now open it," he demanded.

"Leave me alone! Go home! I don't wanna see you!" I yelled.

"Y'all neighbor named Misty Heiress is an FBI informant. If you're selling drugs, she's gonna snitch on you!" I heard him yell.

My heart dropped into the pit of my stomach while I listened to this guy yell outside my front door that I was an FBI informant. Oh my God! I wondered if someone was listening.

Fear-stricken, I hopped out of my bed and raced to the front door and snatched it open. "What the fuck are you trying to do to me?" I said, grinding my teeth.

He pushed me backwards, walked into my apartment, and slammed the front door shut. "I knew I'd getcha ass to let me in after I said that," he said, giving me a grimace.

"So, you think that this is a game? You think that you

can come to my apartment anytime you want and then try to smear my name to my neighbors like that's cool? Yo dude, you got some fucking nerve," I spat.

"Did you think it was cool when that Arab nigga flexed his pistol at me? That nigga tried to play me like a punk or something."

"That's because you wouldn't shut your fucking mouth! You can't walk around and talk to people any kind of way and expect them to deal with it. And what's up with you and this FBI bullshit? I'm not a fucking informant, you piece of shit! And then to almost tell Ahmad that the feds is watching him was reckless as fuck! Do you know that if I wouldn't have cleaned that shit up, he probably would've killed us both?"

"That nigga wouldn't have done shit! See, I'm a nigga from the streets and I don't let no one intimidate me. Whatever I do, I'm man enough to pay the consequences. I don't need to snitch on nobody."

"I'm not a fucking snitch!"

"Then what are you? You ain't no volunteer worker at an old folks' home. You work with the DEA, remember," Terrell said and then he smiled even more wicked.

"Fuck you, Terrell! Get out of my house!" I demanded.

"I ain't going no fucking where," he protested.

I grabbed his arm and tried pushing him toward the front door, but I couldn't move him as effectively as I wanted because he was too big for me. He weighed at least seventy-five pounds more than me.

"Terrell, if you don't leave my apartment right now, I will call the police."

He threw out a compromise. "Give me some pussy and I'll leave."

"Nigga, I wouldn't fuck you with my mother's pussy."

"What, you fucking another nigga?"

"Don't worry about who I'm fucking. Just know that it ain't you, you fucking coward. All you do is run around town, picking up different bitches and talking reckless to people like you're the man. And remember when you used to always get me to tell you how good your dick was? Well, it was garbage. It's little and you don't know shit about how to fuck me. I thought that maybe after a few times you'd get better at it, well it turns out that you didn't. So, when I found out that you were cheating on me, that gave me my out for our relationship because I didn't have the heart to tell you that you weren't doing it for me. Now with all that said, leave my residence now." I waited for his reaction.

He stood there for a couple of seconds like he was try-ing to process everything that I had just said, so to me he wasn't moving fast enough for me. I wanted him to get out of my face now. "Terrell, get the fuck out of my house!" I demanded and then I opened my front door. At one point, I thought he was going to leave after I ripped his heart out of his chest, but then he slammed my front door shut and backhanded me across my face with so much force that I went down to the floor in seconds.

I scrambled to get back on my feet, but I couldn't be-cause Terrell crawled on top of me. "Get off me!" I screamed while I swung at him a few times with balled fists.

"Shut the fuck up, bitch!" he said and grabbed my neck with both of his hands and started choking the air out of me.

I started choking, trying to breathe at the same time. I even tried to use my strength to push him off me, but it wasn't working. "Somebody help me!" I managed to belt out. But it wasn't loud enough because Terrell applied more pressure to my neck.

"Bitch, I said shut the fuck up!" He gritted his teeth. "You said I wasn't fucking you good! You said my dick was whack, you dirty bitch! You trying to attack my man-hood? You gon' die today, bitch!" He continued to hiss as he continued to apply more and more pressure.

At this point, I knew this guy was going to kill me. I knew that in any given second that I was going to die because he had death in his eyes. But something on the inside of me told me to fight. Get this lunatic off you. I don't know how I did it, but I managed to reach up to his face, and I dug my fingers into his eye sockets.

"Ahhhhhh! You fucking bitch!" he screamed while I continued to apply more pressure to his eyes.

I thought his grip on my neck would ease away, but it didn't. He started choking me even harder. "You fucking bitch! You're gonna die!" he screeched as I was losing consciousness.

But then a light came on in my head. *Misty, you gotta stay alive. Your family needs you. You can't let this man kill you. Fight back, girl! You can do it*, I said to myself. And with the last bit of energy I had left in my body, I applied more pressure to his eyes until I felt gobs of blood and human tissue between my fingers. And at that moment, Terrell released his grip from my neck. "You fucking bitch!" he screamed once again after he let me go.

He couldn't see me because of the condition of his eyes so I jumped up from the floor and tried desperately to find my cell phone that I had dropped on the floor when he had first hit me.

"Where is my fucking phone?" I mumbled as I knelt on the floor to look under furniture. That wasn't a good idea because Terrell grabbed me by my hair and snatched me toward him.

"I'm gonna kill you now, you fucking ho!" he roared and that's when I realized that this guy wasn't going to stop until I was dead.

He grabbed me again, but this time he slammed me against the wall. My back landed against and knocked off a medium-sized canvas painting I hung there when I first moved into my apartment. He and I wrestled back and forth. He was trying to choke the life out of me while I was trying to stand my ground.

"You fucking bitch! I'm gon' kill you!" he hissed. It was like he could taste my blood.

Once again it felt like I was losing consciousness. But my mind was telling me to keep fighting. *Come on, Misty, don't let him kill you. Don't let him take your life*, I said to myself and that's when one of the nails the canvas painting had been hanging on scraped my shoulder. I don't know how I did it, but I dragged my back over to the left side of the wall and felt the wall up and down for that nail. Everything seemed like it was going in slow motion. After feeling around the wall a couple more times I finally located the nail, so I grabbed it and wiggled it out of the wall. With a long, utility nail in my hand I lunged my hand toward his face and Terrell screamed on contact.

"What the fuck?!"

I kept stabbing. The more I stabbed him the more his grip lessened, so I kept stabbing him. He swung his fists at me a few times, but I dodged them. A few seconds later, he collapsed onto the floor. I stood there in the dark and waited for him to move, but he wouldn't budge. Then I kicked his feet with mine. He still didn't move.

"Terrell, get up," I said, low enough so no one could hear me but him. Then I kicked his feet again. He didn't utter one word. And that's when panic engulfed me. I dropped the nail on the floor and then I rushed over to the light switch on the wall near the front door and flipped it on.

As soon as the light illuminated the living room, my eyes zoomed in on Terrell's lifeless body lying in a pool of his own blood. The sight of him with his eyeballs gouged out like you'd see in a horror movie made me wonder how I was capable of doing this. I've never put my hands on anyone in my entire life. So, what made me do this? And what am I going to tell the cops? I could end up with a fucking murder charge. But wait, he came here to my apartment and put his hands on me first. The cops might not see it that way, though.

"Oh my God! The fucking cops are going to lock me up for murder and I'll never see the light of day again. What am I going to do? I can't go to jail. Who's gonna bail me out? Or pay for my attorney? I can't go to prison for the rest of my life." I started sobbing as I collapsed on my living room floor.

Then out of the blue, I heard a light knock on my front door. Panic-stricken, I became paralyzed. "Hey, Misty, this is Mrs. Mabel from next door. Are you all right, honey?" I heard her weak little voice from the other side of the door.

I hesitated because I didn't know if it would be wise for me to let her know that I was home. But then, it dawned on me that what if I didn't answer and she decided to call the cops and have them do a welfare check? I couldn't have that, so I said, "Yes, Mrs. Mabel, I'm fine."

"Okay, just checking," she replied and then I heard her tiptoe away from my front door. I let out a long sigh of relief and then I looked back at the fucking mess I just made for myself.

29

PARANOIA AT ITS FINEST

I sat on the floor of my living room for another thirty minutes trying to process what just happened. It was clear that Terrell was lying dead on my living room floor, but the part I couldn't come to grips with was how I was going to clean this shit up. Was I supposed to call the cops and let them take a statement and risk getting my freedom taken from me? Fuck no! I couldn't let that happen. Not today. Not ever!

I finally got off the floor and dragged myself to the bathroom. I tried to avoid looking at my face when I passed by the bathroom mirror, but I couldn't. I had to see what a mess I made. "Oh my God!" were the only words I could utter. Seeing all the blood drying on my face, my hair all over my head, and the blue, black, and purple welts and marks on my neck looked horrible. And that's when it hit me, and a floodgate of tears poured down my face as I examined the condition of my face and neck. I had to wonder what kind of man could do this to a woman? Who would hurt a woman to this degree? And for what? Because she doesn't want to fuck you or be with you? Life is that fucked up for you?

While I stood there trying to figure out what to do, I decided that if nothing else, I needed to call Jillian and have her come over. She'd help me make the right choice. Thank God she answered on the first ring. "Hello," she said, sounding groggy.

"I need you to come over my house right now," I said with urgency.

"What's wrong? Are you all right?" she asked.

"Jillian, I can't talk over the phone. So, please come over here right now."

"Mind if I bring Edmund? 'Cause I'm at his house."

"No, you gotta come alone. And you gotta come now."

"Okay. I'm leaving now," she assured me.

Seconds after I got off the phone, I stripped down to nothing and hopped into the shower. I knew I needed to at least have myself cleaned up before Jillian got here. So, I showered for at least ten minutes and washed my hair. It seemed like moments after I got out of the shower and slipped on a T-shirt and a pair of boy shorts, my doorbell was ringing. I rushed to the front door and opened it slowly.

"What are you doing? Open the door," she said like she was getting agitated.

"Whatever you do, please don't scream when you come in here," I begged her quietly while I continued to pull the door open slowly.

"Girl, move," she said, and then she pushed her way by me. She took a total of five steps before she stopped in her tracks and gasped. "Oh my God! What the fuck! Is that Terrell? And is he dead?" she whispered while she tried to process what she was looking at.

"Yes, he's dead," I whispered, waving my hand to get her to lower her voice.

"What the fuck happened? And why is he dead?" Jillian's questions kept coming.

"He came over here and started attacking me because I didn't want to give his ass any pussy," I told her.

"Okay, I heard what you just said, but tell me how a conversation about pussy turns into a dead nigga on your living room floor?"

"We got into an argument and I told him that his dick was small and that he never fucked me good and he got mad and started choking me. Look at the welts on my neck. He tried to kill me. He was literally taking the breath out of me. So, I started gouging his eyes out and then I stabbed him with a nail I got from the wall," I explained.

"So what are you going to do?"

"I don't know. That's why I called you." I instantly became panic-stricken again.

"Think anyone seen him come here? Maybe one of your neighbors?"

"I'm not sure. But why?"

"With everything we got going on, we don't need this distraction right there," she said, pointing toward Terrell's body. "If we call the cops right now, they're gonna want you to go down to the police station. And who knows . . . what you tell them might make them lock you up with no bond. . . ."

"No bond?!" I gasped.

"Yeah. When people murder other people, they don't get bailed out of jail just like that." She snapped her fingers, startling me with the unnecessary emphasis. "And for the ones that do get bail, they can't afford it because they be asking for like one and two million dollars. So, like I said, with everything we got lined up, we can't let this shit throw a monkey wrench in our plans."

"So, what are we going to do with him?" I asked her.

"We're gonna have to chop his fucking body up and put it in trash bags and take that shit out of here," Jillian replied nonchalantly.

I looked at this bitch like she had just lost her fucking mind. "First, that's disgusting. Second, so you saying that *you're* gonna chop his body up? 'Cause I'm not. My stomach ain't built for that type of shit. I got nausea just by standing here and looking at him."

"No, silly! I'm gonna call my homeboy Tedo. He'll do it," she said confidently as she pulled her cell phone from her purse.

"Hold up!" I tried to snatch her cell phone from her hands, but she was too fast for me and spun out of my reach.

She gave me the side-eye. "Whatcha doing?"

"Do you trust him to come here and do that shit? What if he calls the cops or blackmails us because of this shit?"

"Don't worry about all that. That nigga got plenty of bodies and one more ain't gonna matter. So relax."

"Relax?! How the hell can I relax when I'm standing in my living room next to a nigga I used to be with and now he's dead? You can't even make that shit up."

"Look, I don't know what else to tell you. If you don't want me calling Tedo, then do it yourself because that ain't my cup of tea."

"Are you high?"

"You damn right I'm high. But I still know what's going on around me."

"I kind of figured that," I said and then I grabbed her by the arm and escorted her into the kitchen. I couldn't keep standing there and looking at Terrell. The thoughts in my head started jumbling up in my mind. I couldn't think straight, so I took a seat at my kitchen table while Jillian sat in the chair next to mine. A few minutes later she had Tedo on the phone. "Hey, Tedo, where you at?" I heard her ask him.

"Out here in these streets. What's good?" I heard him say through Jillian's cell phone. He was extremely loud.

"Well, check it out. I need you to come to my cousin's spot asap. We gotta throwaway that we need you to take out, and we ain't gonna be able to do it by ourselves," Jillian instructed him.

"You know how much I charge for that shit, right?"

"Of course I do, which is why we're gonna sweeten the pot in a couple of days when we do that other job," Jillian reminded him.

"A'ight. I'll be there within the hour, so text me the address."

"I'm on it now," Jillian said, then she disconnected their call.

"Are you really gonna text him my address?" I asked. I wasn't feeling that idea at all.

"How the fuck is he going to know where to come if I don't?" she replied sarcastically.

"Why don't you call him back and tell him that you'll meet him somewhere and that's when you get him to follow you here."

"Look, Misty, I'm not doing all of that so stop being fucking paranoid. If you want me to, when he gets here, I'll get him to delete the text."

"All right," I said.

30

I CAN'T BELIEVE MY EYES

Jillian met Tedo outside after he pulled up in front of my apartment building. He had another woman in tow as Jillian escorted him up to my apartment. "I just briefed him so he knows what to do," Jillian said as soon as she walked back into my apartment.

Tedo walked in behind her and the woman with him followed. Tedo and the woman both looked at the condition of Terrell's body like it didn't faze them. Tedo did say, "Where is his eyeballs?"

Jillian chuckled a bit and said, "Somewhere down there."

"I know y'all find humor in this, but I don't. And as soon as y'all can get him out of here, the better."

"Don't get your panties in a bunch, sis, everything is gonna be all right," the woman with Tedo chimed in.

"How long will it take y'all to do it?" I asked her and Tedo both.

"After we get him in a bathtub, it shouldn't take us longer than forty-five minutes," he replied.

"Yeah, that's about right," the woman agreed.

I looked her up and down and saw a heavy-set female gangster with a medium-brown complexion who looked like she wanted to take on the image of a man and had something to prove. She even looked like she could be a female pimp with a stable of run-down-ass prostitutes with drug habits.

After she put her backpack down on my coffee table, she opened it and pulled a slew of items from it. The first thing I saw was a black body bag. She had the fucking real deal. I'm talking about the ones you see on the TV series *NCIS*. The next thing she pulled out of the bag was a small electric saw.

"Hey wait, you're gonna cut him up in pieces?" I wondered aloud. But it was only loud enough for everyone in the living room to hear me.

"How the hell else did you think we were going to take him out of here?" Tedo asked me.

"That saw is going to be really loud. What am I going to tell my neighbors when they start knocking on my walls or the front door this time of the night?" I expressed.

"This saw doesn't make the noise like the ones you use to cut down trees. This is some new and improved shit that butchers use," the woman informed me.

"Are you sure?" I pressed the issue.

"Yes, we're good. No one will hear us," Tedo chimed in while he suited up with a jumpsuit that looked like a suit that a professional crime scene technician would wear. After the chick pulled all her tools out, she suited up in the same kind of jumpsuit.

"Come on, let's put him in the bag," Tedo instructed her immediately after she was dressed and ready to work.

Jillian stood there in awe. "Why are you staring at them like that?" I asked her.

"Because I ain't ever seen nobody do this shit in person. It's always been on TV," she replied while the woman and Tedo picked Terrell's body up and placed it in the body bag.

"Will you be cleaning up the blood on the floor and on the walls?" I asked.

"I got that. That's what I do," the chick said.

"So, what do you want us to do?" My questions continued.

"I guess you can go and take a seat somewhere. We pretty much got everything else," Tedo interjected while the woman zipped up the bag.

Taking Tedo's and the woman's direction, Jillian and I tiptoed around the blood on the floor and headed into the kitchen. I sat down in one chair while she sat down in the next. "I can't believe what the fuck just happened," I spoke out.

"I can't believe it either. I mean, I never in a million years would've thought that you'd be capable of killing somebody."

"Jillian, you're acting like I woke up this morning and said, oh, it's Tuesday, I'm gonna kill somebody today," I responded sarcastically.

"I'm not saying it like that. All I'm saying is that, look at you. You're a small frame woman and Terrell is big as fuck, so how were you able to pull that off? That's all."

"I still don't get it. Terrell brought that drama bullshit to me. I was in my bed, watching TV and about to go to sleep and then he calls me, talking about letting him in. I told him no and for him to go home. Then he starts yelling through the phone and outside my front door, talking about how I'm a fucking FBI informant. So, tell me how you would've handled that situation."

"Look, Misty, I'm not saying that this is your fault. All I was saying was that you're one of those pretty, petite women that doesn't bother anyone. But look at what could happen if you're provoked."

"Look, I see where you're trying to go with this. But it all goes back to the fact that I killed that nigga. And because of it, I gotta get someone to come into my house and clean up behind me."

"Just be grateful that you ain't the one that ended up

dead. The coroners would be taking your body out of here right now in one of those body bags if you hadn't fought back the way you did. So, thank God for that and let's move on from it."

"I wish it could be that easy."

"What do you mean?"

"You know I ain't gonna be able to sweep his murder under the rug that easy. One of his hos or family members are going to start looking for him and that's when the cops are going to start their whole investigation."

"They can investigate all they want. Tedo and April are the best that ever done it. After they leave here tonight, there's not gonna be a trace of Terrell."

"I don't care how good they clean up my place, they could still rat me out," I whispered.

"Misty, Tedo and his people ain't into that snitching shit. That's a code that they live by." Jillian tried to reassure me, but doubt loomed in the back of my mind. There was nothing Jillian could say that would ease my mind.

While I sat there in the kitchen, talking with Jillian, I heard the little buzzing sound coming from the bathroom. They were right. It didn't sound like the industrial-size chain saws. It pretty much sounded like a man's handheld electric shaver. Boy, what a sigh of relief that was.

"Did I tell you that the DEA agent wants me to accept the Arab guy's offer to take me to dinner?" I whispered so that only Jillian could hear me. The last thing I wanted to do was let Tedo and that woman April know the arrangement I had with the DEA.

"So, what are you going to do?" Jillian whispered back.

"I don't have a choice."

"What are they trying to get out of that dinner date?"

"They want me to plant two bugs in his car."

"Oh no, that's not a good idea. What if he catches you? Or finds out?"

"I don't have the answer to that."

"If he finds out about the bug and flips out on you, that could mess up the rest of our plans."

"Don't you think I already know that?" I raised my voice just a tad. She acted like I wasn't aware of the consequences if I did get caught. Those men that Sanjay and Amir were dealing with were some ruthless people. But what other options did I have? "Jillian, let's not talk about that anymore. I'm getting more and more upset just by the mere thought of it."

Jillian threw her hands in the air. "Okay. I won't say nothing else about it," she said nonchalantly.

She and I sat there at the kitchen in silence for the next few minutes until her cell phone rang. "Hello," she answered.

I knew it had to be her lame-ass boyfriend Edmund calling her this time of the night, so I sat there quietly while she talked to the clown. "Oh baby, I'm so sorry. I forgot. But don't worry, I made it here safely. And I'm sitting here with her now."

After hearing the first couple of words uttered from her mouth, I knew she was apologizing to that nigga because she didn't call him and let him know that she made it to my apartment safely. I say who cares if he wants to know her every move? He's a fucking joke. He sits around his mother's house and waits for Jillian's unemployment check to come in the mail so they can stock up on prescription drugs that will hold him over until he can get the next one. I say throw his ass on a deserted island and leave him there.

"I don't know how much longer I'm gonna be here," she told him.

"Tell 'im I'm in a fucking crisis and that you'll see his ass tomorrow," I blurted out. The sight of her trying to appease that nigga was irritating the fuck out of me.

"She didn't say anything, that's the TV," she lied.

"Don't lie to him," I said louder. I wanted him to hear

me so desperately. I mean, will she just take her fucking titty out of his mouth and stop breastfeeding him already? Make that nigga be a man for once in his life. It was bad enough that he lived at home with his mother, rent-free.

"Okay, I'll let you know either way," she said, and then she ended their call.

"When are you going to leave him? You can do so much better! He is a fucking bum!" I said.

"He's not all that bad," she replied as she laid her cell phone down on the table in front of her.

"Jillian, he's unemployed, he lives with his mother, he doesn't have a car, and he uses prescription drugs that you provide for him. It can't get no worse than that."

"Misty, he really has a good heart. And he's faithful to me."

"He has no choice. He can't find anyone else that would treat him as good as you do."

"You don't know him like I do. Because if you did, you wouldn't judge him the way you're doing now." Jillian turned her attention toward her cell phone that she had started playing with.

"Look, I'm sorry," I started off saying, "I just don't want you wasting your life away on a man that doesn't appreciate what he has. I mean, look at all the time I wasted on Terrell. I can imagine where my life would be right now if I had left him the first time we broke up. I'd probably be married with kids. Picture me with a little girl and a little boy. Maybe even a set of twins."

"Yeah, I can see you with kids. You'd be a good mother too."

"You think so?"

"Of course. You're a good daughter and cousin. You're always making sure everything is good."

"I guess I do have motherly ways, huh?" I said, giving Jillian a half smile. Thinking about how my life would've been if I had made better choices took me away from what was really going on around me. But it only took a voice from another room to bring me back to reality. "No, hold it like this," I heard Tedo say from the bathroom.

"I wonder how far they've gotten?" Jillian wondered aloud.

"I was just thinking the same thing."

"I'm gonna go in there and check," Jillian suggested and then she stood up from the kitchen chair.

"Be careful," I told her while I watched her leave the kitchen.

In a few seconds I heard Jillian say, "Oh my God! I can't do this." And she was right back in the kitchen with me. She took a seat and buried her face in her hands.

"What happened?"

"I couldn't stand there and watch them with all the damn blood, with the legs and arms and shit. My stomach couldn't take it," she explained after she removed her hands from her face.

I let out a long sigh. "I hope they're able to get all that blood and shit up."

"Don't worry, they will," she assured me.

31

BODY PARTS

It took Tedo and April over an hour to chop up Terrell's body and place the pieces in the bags. When they were done with it, April got me to fill up a bucket of cold water and hand it to her. She took it and applied some solution to it and then she went in the living room and started cleaning up the blood and whatever tissue remains I pulled from Terrell's body. It took her another hour to do that.

While she was doing that, Tedo started loading Terrell's body parts into his car. I watched him as he shuffled the bags into the back of his car, but at the same time watching my neighbors' apartments to see if anyone was watching Tedo and wondering what he was doing this time of the night. So far, the coast looked clear.

Immediately after April wiped everything on the surface clean, she instructed me to get rid of all my paintings and wall décor asap. "The solution I used to clean up your floor and walls made it so the blood won't show up if a homicide detective came here and used one of those UV lights. But it would show up on everything else, like the stuff you have on the wall."

"What about my furniture?"

"It's leather, so you're good. I gave it a good wipe down so I wouldn't worry about that," April assured me.

"All right," I said while I stood in the middle of the living room floor surveying everything on my walls.

"What about her hardwood floors?" Jillian chimed in.

"I tackled that. She's good. It won't show up," April told Jillian. "Oh yeah, you may wanna get rid of all the towels and the shower curtains in your bathroom too, because some of homeboy's blood may have splattered on em," she continued after she turned her attention toward me.

"Ready?" Tedo said as soon as he walked back into the house.

"Yeah, as soon as I take this jumper off," she told him.

"Everything a'ight on y'all end?" Tedo said as he looked at me and Jillian.

"Yeah, I'm good," Jillian replied.

I nodded my head.

"Everything still good with that job coming up?" Tedo continued.

"Yeah, everything is good on that end too. I told Misty we were throwing me a bigger cut because of this," Jillian explained.

"A'ight good. So, I'll hit y'all up later," he said.

"Cool," Jillian said.

"Thanks," I said while I watched him hold the front door open for April so she could exit. Right after they closed the door, I walked over there and locked it. And then I walked over to the living room window and peered through the blinds to see any other movement outside other than Tedo and April. More importantly, I need to see if there was movement coming from any of my neighbors' curtains or miniblinds, and when it seemed like everything was quiet, I took another look toward the parking lot while Tedo was driving away and noticed that Terrell's car was parked three cars over. Once again panic stricken, it felt like I was about to have a panic attack and Jillian noticed it too.

"What's wrong? Who's out there?" she asked me. I could heard the alarm in her voice.

"I forgot that Terrell's car is parked outside."

"Oh shit! What are we going to do?" Jillian asked me.

"I don't know."

"Where are his keys?"

"I don't know. Maybe Tedo and April got em. Just call them."

"All right. Hold on," she said and started dialing his number.

"He's gotta have em." I continued to talk while I waited for her to get him on the phone.

"Hey, Tedo, did you by any chance find homeboy's car keys?" Jillian asked him and then she fell silent.

"Oh, okay. Thanks, man. I'll talk to you later," she said and then she ended the call.

"What did he say?"

"He said he put 'em on bathroom sink."

I let out a long sigh. "Thank you!" I said and then I headed to the bathroom.

Right after I grabbed the keys to Terrell's car I got Jillian to follow me in her car so I could find a perfect spot to ditch his vehicle.

After driving for thirty minutes, I finally decided to drive Terrell's car into the swamp on the back roads of Chesapeake. This property belonged to the city of Virginia Beach, so no one was allowed on it. The water was green and muddy with tons of trash and debris. I figured if his car was ever found, it wouldn't be recognizable and they would never recover any of my DNA in the vehicle because of the water.

"Take me home," I told Jillian as soon as I got back into her car. She smiled at me and drove off.

I'm normally a silent thinker when I'm in a car going from point A to point B. If she wouldn't have sparked up a conversation with me during our drive back to my place, the entire drive would've been silent.

"Can you believe it's almost three o'clock in the morning?" she started off.

"No, I can't. It has been one long day," I commented. "And as soon as I get home, I'm gonna jump in my bed. Don't know if I'm going to get any sleep after all the shit that happened tonight, but I will try," I continued.

"Well, I'm tired so I'm crashing on your sofa as soon as I walk through your front door."

"Lucky you," I said, and then I turned my attention to the houses and cars we passed. "Did Tedo tell you exactly how much he wanted for cleaning my apartment?" I asked her while my focus was still on the cars and houses we passed.

"He just wants an extra 30K of pills so he can look out for April."

"What do you think they're gonna do with his body?" I wanted to know.

"He gotta uncle that works at a funeral home that does cremations. That's where Tedo takes everybody's body. Whether he killed them or not."

"Are you kidding me? He does that shit on a regular?"

"Yeah, and everybody knows it too. Tedo gets calls like this all the time. If he ain't selling drugs, killings niggas, chopping up their bodies and cleaning spots up. He's like an all-purpose kind of dude."

"Don't you think that's kind of sick? I mean, you're listing his credentials like he's a scholar or something."

Jillian chuckled. "No, I'm not. I'm just telling you all the shit he does. That's all."

"Do you seriously think that he won't rat me out later on down the line? I see on the ID channel all the time where people would ride for you and won't snitch you out.

But ten years down the line, their prison time is getting to them and that's when they start singing like a bird."

"Nah, that ain't what Tedo is about. You're good, so stop worrying."

"What about you?"

"What do you mean? What about me?"

"Look, I know you love your man and all, but you know you can't tell Edmund, right?"

"Yes, I know that."

"Jillian, you promise? Because I know how you get when you and him laid up in the bed having pillow talk and then it slips out. Do you know what that would do to me if that happened?"

"Nothing is going to happen, so stop being paranoid. You know I got you."

"You promise?"

"Yes, I promise."

When Jillian and I finally got back to my apartment, she did just like she said that she would do. She crashed down on my sofa not even three minutes after walking into my apartment. I ventured off into my bedroom, got into my bed, and was only able to get two hours of sleep. I woke back up at five thirty in the morning.

I got out of bed and went into the living room and noticed that Jillian was still asleep, so I went into the kitchen, made me a cup of hot tea, and then I took it back into the bedroom with me. I watched the news over and over for the next two-and-a-half hours until Jillian woke up and joined me in my bedroom. "How long have you been up?" she asked me after she crawled onto my bed.

"Two, three hours now, I think," I replied immediately after I swallowed the tea that was in my mouth.

"How are you feeling? Feeling any remorse or regrets right now?"

"Of course I am. All morning I've been replaying everything that happened last night and have been beating myself up because I really could've prevented what I did from happening."

"I understand what you're saying, but you can't do that to yourself. It will drive you crazy."

Feeling the regrets that Jillian had just mentioned gave me an overwhelming burst of emotional pain and I broke down in tears. "Why didn't he just leave me alone? Why didn't he just stay at home and not bother me? We've been broken up for the past couple of months and he couldn't get it through his head that we weren't getting back together." I sobbed uncontrollably. Jillian moved her body closer to mine and embraced me.

"I know it doesn't seem like you're gonna get past this, but you will," she said as she massaged my back with one of her hands.

"What's gonna happen if the cops find out about it?"

"They won't, so stop saying it."

"Whatever happens, please don't turn your back on me."

"Misty, you're talking crazy. I would never to do that to you. You're family. You're blood."

"You can't tell nobody. Not even Grandma or Edmund."

"I won't. I promise."

Jillian stayed with me for another hour in my bedroom, trying to console me. It seemed like it worked, but as soon as she left my apartment, I released another floodgate of tears from my eyes. I wanted to crawl underneath my blanket and shut myself off from the rest of the world and hope that they forgot all about me. But I knew this scenario was a bit far-fetched, so I lay there in my bed until I got a phone call from Agent Sims. My heart started pumping erratically. Was he calling me to say that he knew about Terrell's murder? And that he was about to take me into custody? Whatever it was, I wasn't ready for it.

"Hello," I said.

"Hope you had a good night's sleep because we've got to make something happen today," he replied.

"What are you talking about?" I asked him, needing him to tell me what he was referring to.

"I'm talking about the dinner date with Ahmad. You gotta make that happen today," he insisted.

"And you need this done today?" I asked him, even though I knew the answer. I just needed him to talk more so I could get a gauge on his mood.

"We've already discussed this."

"All right, don't pressure me. I'll make it happen," I assured him, but at the same time feeling sick to my stomach for the emotional and physical turmoil I experienced last night, trying to prevent Terrell from killing me.

"What time does your shift start today?"

"In a couple of hours."

"You're still going to wear the body camera we furnished you with, right?"

"Yes,"

"Okay. Well, look vibrant. Chop! Chop!" he said.

Instead of commenting I disconnected our call. I wasn't in the mood to hear all that unnecessary excitement. There was nothing to be excited about. People were dying around us and he wasn't to be happy about it. Well, I say fuck him! And as soon as I was done with this whole thing, I was getting out of here. Move far away from all of this bullshit! I wanted a normal life and this wasn't it.

Amir was inside the pharmacy when I walked through the front door. As usual I spoke first, like I always do, and then I went on to do my same routine. "Have you spoken to Sanjay?" I asked him, just to get a reaction from him. I also needed to get his reaction on camera so Agent Sims and the rest of those idiots could see that I was doing what I was instructed to do.

He turned around and snapped at me. "Why do you

want to know that?" This guy even pointed his finger at me too. Had I hit a nerve?

"What the hell is wrong with you?" I stood my ground.

"Stop asking me questions about my brother. What I do and he does is none of your business. So don't ask me about him anymore," he spat. I could see the veins bulging in his temples.

"No problem. But will you at least tell him I said hello?" I continued, hoping what I had just said would send him over the edge.

"I'm not telling him anything. Now leave me alone about him and get back to work," he instructed me and then he turned back around to his computer monitor and started typing away.

I shook my head in disgust because this idiot thought that he was intimidating me by getting loud and pointing fingers at me. If he knew that I had just killed my ex-boyfriend because that bastard put his hands on me, he'd think twice before he talked to me like that ever again.

Instead of feeding into his bullshit tactics, I logged into the system and once again started processing our online prescription orders. I couldn't believe that we didn't have a lot of them because it was the first of the month, and our elderly clientele spends the bulk of their social security checks refilling their meds. But for some reason, that wasn't happening today. So I turned around toward Amir and asked him if he knew why we didn't have an influx of online orders today.

He turned toward me and said, "Don't ask me anymore questions. Just process the orders that are there. Now, if you give me anymore problems I will fire you today."

I swear, I was seething on the inside because of the way this asshole was talking to me. He didn't have to speak to me like that. I only asked him a simple question pertaining to this fucking store. Well, if he didn't give a fuck about the sales, then I didn't give a fuck either.

While I carried on with what I was doing, the front door of the pharmacy opened. I looked up and saw one of our faithful customers named Mr. Childress entering. But when I saw Ahmad walking into the pharmacy behind him, my heart skipped a beat. He gave me a huge smile as he walked toward me. He seemed happy to see me, but when I looked back at Amir through my peripheral vision, he had a very different expression. I could tell that he wasn't at all happy to see Ahmad walking toward us.

"Hi, Mr. Childress, how can I help you today?" I asked the elderly guy.

He handed me his prescription document. "It's a beautiful day outside. You should be out there rather than in here," he commented.

"That's why I'm here to take her out to lunch," Ahmad walked up behind him and said as he stepped behind the counter where Amir and I were.

Amir's facial expression went from frustration to rage. "Ahmad, we have a lot of work to do today."

"Well, hire someone else to do it, because she's going out to lunch with me."

I kept my back slightly turned toward Amir, pretending to process Mr. Childress's meds, but I watched Amir's demeanor through my peripheral vision and he was not a happy camper. He was slow to speak after Ahmad told him to hire someone new. I can't believe that I started feeling sorry for the moron, so much so that I jumped to his defense. "He's right, we do have a lot of work to do," I chimed in. I knew this wasn't a move the DEA agents wanted me to make, but it had started getting really awkward in his store.

"I'm with the fella here. Take her out and show her a good time," Mr. Childress interjected.

"See, this gentleman knows what he's talking about." Ahmad smiled as he pointed to Mr. Childress.

"She goes to lunch in an hour. Can you wait until then?" Amir asked Ahmad passively.

"No, I can't wait for another hour. I'm here now." Ahmad pressed the issue. And as badly as I wanted Amir to stand up to Ahmad like he does to me, I was enjoying the way he was being pushed around. He was a fucking coward and Ahmad made that known.

"All right. All right. She can go," Amir finally agreed. But he knew he really didn't have a choice any way you looked at it. Amir feared Ahmad, and if you wanna know the truth, I feared him too. The thought of going somewhere with him alone was frightening in itself. But I knew that I had to do it, so I started preparing myself mentally for this venture.

Ahmad stood there next to me, literally looking over my shoulders while I worked on the customer's order. I felt so uneasy. It felt like he could see the wire I was wearing and that at any moment he was going to brush against me to confirm his suspicion. I swear, I wanted to just fall out on the floor right then and die. This guy was giving me so much anxiety and at one point it felt like I couldn't breathe because my life was being sucked out of me. But I knew that I had to play it cool. I had to maintain control of my actions, do what I was told and this too shall pass.

It only took me ten minutes to fill Mr. Childress's order and after I handed it to him, he smiled at me and then he looked at Ahmad and said, "She's a beauty, so take care of her."

Ahmad smiled back at Mr. Childress and said, "Don't worry. I will."

32

WHAT'S FOR LUNCH?

"Are you ready?" Ahmad asked me immediately after I handed Mr. Childress his medicine. I wanted to tell him to haul ass, but I couldn't speak. Per Agent Sims's instructions, I had to spend some alone time with this evil and murdering motherfucker, long enough so that I could set up a bugging device in his vehicle. Sounded like a suicide mission to me.

"I need to use the ladies' room first and then I'll be ready," I told him and then I walked off. I grabbed my purse from my cubby and took it with me to the restroom. Right after I closed the door I locked it to make sure that no one came in behind me. I couldn't risk Amir or Ahmad catching me while I removed the body cam and wire from my body. I knew I wouldn't leave this pharmacy alive if that happened. I had to be on point with every step I took with these dudes. They're mafia cats and I can't measure up to that. They have game passed down from one generation to the next. I only know that nigga Tedo and I haven't been knowing him long. So, what do I have as far as street credibility? Nothing or no one.

The body camera and wire slid off with ease, so I stuck

them into a small pocket in my purse and then I zipped it up. I wanted to make sure that the bugs that Agent Sims gave me to put in Ahmad's car were still tucked away in my purse and that they were accessible when I needed to pull them out. When I saw that they were still in the place I put them, I closed my purse back up. Right when I was about to walk back out of the bathroom, I remembered that I needed to call Agent Sims and let him know that there'd been a change of plans. Thank God, he answered on the first ring. "We just saw Ahmad go into the pharmacy, so how's everything going? Are you okay?" Agent Sims asked me.

"He came to take me to lunch instead of dinner," I whispered.

"You're going, right?"

"Yes, that's why I'm calling you."

"Don't forget that this is your chance to stick the bugs into his car. One in the front seat and one in the back," he instructed me.

"I know. I know," I whispered once more.

"Well, be careful. But don't worry, because me and the other agents will be with you every step of the way." Agent Sims tried to reassure me, but I knew this was straight bullshit. All he cared about was this stupid-ass case. I bet if he knew that I killed Terrell last night, he'd tell me to plant the bugs and then meet him at the station so he could lock my ass up. It's all about them and nothing else. Bastards!

Ahmad was waiting for me behind the counter when I exited the ladies' room. Amir was standing there next to him with a mean grin on his face. I know he wanted to call me every bad name in the book, but he knew Ahmad wasn't going to have it.

Ahmad beamed. "You ready?"

"Yes, I am," I replied. But inside I wasn't. This guy scared me to death. I felt like at any minute he'd pull out his gun and shoot me. That's not how I wanna leave this earth.

Ahmad walked me outside and escorted me in the direction of his car. When he hit the car alarm, I saw the headlight flicker on a Maserati SUV. Its exterior was black with black tinted windows, and when he opened the passenger-side door, I noticed that the interior was all black as well; the only other color I saw was the brown wooden finishes on the dashboard and around the steering wheel. The car was immaculate.

"Do you eat Indian cuisine?" he asked me after he started the ignition.

"No," I said. I was extremely nervous sitting in this car with this man. I swear, it felt like he was going to take me somewhere, kill me, and dump my body underneath the Berkley Bridge.

"Great, because I'm going to take you to my family's restaurant on Military Highway, called Indian Delight. Have you eaten there before?"

"No, I haven't."

"Good. Because I'm gonna get my cousin to prepare you something that you're gonna love," he said with enthusiasm as he pulled away from the pharmacy parking lot.

One minute into the drive Ahmad decided that he wanted to ask me a slew of fucking questions. I didn't know if he was just trying to have a general conversation or he was probing me for something. I played along with him anyway.

"Has your ex-boyfriend been harassing you lately?" he didn't hesitate to ask me.

I swear, I was about to fucking shit on myself when he inquired about Terrell. What made him do that? Did he know that I killed him? If he did, then that meant that's he'd been watching me. And if he'd been watching me, he'd seen the DEA agents. Oh my God! He was getting ready to take me somewhere and kill me. What had I gotten myself into?

"Don't tell me you guys are back together, because if you are, then I'm gonna be jealous," he continued, and then he chuckled.

"No, we're not back together. I would never get back into a relationship with him," I finally answered.

"Good. He doesn't look like your type anyway."

"Everyone says that," I replied nonchalantly while I watched the birds flying around in the sky. My mission was to avoid eye contact with him at all costs.

"How old are you?"

"I'm twenty-nine."

"No kids, right?"

"Right, no kids."

"Never been married?"

"Nope."

"Why not?"

"Because I'm not the marrying type. I like my independence," I lied. I was trying everything in my power to be the opposite of what he deemed attractive. All I wanted was for this lunch date to be over and done with.

"I think you are. You're just trying to be modest."

"Can I ask you something?" I interjected.

"Sure."

"Why do you really want to take me out to lunch?"

"Because you're beautiful and I like being in the company of beautiful women."

"So, you're expecting for me to have sex with you after you take me out to eat?"

"No, of course not. I'm not that type of guy. There's a few nice guys left in this world, you know."

"I'm sure there are . . ."

"But you haven't found one yet, right?" He finished my sentence.

"I guess so." I gave him a half smile.

"I see you over there smiling. But I know that you can do better than that."

"Maybe on another day," I told him, and then I changed the course of our conversation. "What's gonna happen after we have lunch?"

"I take you back to work."

"That's it? You're sure you're not going to ask me to show you how to get to my apartment?"

"No, because I already know where you live," he replied. And when he said that, it felt like a lightning bolt struck me directly in the center of my heart. He knew . . . He knew that I was doing business with the DEA. And he knew that Terrell had been to my apartment several times, when in fact I told him no. *What am I going to do now? Should I open the door at the next traffic light and jump out? Would Agent Sims rescue me from the side of the road? Or would that derail his investigation so he leaves me there?* I hate when I got to make decisions on this level. I can't ever get it right.

I cracked a half smile and said in a teasing manner, "Don't tell me I got a stalker on my hands."

"Of course not. I got your home address from your employee file at the pharmacy."

"Oh yeah, my bad!" I chuckled, trying to make light of the situation.

"Well, we're here," he said as we pulled into the parking lot of the restaurant.

I looked at the building and the scenery around it and realized that I had seen this place before. After Ahmad got out of the car, he walked around to the passenger side and opened the door for me. I can't remember the last time I had my car door opened for me, so it was something different. I thanked him and then we both headed into the restaurant.

The lighting and music created a great ambiance. I didn't

know whether to enjoy it, or keep my guard up because of the job I had to do. "We're gonna eat over here." He pointed to a booth in the far corner of the restaurant. After I sat down, he excused himself and went into the kitchen. I pulled out my cell phone and called Jillian to tell her where I was. "Hey, are you at home?" I asked her.

"Why? Whatcha need?"

"Remember I told you that that guy named Indian Delight asked me to go to dinner with him?"

"Yeah, what happened?"

"He came and got me and brought me to his family's restaurant so I could eat lunch with him."

"You fucking kidding?!"

"No, I'm not. I'm sitting in a restaurant called Indian Delight that's on the corner of Virginia Beach Boulevard and Military Highway."

"I know where that is."

"Good, because if I come up missing between here and back to the pharmacy, you know who's got me," I instructed her.

"Just be careful."

"I will."

Ahmad came back out of the kitchen about eight minutes later and he had two plates of food with him. And when he set those plates of food on the table in front of me, I was impressed at what I saw. "You cooked this?" I asked him.

He smiled. "Yes, I did. I did it for you," he replied.

"What is it?" I wondered aloud.

"This first plate is salmon makhani, which is salmon cooked in a tomato and cream sauce. It's one of my favorite dishes. And this second plate is paneer makhani, which is chunks of cheese cooked in the same tomato and cream sauce. Sometimes I'll eat the cheese in spinach. It's good both ways. Try some," he insisted after he sat down on the other side of the booth.

I picked up my fork and tried the salmon dish and I have to admit that it was good. It was so good that I ate another forkful of it. "This is really good," I said between chews.

"Try the cheese dish."

Without saying another word, I dug into that dish too and loved it so much. I covered my mouth, still chewing my food, and said, "I could eat this every day."

He smiled. "I'm glad that you like it."

Ahmad and I ate every morsel of food on both plates and chitchatted the entire time. I let my guard down. For the first time around this guy, I wasn't afraid. He wasn't intimidating. Our connection seemed genuine. He made me feel okay with sharing the same space with him.

Our lunch date lasted for a little over an hour. I've gotta be honest and say that I had a really nice time. In fact, I wasn't ready to go back to work when we exited the restaurant and got back into his SUV. I didn't tell him that, though. I kept my game face on and reminded myself to stick with the plan.

On the way back to the pharmacy, I started panicking because I knew that if Ahmad dropped me off without getting out of his vehicle, then I wouldn't be able to plant the wiretaps underneath the seats. I figured that I needed to do something and do it quick, so I said, "Hey, Ahmad, could you stop off at this gas station coming up on the right?"

"Sure. What do you need?" he wanted to know.

"I want some gum really bad. I can still taste the garlic from the naan."

"No problem," he replied and made the detour.

"Could you go inside and get it for me? My stomach is full and I can't move an inch," I lied.

"What kind do you want?"

"Anything with mint."

"Okay. I'll be right back."

Immediately after Ahmad got out of his vehicle I watched

him walk into the convenience store, and when the door to the store closed behind him, I sprang into action. With an increased heart rate, I grabbed the bugs from my purse and placed the first one underneath my seat. But as soon as I tried to stick it to the bottom of my seat, it fell down on the floor. I panicked. My hands started shaking and I couldn't concentrate because of trying to keep my eyes on the door of the store and making sure I installed the wire correctly. After three tries, I finally was able to stick the bug underneath my seat without it falling again. But by the time I grabbed the second device so that I could place it underneath the back seat, Ahmad was coming back out of the store. Petrified that he might see the wire in my hand, I stuck it back into my purse right before he opened the driver-side door. "I gotta Trident. Is that okay?" he asked as he got in.

"Yes, it's perfect. Thank you," I told him as I took the gum from his hand.

"Want one?" I asked after I opened the pack.

"No, but thank you."

I pretended to savor the taste of this minty-ass piece of gum. The mint in it was too strong and it was throwing off the flavors that were lying in the creases of my tongue from the salmon and cheese makhani. There was no way in the world that I was going to be able to put the other bugging device where I was instructed to. I hoped the one I did put in place worked, because if not, I knew I wouldn't hear the end of it.

The moment after Ahmad drove up curbside to the pharmacy, he thanked me once again for the lunch date. He even expressed that he wanted to see me again, so I suggested that we needed to play it by ear. But before I got out of his SUV, I said, "You know I'm gonna get a lot of flak because of this lunch date with you."

"From who? Amir?"

"Yes, he's gonna chew me out as soon as I walk into the store."

"Oh no, that's not gonna happen. Come on, let's go inside together," he instructed me.

Just like that, Ahmad escorted me back into the pharmacy and laid it on thick when he and Amir came face-to-face. "Listen to me, and listen to me good, I don't want you to say anything to her about going out to lunch with me. I don't want you disrespecting her. And don't threaten her about anything. If she comes back and tells me that you made her feel uncomfortable or that you disrespected her, then I'm gonna deal with you accordingly. Got it?"

Amir nodded in agreement.

Right after he laid down the law to Amir, he turned toward me and winked. I gave him a half smile because I saw the way Amir was looking at me through his peripheral vision. I knew that if that man didn't like me five minutes ago, then he hated my guts now. There was a new sheriff in town.

33

COVERING MY TRACKS

Thankfully, the rest of my time at work today ended quickly. But that was not the important issue here. I couldn't get my mind off the bug I put in Ahmad's truck earlier. I was consumed with that all day. Every time someone walked into the pharmacy I thought it was Ahmad coming back to question me about the bug device. At one point, my stomach was gurgling so badly that I thought that I was going to shit myself. I don't know how I made it through the rest of the day.

I went straight over to my grandmother's house from work. I called Jillian in advance and told her to meet me there because she was over at her lame-ass boyfriend's mama's house. Surprisingly, she got there before I did. She met me outside as soon as I pulled up curbside.

"What's up? Are you all right?" she wondered aloud after I got out of my car. We both found a spot and leaned against the trunk of my car.

"Yeah, I'm good. Can't believe that I got through today without getting killed. And when I tell you how nervous I was around that guy at certain times during the lunch date, you wouldn't believe me."

"How was the Indian food?"

"It was really good. He was so accommodating. I mean, he was so freaking nice to me. The way he treated me was like night and day from the way he treated Sanjay and Amir."

"You wanna fuck him, don't you?"

"No, Jillian. I don't. I'm just telling you that I saw another side to this guy. And if I didn't know the evil side of him, I would go on another date with him if he asked me to."

"Well, has he asked you?"

"No. And I'm glad too. I think he didn't ask me because he had to straighten Amir out about me, so that probably threw him off track."

"You know you better be careful with that guy. I know he's a perfect guy while y'all are together. But let's focus. We're gonna rob him and all his buddies. So, take that fairy-tale bullshit out of the equation because we got a job to do."

"Come on, Jillian, you don't have to tell me all of that. I already know. It's just that I wish things were different. I wish that I wasn't knee deep in all of this bullshit. Sometimes it feels like I'm drowning."

"I'm sure it does. But look at it this way—after tomorrow we're gonna make a lot of money, you aren't gonna have to work at that shit hole anymore. You can tell everybody to kiss your ass and keep it moving."

"What about Terrell?"

"What about him? You ain't gotta deal with that loser anymore either. His body is now ashes and his car is in the bottom of the dismal swamp. Now it can't get no better than that," Jillian said and cracked a smile.

"I can't see why you find this humorous."

"Face it, Terrell was a self-absorbed, narcissistic-ass nigga. All he ever cared about was what he wanted. What he had to have. And that was it. Trust me, the world is better off without him."

"I hope I don't go to hell for what I did to him."

"Go to hell! Misty, you were defending yourself. If you hadn't stopped him, you'd be dead and not him. You had to protect your life, and killing him was something that had to happen. Case closed."

"I hope April and Tedo never rat me out."

"Trust me, they won't," Jillian tried to reassure me. "So, I hear your mom's birthday is today?"

"Oh shit! Damn, I haven't even called her," I said and pulled my cell phone from my purse, which was still in my car. Jillian stood there while I talked to my mother on the phone. "Mom, I'm so sorry that I didn't call you much sooner. Today was a very busy day at work. And I'm just now leaving. So happy birthday."

"Thank you. So, where are you?"

"I'm getting in my car as we speak. Why? Is anything wrong?"

"No. Are you still coming?"

"Yes, I'm coming right now."

"Okay. See you then," she told me and then she hung up.

Immediately after I got off the phone with my mother I let out a long sigh.

"You better hurry up and get over there," Jillian teased me.

"I swear, I don't feel like going anywhere but home."

"You know you'll break her heart if you don't go over there and spend her birthday with her."

"I know. I know. Damn! Why couldn't it be on another day?"

"Well, it's not. Now get your butt into your car and ride over there. Call me when you're on your way home."

"Okay. I will," I assured her and then I hopped back into my car.

Being mentally broke down wouldn't be a good enough excuse for me not to show up to my mother's birthday dinner. It would crush her heart if I did. So, I'm gonna put an H on my chest and take one for the team.

My mother was so happy to see me walk through the front door of her house. This was the first time in months that I'd seen her smile. After she gave me a kiss on my cheek, she escorted me to the dining room, where she had all her food set out on the table and a beautiful flower centerpiece. Her boyfriend was already sitting at the table when I walked into the room. He spoke. I spoke back, and then the festivities started with my mother sitting at the head of the table. She was smiling from ear to ear.

"I am so happy that the two people I love are here with me and celebrating my fifty-fifth birthday. I don't know what I would do without you two. I love you!" she said.

"I love you too, Mama." I chimed in.

"I love you too, babe," he said.

Like she had promised, she baked a lasagna and it was delicious. I didn't have a huge appetite, but I knew that if I hadn't eaten everything on my plate, my mother would've went ham on me. "I'm glad you're enjoying your food," she said to me.

And that's when it hit me that I didn't bring the birthday cake. "Mom, don't kill me, but I forgot your birthday cake."

"It's okay, baby. Carl picked up one of those ice cream cakes when he came from work this morning."

I looked over at Carl and thanked him for saving me from the cake mission. He smiled at me and told me everything was good.

I noticed that Carl wasn't much of a talker, because as soon as he finished eating his food, he got up from the table and retreated to the den to watch TV. That left me and my mother alone, so this was prime time for her to pile a load of questions on me.

"Have you spoken to your grandmother today?" she started off.

"No. Have you?"

"Yes. She called me and wished me a happy birthday."

"That's was nice. Did she say anything else?"

"Well, she said that she wished she could come by and see me, but the new medicine that the doctor put her on makes her sleep a lot, so she needed to be home."

"Is that all she said?"

"Well yeah, because the rest of the conversation was about the government shutdown. And how she was sick of our new president. And you know when she starts talking about what's going on in the news, I tend to shy away from those topics. I think she does that to avoid talking about the real issues that involve her and me. I would say my brother too, but he's no longer here, so I'll just say us."

"Why don't you guys go to counseling, Mama? You and Grandma need a mediator. Someone who's not going to be biased," I suggested.

"No, honey, I'm old-school. Black families in my generation don't get involved with counseling. We sit down and deal with the problems head-on."

"If that's how y'all do it, then what's the problem? Why haven't the issues been resolved?"

"Because your grandmother can be a little stubborn."

"Look, Mama, enough is enough. Y'all gonna have to bury this mess before someone in this family dies. And if that happens, that means that things never got resolved and then you're gonna be beating yourself up that the other person is gone and you didn't get a chance to say you love them."

"I'm ready to do that now, but your grandmother isn't." My mama continued placing the blame on my grandmother. I sat there at that table with her for at least thirty minutes, trying to convince her that life is too short so we need to cut all the nonsense out and start loving on each other. It bothered me that she and my grandmother weren't on the best of terms. I loved them both, so this mess had to stop.

34

THE DAY OF THE HEIST

I lost another night of sleep. I thought I'd be able to get at least six hours, but I was fooling myself. With the robbery that was going to go down tonight, I couldn't think about anything else. Moments after I got dressed, Agent Sims and his partner showed up at my front door. "Are you ready?" he asked while we stood in a huddle at my front door.

"As I'll ever be," I told him.

But then something happened that threw me off track when Agent Sims and his partner started sniffing the air around us. "Do you smell that?" he said.

"What smell?" I spoke first while a nauseating feeling came over me. I knew what he was talking about. I knew he smelled that formula April used to clean up Terrell's blood. I just stood there and acted like I didn't know what they were talking about.

"You haven't killed anyone in here in the last couple of days, huh?" Agent Sims asked me in a joking manner.

Agent Montclair burst into laughter. "That's funny!"

I laughed too. If only he knew the truth.

"Look, I would love to stand here all day and joke

around with you guys, but I've got to get to work. So, say what you gotta say so I can get out of here," I told them. The real reason I wanted them out of here was because if they'd stayed around any longer, they'd probably figure out that twenty-four hours ago, I actually did have a dead body lying on the floor right where we were standing. I thank God that they were more consumed with the case dealing with Sanjay and Amir, because if they weren't they'd be handing me a search warrant rather than a camera and wiretaps. Agent Sims and I went over a few more things and then he left. Boy, was I glad to see them go.

I left my apartment about thirty minutes after the agents left. The past couple of days I'd suited up with the wire and the camera before I left my apartment, but I couldn't do it today. I had to stop by my grandmother's house to talk to Jillian about last-minute preps, so having the wire and camera in place would've been the stupidest thing that I could do. Got to be careful not to let the left hand know what the right hand is doing.

When I reached my grandmother's house, Jillian was front and center. She was dressed and ready to go. "Talked to Tedo today?" I asked her after I walked into the house. I made sure we talked in a whisper, because my grandmother had some good ears.

"Yeah, I talked to him about an hour ago. He's ready whenever we are," Jillian assured me.

"Good, because I want this thing to run smoothly. You know the DEA agents are going to be parked down street from the pharmacy, so you gonna walk in the store like you're a customer."

"I know that already."

"I just want to make sure everyone is on the same page," I told her.

"Don't worry, everything is gonna be all right."

"All right. I'm holding you to that," I said, and then I made my way back out of the house.

* * *

Amir was standing in his usual spot in front of the computer monitor.

"Has today's shipment come in yet?" I asked him as soon as he looked up from the computer.

"No. They are late."

I looked down at my watch and noticed that it was eleven o'clock in the morning. Normally the UPS driver would be here around nine o'clock, so to see that he was running behind schedule made me feel uneasy. "Do I have a lot of orders to fill today?" I asked him.

"We have a few," he replied. His tone was really calm. He did not act like he had a chip on his shoulder or anything. I was thinking Ahmad put the fear in his heart to the point that he didn't want to waste any negative energy on me. For the first time since Sanjay had been gone, I felt a little easier.

One hour into my work, I realized that I had forgotten to put the wiretap devices on my body, so I grabbed my handbag and raced to the ladies' room. But when I got there I realized that I didn't have enough tape to put the wires back in place so they wouldn't be visible through my shirt. "Fuck! I don't have enough tape. What am I gonna do?" I said and then I sighed heavily. "Fuck it! I'm just gonna have to wear the camera and that's it," I continued.

When I walked back out of the ladies' room I noticed that the UPS driver had finally come to deliver the orders Amir put in a few days ago. He and I spoke to each other while I headed out the front door. I walked outside so that the agents could see me and know that I was okay, despite the fact that they couldn't hear me through the wire. After I stretched out my arms, demonstrating that I was tired but okay, I turned around and walked right back into the pharmacy. The moment I stepped over the threshold, the UPS driver was walking toward me. I stood there and held the front door open for him so he could leave. "Have a nice day," he told me.

"You do the same." I replied.

Immediately after I walked behind the counter where Amir was standing, I said, "Want me to unpack the boxes and put everything in the supply closet?"

"No. Leave them by the wall. I will get them later," he told me, not looking up at me once.

I swear, Ahmad really had this guy shook. He didn't even want to look at me anymore when he was talking to me. I was loving this because he was a fucking coward and he had no respect for anyone. I was glad to finally see that I was getting some. Couldn't say how long it would last, but at this point, who cares. I was there to do a job and that's it.

I think in the last thirty minutes I looked at my wristwatch over a dozen times. I was plagued with anxiety and fear of the unknown. I was an emotional wreck. And I couldn't get a grip on myself. I just wished today would hurry up and be over so I could go on about my life. This shit right here was for bitches that like drama in their lives. Not me.

For the next several hours, only a few customers here and there came in to get their prescriptions filled. So there was an awkward silence that filled the room every time it was just Amir and I standing there. It was obvious that he had a lot of shit on his mind because I had a lot on mine as well.

Thinking about Terrell's accidental death for one. One part of me felt like I was going to be all right. But then the other part of me became scared shitless when I thought about the possibility that the cops were going to find out that I killed him. I see it on TV all the time. Murders become cold cases, and then ten to fifteen years later some new detective comes along and solves the case. I could be one of those people. I couldn't spend the rest of my life in prison, especially for something that I didn't mean to do. He violated me and he got dealt with. End of story.

Now as far as my mother is concerned, she's going to self-medicate on alcohol for the rest of her life. She doesn't believe that she has a problem, so there's nothing I can say to make her feel any different. All I can do for her is just love her unconditionally. That's it. And if she finally figures out that she does have a problem, I'll be there for her as well.

My cousin Jillian, on the other hand, has a lot of demons. She's a sweetheart, but she's a lost soul. I think allowing my grandmother to baby her gives my grandmother purpose. And in return, Jillian babies her loser boyfriend, Edmund. It's like a domino effect. Because I'm sure Jillian feels like she's on this earth to take care of and nurture a lame boyfriend. For the life of me, I can't understand the enabling characteristics that my grandmother and my cousin share. I've never been the type to enable a person, like my mother for instance. I don't hold her hand or downplay any of her problems. I like to deal with things head-on. Now, I didn't do that in my relationship with Terrell, which is why I kept taking him back. I know that if I hadn't done that, I wouldn't have wasted so much time and would be further along in life. Tomorrow was going to be the start of a new day for me. And I wouldn't let anyone stop me.

Lunchtime rolled around and Amir made me aware of it. It almost sounded like he wanted to kick me out of the pharmacy. "It's time for you to go to lunch," he said. This time the motherfucker looked at me head-on. All the other times, he kept his head hung low. I guess he grew some balls.

"I'm not going out today. I brought my lunch with me." I lied because I knew what he was doing. He was about to take those prescription drugs out of here and he didn't want me nowhere around while he did it.

"I don't care if you brought your lunch with you. Take it outside and eat it in your car," he protested.

"I don't eat in my car."

"Go next door to Starbucks. Eat it in there," he instructed me. He wasn't playing no games.

"Sanjay never made me leave outta here during my lunchtime. He let me have lunch wherever I wanted it."

"But he's not here anymore. I am your boss. So you have to listen to me. And I say leave," he demanded.

"Why do you have to be so rude? All of the anger is not necessary," I told him while I began to log myself out of the system for my lunch break.

"I am not rude. And I am not angry. You just have to listen to me. That's all."

"Yeah, whatever," I said, and grabbed my purse from my cubby.

Instead of going out the front door, I made a detour and went to the ladies' room. I needed to prolong my exit to see what was going on, because Amir was being tight-lipped about it. After I locked the bathroom door, I pulled out my cell phone and called Jillian. "Hey where are you?" I whispered.

"I'm still in the house."

"You need to get down here. Because something isn't right."

"What do you mean?"

"First off, the deliveries came late. And then when my lunchtime rolls around, Amir wants me to leave the store. He literally told me to get out of the store while I am on my lunch break. So I know something is about to happen."

"All right, I'm gonna call Tedo now, and then we'll be on our way up there."

"All right. Hurry up," I said, and then I ended the call.

I stayed in the bathroom for another five minutes and pretended that I had to use it just in case Amir found out I was in there. I thought that at any moment he was gonna come knock on the door and tell me I needed to get out. That's when I would've hit him with the *I got diarrhea* excuse. Didn't know if it would work, but I was gonna use it.

I looked down at my wristwatch and noticed that a total of eleven minutes had passed. I heard nothing outside the door, so I stood there quietly, counting down the time that my cousin Jillian would call me and let me know that they were outside.

Another five minutes passed, so I had been in the bathroom for total of sixteen minutes, and nothing had happened. No voices or nothing came from the other side of the door. But when I was about to call Jillian back, that's when I heard a couple of voices. When I went to crack open the door I heard the voices more clearly and realized that they were a husband-and-wife couple that normally got their prescriptions filled in our pharmacy. So I closed the door and called Jillian. "Hey, where are you?" I asked her.

"I'm parked like a half a mile away from the pharmacy."

"Why are you parked so far away?"

"Because I don't want your people to see me."

She meant the DEA. She remembered that we couldn't tip off Tedo that I was working on both sides. "Okay, well stay there until I tell you different," I instructed her.

"Okay," she replied.

Instead of hanging around the bathroom for the rest of my lunch break, I tiptoed out of the bathroom all the way to the front door, so Amir wouldn't see me. I knew he would look up at the front door if I were to push it open, due to the fact that it had a chime bell on it, so I pushed it open like I was coming back in from the outside. Amir looked up at me. "Your lunch break isn't over," he said to me.

"Yes, I know. I have to use the bathroom," I lied and walked back in the direction of the ladies' room.

"Wait a minute, help Mr. and Mrs. Todd with their prescription," he instructed me.

"Sure. But do you want me to clock back in while I'm doing that?"

"Just go ahead and clock back in, because I've decided to close early."

"Really? What time?"

"At three."

"But that's thirty-five minutes away."

"Yes, I know. When you came back from your lunch break I was going to send you home for the rest of the day," he said sarcastically.

"Why didn't you tell me this before?" I pressed the issue because he was fucking up my plans.

"Listen, just do your job and fill their prescription and go home after that."

"Sure. No problem," I snapped back. The elderly couple waiting for their prescription to be filled looked at Amir like his mind was going bad. I mean, who talks to a woman the way he does? I ignored him this time around because I had bigger fish to fry and he was going to be one of them.

While I was processing the couple's prescription order, I pulled my cell phone from my pocket and texted Jillian, letting her know what was going on. She texted me back a couple of seconds later, letting me know that she was en route. "I'm gonna walk over to Starbucks and get me a cup of coffee," I heard Mrs. Todd say to her husband.

"Okay. Well I'll be over there when I'm done here," he told her.

"All right," she said and exited the pharmacy.

After I handed our last customer his prescription, I escorted him to the sliding glass doors and watched him exit the building. While the doors were closing, I was caught off guard when three Middle Eastern men that I had never seen before appeared out of nowhere and walked into the pharmacy like they owned the place. They pushed their way by me like I wasn't standing there. "I'm sorry, but we're closed," I told them, puzzled by why Ahmad wasn't walking in with these guys. Not knowing what to do, I watched them as they headed to the back of the pharmacy where Amir was packaging up two large orders of Vicodin and Percocet that he planned to get rid of after we closed tonight.

I wanted to yell to the back of the pharmacy to forewarn him that the men were headed in his direction, but I was distracted when my cell phone started vibrating in my pants pocket. I pulled my cell phone from my pocket and noticed that it was Jillian calling me. I quickly accepted the call and turned my body to face the front door. "Hello," I answered quietly.

"Is everything still good?" she asked me.

But before I could answer her, I saw the reflection in the glass door of someone standing behind me. Startled at the sudden appearance, I turned around. "Oh my God! You just scared the shit out of me," I said, muffling my cell phone against my chest.

"Who are you talking to?" the Middle Eastern–looking guy asked me.

"My cousin," I told him.

"Tell your cousin that you're gonna have to call her back," he instructed me.

I was confused as to why he wanted me to end my phone call. I wanted to fight him on it, but I didn't. Instead, I placed my cell phone back up to my ear and told Jillian that I would have to call her back.

"But wait," I heard her reply right before I pressed the End button.

"Give it to me," he demanded as he held out his left hand.

"Is there something wrong?" I questioned him. Asking me for my cell phone was a weird request.

"Just hand it to me," he demanded and snatched it from my hand. "Did you lock the door?"

"Wait, what are you doing?" I heard Amir yell from his station in the back of the pharmacy. And then I heard a slew of medicine bottles and boxes fall to the floor. I turned my attention to the back of the pharmacy. But I couldn't see anything. Amir's workstation was out of view from where I was standing.

Not knowing what was going on in the back of the pharmacy spooked me. "Look, I don't know what's going on back there and I really don't care," I started off. I needed this guy to know that I wanted no parts of him nor those other men in the back. As far as I knew, our plans to rob the pharmacy had been botched. Ahmad wasn't here nor his partner. "So, if you'll let me get my purse from the back, I will leave immediately after."

"You aren't going anywhere," he told me in an eerie tone, and then he grabbed me by the collar of my sweater. Acting off mere instinct, I tried to yank my sweater back from him as I took a couple steps backwards, simultaneously jolting my body hard enough for this guy to release the grip he had on me. Immediately after he lost his grip, I turned my back toward him so I could make a run for it. But as the door slid open, I was stopped in my tracks by yet another human being. "I'm not too late, am I?" Tedo asked.

Tedo pulled out his pistol, locked and loaded, with a silencer at the end of it, and pointed it directly at the Middle Eastern guy's head and fired. The guy instantly hit the floor behind me. I didn't look back to see him, but I heard the thud and knew it all too well. Terrell's lifeless body fell the same way after I stabbed him to death.

"Where is Jillian?" I asked him.

"She's in the car. It's parked behind the store," he answered me. "Who else is in there?"

"There's two other guys in there. But you need to go to the back because that's where they're taking the boxes of pills to."

"Are there any more customers in there?" His questions continued.

"No."

"A'ight, well I'm gonna push those dudes out the back door so I can make sure we get everything," he said.

"Okay," I said. But I really wasn't concerned about anything he was talking about. I wanted to find Jillian and make sure she was good because I knew the DEA was a block down the street.

While Tedo headed into the pharmacy through the front door, I casually walked around the building, giving off the impression that everything was fine because I knew once again that the DEA agents were watching the front of the pharmacy. As soon as I got around the corner of the building, I raced toward where Jillian had parked her car. It took me about ten seconds to get to the back of the building, so when my eyes landed on the taillights and the trunk of her car, they lit up. I saw Jillian sitting behind the steering wheel looking like she was waiting for the back door of the pharmacy to open. Parked in front of her car was Amir's car. It wasn't running and no one was inside of it, but I knew Amir would be coming out that door any minute now.

As expected, the back door of the pharmacy opened and when it did it flew open like a bomb had just exploded. I stopped in my tracks and watched as Amir and another Middle Eastern–looking guy bailed out the back door.

They were both carrying boxes filled with prescription drugs. Amir raced by Jillian's car with his box in tow, but the other guy running behind Amir turned toward Jillian, aimed his gun at her and shot it twice. The flash from the bullets sparked, one after the other. Jillian sat there in the driver seat while the window shattered into pieces. My heart collapsed into the pit of my stomach.

"Noooooooooooo!" I screamed and made a dash toward her.

While I was running toward her car, Tedo and another guy ran out the back door of the pharmacy. For a brief second Tedo looked at Jillian's car and then he looked in my direction and saw that I was crying hysterically. "They shot Jillian!" I screamed.

Without thinking about it, Tedo and his homeboy aimed their guns at Amir and the other guy and started busting shots at them. Amir looked like he got hit first because he fell down to the ground and all the contents in his box scattered on the ground. "Get those motherfuckers! They shot my cousin. They shot her!" I screamed while I cried uncontrollably.

BOOM! BOOM! BOOM! Pop! Pop! Pop! Tedo and his homeboy returned fire on Amir and his henchman.

"Jillian, come on. Get up. I gotta get you to the hospital," I sobbed while I tried pushing her to the passenger side of the car. Her body was too heavy to move and she wasn't responding. I panicked even more. "Come on, Jillian, get up. We gotta get you to the hospital," I yelled. But once again I couldn't get her to respond. Her body just lay there, limp.

Pop! Pop! Pop! I heard more gunfire. Then the back door of Jillian's car opened. I looked up and saw Tedo throwing a box into the back seat. "We gotta get her to the hospital, but I can't move her. Her body is too heavy!" I screamed.

"She's dead. We can't help her," he yelled at me and

then he ran away from the car. A couple of seconds later he came back with another box and threw it into the car. "They got Rick. We gotta go now!" He climbed into the front seat and proceeded to push Jillian out of the car. "Help me get her out of here. We gotta go," he yelled at me.

"No, we can't leave her," I yelled back at him. But my words fell on deaf ears because he shoved her one good time and she fell down on the ground over top of me. Moments later, Tedo put the car in reverse and started backing it out of the one-way road. I couldn't believe that he was leaving us like that. But unfortunately for him, he didn't get far. When I looked and saw the black van barreling toward Tedo, I knew he wasn't going anywhere.

BOOM! BOOM! BOOM! BOOM! More shots rang out, aimed at the black van Agent Sims and the other agents were in. Seconds later, the agents returned fire at Tedo. I thought Tedo would've put Jillian's car in drive and tried his luck driving back in my direction to see if he could hop one of these gates behind the pharmacy, but he didn't. He pressed down on the accelerator and tried pushing the van backwards with Jillian's car, but it wasn't powerful enough to handle the weight of the van. So I figured that Tedo would stop the car and give up, but he went all in and so did the DEA agents. *BOOM! BOOM! POP! BOOM! POP! POP! BOOM! BOOM! POP! POP!* Within a matter of twenty seconds, Jillian's car was riddled with over thirty bullets. And when the car stopped moving, I knew Tedo was in fact dead. There was no one left alive but me.

35

THERE'S MORE AT STAKE

I had no idea where to go from here. I was lying in a pool of my cousin's blood and everything around me had crumbled. I was feeling a ton of different emotions right now but I couldn't describe the first one. I rocked my body back and forth while I cradled my cousin's head in my arms.

"I am so sorry, Jillian. I know we shouldn't of did this, because you'd still be alive." I continued to sob as I rocked her.

Off in the distance I saw the two ambulances scurrying toward me while Agent Sims talked to a couple of other agents. He looked over at me twice, and after standing there in his huddle, he started heading my way with two paramedics in tow. As soon as he got within arm's distance of me, he stood there and told me that I had to let Jillian go so the coroner could carry her body away. I sat there with my face saturated with my tears and protested a little because I knew that if I let her go, I'd never be able to hold her like this again.

Finally, after a few minutes, I released her to them and then Agent Sims helped me stand up on my feet. "Come on, let's walk over to the ambulance," he instructed me, pointing to the vehicle. "After we get you cleaned up, we're gonna have to have a serious talk."

I didn't respond to him. I couldn't think about anything but Jillian. She was my everything. She was like my sister. Our bond was unbreakable. So, to know that I would never get to see or talk to her again tore me up inside. This had to be a bad dream.

While one of the paramedics checked me for signs of trauma or injuries, Agent Sims stood there with a look of disappointment on his face. "I know you're hurt because you just lost your cousin, but I have to ask you, what happened out here? Why are there five dead people thrown in the middle of my investigation?"

In my head I tallied the five people he was talking about so I could give him a definitive answer. I knew my cousin Jillian was one, Tedo was number two, Tedo's homeboy was three, the Middle Eastern guy that tried to take my cell phone at the front entrance of the pharmacy was number four. Now there were two people left, one being the third Middle Eastern guy that entered the pharmacy and the last person would Amir. "Who's still alive?" I asked him.

"Amir. He's still alive," Agent Sims answered.

My heart rattled at the sound of Amir's name. I couldn't believe it. I thought he was dead. I saw him when he fell down on the ground after he was shot. "You know he's the one that killed my cousin," I lied. I mean, cause how dare he still be alive and my cousin wasn't? He didn't value life. He was a mean motherfucker from the pits of hell.

"How do you know that?" Agent Sims's tone was harsh.

"What do you mean, how do I know? I saw him point his gun and fire at her. The other guy that was with him shot her too." I gritted my teeth while the female paramedic started wiping away the blood from my face and arms.

"What was your cousin doing here? Why does your cousin's car have boxes of prescription drugs in the back seat? Are you embroiled in what looks like another prescription drug heist?"

"No! That's not what this is."

"Then what is it, Misty? Why are all these people dead?" He wouldn't let up.

"I don't know," I spat.

"You know something, and if I find out that you orchestrated this whole thing, I am going to lock you up for a long time. You're looking at twenty years. So, you better take the time now to figure out what you are going to do," he yelled at me. He said to the paramedic, "When you're done with her, escort her to one of the squad cars and put her ass in the back of it."

"Oh, so now you're arresting me?" I yelled back at him as he walked away from me.

"You better worry about what you're gonna tell me, because if I talk to Amir and he wants to help with this investigation, then you're gonna get the shorter end of the stick," he yelled back at me without turning around.

I began to wrestle with how I was going to go at this thing head-on. From the looks of things, they had me as a culprit. And there was no way I could pretend that I didn't know anything about this robbery gone bad. Amir disliked me, so it would be a no-brainer to get him to talk. *But will he?* was the question. And if he decided to, then what was I going to do?

After the paramedic cleaned me up as much as she could, she and another paramedic escorted me to a patrol car and placed me in the back of it. I sat there with hurt in my heart and sorrow on my shoulders because I knew that my grandmother was going to lose it once she found out what happened to Jillian. My world had turned upside down.

* * *

The police officer assigned to the car I was in took me to the DEA office in downtown Norfolk twenty minutes later. I was shocked that I wasn't handcuffed. I was even more shocked that when I was escorted inside the building, I saw the same two cops that wrote the robbery incident report down there talking to another set of DEA agents. After realizing that this shit was about to get real, I just shook my head because I knew that I was going to spend tonight in jail.

The cop turned me over to a female DEA agent. Immediately after she searched my body, she placed me in an interrogation room. "Want anything to drink?" she asked me.

"No, I'm fine," I told her.

"Well, just let me know if you do," she replied and then she left me in the room and closed the door. When I heard it lock, that was more confirmation that I wasn't going anywhere. And all I could do at that moment was come up with a plan, because it was now everyone for themselves.

36

READ ME MY RIGHTS

I couldn't believe these motherfuckers had me in a damn room for over an hour and no one had come in to say anything. What type of games were they playing with me? They were treating me like I was a hardcore criminal. I had never in my life been arrested or hurt anyone. So, why were they doing me like this? Was this their way of making me sweat? Was this one of their tactics, where they kept me isolated for a long time, shutting me out from everyone, giving me time to assess my situation and come to the conclusion that I needed to cooperate with them? Well, it was working.

Two hours later, Agent Sims and Agent Montclair finally showed up. When they walked in the room, they took a seat in front of me and started throwing questions at me, one at a time.

Agent Sims started off. "We just left the hospital and Amir was shot twice, but they weren't life-threatening injuries, so he will live. Before we left him, he told us everything we need to know about what happened today."

"Then why are you here wasting your time with me?" I replied.

"Because we wanna give you a chance to tell your side of the story. Why did your cousin and those two guys she brought with her try to rob the pharmacy? And what was your role in it?" Agent Sims continued.

"My cousin wasn't there to rob the pharmacy. She came up there to see me." I started lying, hoping they'd buy into it.

"If she came to see you, then why was she parked in the back of the pharmacy? That's where all deliveries are made, right?" Agent Sims pressed me.

"Yes, it is."

"Well, so then why was she back there?"

"I don't know."

"It's because you told her to go back there, right?" Agent Sims snapped.

"No, I didn't," I replied calmly. I knew I needed to maintain my composure. I needed to win this interrogation. My freedom depended on it.

"Well, what did you tell her?"

"I didn't tell her anything."

"Then why was she there?"

"I said I don't know." I placed my face in the palms of my hands. I needed to hide my face. I didn't want to face the reality about what happened today. I just wanted this whole thing to go away.

Agent Sims slammed his left hand on the table. "Misty, tell me what the fuck happened out there today! Why did five people end up dead in the middle of my fucking investigation?"

"I told you that I don't't know. Why don't you ask Amir? He and the other guys with him are the ones that shot and killed my cousin. He was the one that was taking prescription drugs from the pharmacy to pay his debt. So, talk to him. He has all the answers to your questions!" I roared, while I visualized my cousin's lifeless body.

"We know you have answers too. So, cut the shit. And

think back to the other morning when two police officers came by and took the robbery report for the other shipment of opioids that were stolen. They spoke to you and Sanjay. And considering the fact that you walked into the pharmacy before Sanjay, they believe that you had a hand in that robbery."

"That's bullshit! Sanjay was using those drugs as payment to Ahmad and that other guy, and you know it. You said it yourself."

"Misty, tell us, what was your cousin doing parked in the back of the pharmacy? And why were those two street thugs with her too?"

"I need to call my lawyer," I said.

"Oh sure, you can call your lawyer. And when you get him or her on the phone, let them know that you were working with us on an ongoing investigation prior to this incident and that you're a suspect in two robberies."

"Are you done?" I asked sarcastically. I wasn't feeling any of the bullshit he was saying.

"No, I'm not done. My partner and I know that you planned to have your cousin and those two street thugs rob the pharmacy. But the robbery was botched. I also know that after I prove my theory, I am going to have the judge throw the book at you. When I'm done with you, you won't ever see the streets again."

"What the fuck do you want me to say?" I yelled while my tear ducts opened up like the floodgates. I broke down. "That I set Amir up to get robbed by my cousin's friends? And that she wasn't supposed to get shot and killed? Well guess what? That's exactly what happened. I fucked up. And now I can't take none of it back." I continued to sob.

Agent Montclair handed me a box of tissues. I thanked him and then I took a couple of them to wipe my face.

"Now see, was that hard?" Agent Sims asked me.

I didn't wanna answer his question. The only thing I wanted to do now was call my grandmother to let her know what happened to Jillian. But what was I going to tell her? Would I tell her that it was my fault? Or would I tell her that Jillian acted on her own with this? I had yet another decision to make.

"I need to use the phone to call my grandmother. She needs to know what happened to Jillian," I told him.

"We already have a car en route to your grandmother's house now."

"No. Tell them to turn around. I need to be the one to tell her," I insisted.

Agent Sims looked at Agent Montclair and instructed him to call off the home visit with my grandmother. "Would you like for us to take you there to speak with her?" Agent Sims offered.

I couldn't believe how fast he went from an asshole to a sympathetic human being. I took him up on his offer and about ten minutes later, we were on our way to see my grandmother. During the drive Agent Sims started plotting how he was going to use me to wrap up his investigation with Amir and Ahmad. "We're gonna need you to testify in front of a grand jury after we make our arrests," he said.

"Testify?! You said that all I had to do was plant the bug in Ahmad's car and that's all I would have to do," I argued.

"That deal is off the table. You're knee deep in this investigation now. There's so much at stake at this point."

I let out a long sigh. "I knew this bullshit was going to happen."

"If you had done what we told you to do, then none of this would have happened. Your cousin would probably still be alive right now too. How do you think your grandmother is going to react after you tell her that you had a hand in your cousin's murder?"

"Leave me the fuck alone, already. See, you think this whole thing is a game. But's it's not. I lost someone very important today and all you wanna do is sit there in the front seat and mock me? That's fucked up!"

"Misty, I'm sorry, but you can't blame no one but yourself. You could've prevented all of this if you had just stuck to our plan. Not yours," Agent Sims pointed out.

"I'm done talking about it," I replied and then I turned my focus to the birds flying in the sky. They looked so fucking free! I swear, I would do anything right now to be free. But that opportunity was gone.

37

DON'T BLAME ME

My grandmother was sitting in her normal spot in the living room when the agents and I walked into the den. I introduced them and before I could tell her why they were there with me, she already knew. "I saw the news so just tell me where they took her body?" she asked Agent Sims.

"She's down at the coroner's office," Agent Sims replied.

"Did you get the men that did it to her?" My grandmother pressed the issue.

"Yes, ma'am, we did."

"So, what happens now?" she wanted to know.

"We're gonna seek justice for your granddaughter. But in doing so, we're gonna need Misty to help put the guy that shot Jillian, and his crime family, in prison."

My grandmother looked at me and said, "How do you feel about it?"

"I don't have a choice, Nana," I told her.

"Oh, you have a choice. We all have choices. You just got to figure out which one works for you," she corrected me. "Have you spoken with your mother?"

"No, ma'am. You're the first person I talked to since the incident from earlier."

"Well, then you need to call her."

"I will," I assured her.

"Ma'am, will you excuse us?" Agent Sims said, and then he grabbed me by the arm and escorted me off to the front of the house. Before he could utter one word, my cell phone started ringing. When I looked down at the caller ID the text on the screen said, *Unknown*. I looked up from my cell phone at Agent Sims.

"Who do you think that is?" he asked me.

"I don't know."

"Answer it and then put it on speaker."

"Hello," I said after I took the call.

"Misty, this is Mrs. Faye, Terrell's mother. Have you seen or heard from Terrell?"

My freaking heart sank to the pit of my stomach. "No, ma'am. I haven't talked to him in a couple of days," I lied, but at the same time trying to keep a straight face in front of Agent Sims.

"Well, that's strange because I talked to him the other night and he said that he was going over to your house to talk to you about something."

Listening to her tell me what Terrell told her got me hot around the collar. It felt like I was falling into a trap. But I knew I couldn't, especially with Agent Sims standing right there in front of me. I also knew that I had to hurry up and get this lady off the phone before I triggered Agent Sims's mind to think back to that smell inside of my apartment. "Listen, Mrs. Faye, I haven't talked to your son in a couple of days. But if he calls me I will let him know that you're looking for him. Okay?" I finally said.

"But—" she started to say, but I cut her off.

"Have a nice day." And then I disconnected her call. "I can't believe she had the nerve to call me, especially after she's shown me on many occasions that she doesn't like me," I explained, hoping to throw Agent Sims off track. I needed him to focus only on this Amir and Ahmad case, not Terrell.

"So, you were saying," I said, giving him the floor back so he could tell me what he brought me out in the hallway to say.

"I think it would be best if you stay with your grandmother tonight while myself and the other agents can figure out how we're going to move forward with this investigation. And besides, I'm sure your grandmother is going to need someone to keep her company now that you guys lost your cousin and granddaughter."

"I had already decided that I was going to stay with her tonight. My cousin was all she had. And the fact that my mother and my grandmother don't have a relationship, it's a no-brainer for me to be with her."

"Are you going to let your mother know what happened?

"Yes, I'm gonna call her in a few minutes," I told him. "So, tell me, when am I gonna be able to get my car? Remember it's still at the pharmacy."

"One of the city's tow trucks is gonna bring it here before the night is over," he told me.

"What's gonna happen with the pharmacy?"

"We've closed it down. And all the prescription drugs that Amir tried to take out of there today will be sent to our evidence department so that it can be processed and evaluated."

"What did you guys do with my cousin's car?"

"It's been towed to our government garage to be processed too."

"But why?"

"Because it was used in the commitment of a crime."

"Will we ever be able to get it back?"

"Yes, I'm sure."

While Agent Sims and I continued to go back and forth

regarding this fucking case, someone started knocking on the front door. I gotta admit that it startled me because my grandmother never has any guests. I looked through the peephole and saw that it was Jillian's boyfriend, Edmund. And boy, was I dreading to see or talk to him.

"Who is it?" Agent Sims whispered.

"It's my cousin's boyfriend," I reluctantly replied.

"Are you gonna answer the door?"

Without responding to his question, I reached for the doorknob and opened the front door. Edmund stood there looking like a lost soul. He didn't hesitate to ask me about Jillian. "Is she all right?" he asked me.

I shook my head. "No."

"So, it's true? She's dead? I saw her car all banged up on TV."

"Yes," I replied softly, barely opening my mouth.

"Oh my God! Nooo! Don't say that, Misty. Where is she? I need to see her," he said as he paced back and forth on the front porch while he rubbed his head in circular motions with both of his hands. He looked like he was about to unravel.

"Edmund, just come in the house and go in the den with my grandmother," I insisted.

Edmund took my advice and came into the house. While he was walking down the hallway toward the den, I heard him starting to cry. A few seconds later, I heard him say, "Mrs. Torrey, what are we going to do without her?"

"God will make a way, baby. It will be all right," I heard her tell him.

"Look, Agent Montclair and I are going to leave for now. But I will be calling you in the morning," he assured me.

"All right," I replied.

"Montclair, let's get out of here," Sims called out.

Moments later, Montclair came walking down the hall toward us. "Take care of your grandmother," he said.

"I will." I opened the front door for them to leave.

Agent Sims looked back at me and said, "If you hear from Ahmad, call us immediately and let us know."

"Do you think he'll try to call me, especially after everything that happened today?" I wondered aloud.

"You never know."

"Well, in that case I guess I will."

"Just be careful."

"I will."

I locked the front door after the agents left and then I went back into the den where my grandmother and Edmund were. He had his face buried in the palms of his hands when I entered the room.

"I know your heart is heavy, but God is going to carry you while you can't carry yourself," my grandmother said.

"Mrs. Torrey, we were gonna get married," he announced.

"But that wasn't in God's plan for you two. So, just count it all joy," she concluded as I took a seat on the sofa next to Edmund.

"What happened, Misty? The news said that she was at your job and got shot while she was sitting in her car. And then they said that somebody she was with tried to drive off, but the police stopped him by running into her car."

"Edmund, I don't know all the specifics. We're still trying to figure out all of that stuff now."

"The news said that she was with Tedo. And Tedo was the one driving her car."

"Who is Tedo?" my grandmother asked.

"Some guy she knows," I answered.

"Why was he driving her car?" My grandmother pressed the issue.

Edmund looked at me like he was waiting for me to answer my grandmother's question. And when I hesitated to speak, Edmund blurted out, "Because they were going to rob Misty's job and take a shipment of drugs that had just been delivered."

My grandmother looked at Edmund and then she looked at me. "Is he telling the truth?"

"No. That's not entirely true," I managed to say.

"What do you mean that's not entirely true? Everything I just said was true," he yelled at me, and then he turned his attention toward my grandmother. "Mrs. Torrey, Misty and Jillian made plans to rob the pharmacy with a couple of guys. I told Jillian not to go. Just let the guys do it. But no, she wanted to be like a getaway driver of some sort. So, after arguing with her about going, I finally gave up because she said she had to be there. And now look at her. She's dead! And no one can bring her back."

"Is that true?" my grandmother asked me. Her eyes grew in size and it looked like she could see through me.

"No, he's lying, Grandma. Jillian and I didn't plan anything. It was all her idea," I protested.

"I don't care whose idea it was. You should've stopped her. She's the little cousin, not you. And I am so disappointed in you right now. I can't believe you let your cousin go out there in a line of fire like that."

"But Grandma—"

"But Grandma, nothing. You are just like your mother. All you care about is yourself."

"That's not true. I loved Jillian. She was like my best friend." I started sobbing all over again.

"Oh, don't feed me those tears. Best friends and family don't do what you did to your cousin. You knew what she meant to me, and now you take that away? I want you out of this house right now!" she roared.

I swear, I'd never seen my grandmother like that. She never got that angry when she and my mother stopped talking. So, I didn't know where this was going to end.

"Why don't you tell *him* to leave? He's the one that got her hooked up on prescription drugs." I pointed toward Edmund.

He jumped up on his feet. "That's a lie. You did that. Bringing her all those different drugs from your job."

"Edmund, so you're gonna stand there and point fingers at me? Let's talk about how you used her to buy prescription drugs and how your lazy ass don't work in a pie shop. You're the reason why she couldn't kick her drug habit. You got her running around here like a freaking crackhead. Doing favors for other people so that y'all could get high. But you wanna blame me," I snapped. This loser had me pissed. Got the audacity to act like I was bringing my cousin down. She was my heart. I tried on many occasions to get her to stop using drugs, but this loser always talked her out of it.

"Misty, just get out of my house. I'm done with this conversation," my grandmother spat. Hearing her tell me to leave, hurt me to the core. She was like my second mother, so for her to choose Edmund over me was heartbreaking.

Without saying another word, I grabbed my purse and walked out of the house. I didn't have any mode of transportation because my car was still parked at the pharmacy. I did have Uber, though. So that's what I used to get as far away from this place as fast as I could.

I got my Uber driver to take me to my mother's house. But I asked him to make a detour to Colonel Street to see if my car was still there. Surprisingly, it was, so I got the driver to leave me there. He made sure I got into my car safely before he pulled off. I thanked him and then we went our separate ways.

The drive to my mother's house was short. I dreaded going over there for fear that she was going to blame me for what transpired earlier today. If I had to go through another verbal beating from a family member, I would lose my damn mind. I'd also leave the state and never come back.

When I pulled up curbside to her house, I called her

from my cell phone. "Hey, Ma, it's me, Misty. Are you in the house?"

"You know I am."

"I didn't see your car. That's why I asked."

"It's parked in the garage."

"I'm outside. Open the door," I instructed her while I was getting out of my car. She met me at the front door. She seemed happy to see me.

"Are you okay?" she asked me as I entered the house.

I waited for her to close the door and lock it and then I said, "Jillian was shot today and now she's dead." My eyes teared up and then the floodgates opened. My knees started buckling so my mother grabbed me by the arm to prevent me from falling. "Hold on, I gotcha," she said and held on to me tight. "Come on and let's go to the living room," she continued and escorted me down the hallway. Her boyfriend was in the living room watching TV when we entered.

"Hey, what's up? Is everything all right?" he wanted to know, taking his full attention away from the television.

"My niece Jillian was killed today," my mother told him.

"Did this happen on Colonel Street?"

"Yeah," I finally said, tears saturating my face while my mom helped me sit down on the love seat across from her boyfriend.

She sat next to me. "What happened?" she asked while she wiped my tears from my face with the back of her hands.

I knew I couldn't tell her the whole truth, for fear that she'd treat me the way my grandmother did, so I fabricated my story a bit. "Jillian came up to my job to see me. And when she got there she had a couple of guys with her. Next thing I know, both of the guys tried to rob the pharmacy with guns they had, and Jillian got caught up in the crossfire."

"What would possess her to bring guys to your job and rob it?" my mother wanted to know.

"Mom, I don't know." I lied once again.

"Misty, do you know anything about the robbery?" My mother pressed the issue.

"No, Mom. The only thing I can think of is that they talked her into doing it. That's it."

"So, who shot her?"

"Two guys from the pharmacy," I said, leaving that answer with a huge gray area. I mean, I can't say the owners were involved with a mafia group. She would lose her mind if I did.

"Why would two guys from the pharmacy shoot her? That's strange." She wouldn't let up.

"Mom, I don't know. The police are investigating it now," I told her, giving the impression that I didn't really wanna talk about this subject.

"How's your grandma taking the news?" my mother wanted to know.

"She's upset. Jillian's boyfriend told her that it's my fault that Jillian got killed."

"What did she say to you?"

"She told me that she was disappointed with me and for me to leave her house now." I continued to sob.

"So, she believed him?"

"Yes, Mom, she believed him and that hurt me to the heart."

"I told you how she was. She's treating you just like she treated me when she had to choose between me and my brother."

"But that's not fair, Mom."

"She's not fair, Misty. I've told you how she was from day one."

"I know. But she shouldn't be like that to me. I go to visit her and do things for her that Jillian didn't do."

"She doesn't care about that," my mother interjected.

"What am I going to do about Jillian? I'm not gonna ever see her again." I changed the subject, sobbing more intensely.

My mother embraced me hard. "Go ahead and cry. Let it out," she encouraged me.

I sat there in her arms for what seemed like forever. For the first time, I had my mother sober and alert. Not only was she showing me love, she made me feel like I was a priority. It couldn't get no better than this.

For the next hour or so, she continued to talk to me and offer me words of wisdom to make me feel better. I had no idea what direction my life was going to go, but for right now, things were okay because my mother was in my ear telling me that things would get better.

38

FLESH & BLOOD

I ended up staying at my mother's house the rest of the night. I slept in my old bedroom and it felt good to do so. When I woke up her boyfriend had just come in the house from his overnight shift, so he spoke to me and then he disappeared into my mother's bedroom.

"Want something to eat?" she asked me the moment I stepped foot into the kitchen.

"I really don't have an appetite. But I could definitely use a cup of hot tea," I told her.

"Coming right up," she replied and grabbed a coffee mug from the cabinet. She had a teapot on the stove that was already prepared, so she poured me a cup. When I tasted it, it was the green tea that I loved.

"Thank you, Mom," I said after I swallowed it.

"Are you sure you don't want me to fix you an egg sandwich or some oatmeal?"

"No, I'm good," I assured her.

"When you talked to your grandmother, did she say when she was going to start the funeral arrangements?"

"Mom, she was just killed yesterday."

"Well, are you going to call her and find out?"

"She doesn't want to talk to me. Why don't you call her?"

"I'll call her if you want me to. But if she starts bitching about you having something to do with Jillian's murder, then I'm gonna unleash the venom on her. I'm warning you now."

"Mom, please just try to get along for Jillian's sake," I begged her.

"I'll try. But I'm telling you right now, if she starts going on and on about you, then I will remind her that Jillian was the drug addict, not you," she vented.

I let out a long sigh. I tried compromising. "Please try not to say that. Do that another time."

"I'll be nice for you. But she needs to be nice as well."

"All right, Ma. Just try . . . please. That's all I ask." I just wanted this conversation to be over with.

She and I continued to talk about how I was going to move forward with everything going on, and then my cell phone rang. When I looked down at the caller ID I noticed that it was Agent Sims calling me. "Hello," I answered.

"Good morning,"

"Good morning."

"What time do you think you could meet me downtown at my office? We have a ton of stuff to go over and your presence is needed."

"Give me a couple of hours and I will be there."

"Okay. I will see you in two hours," he agreed and then we disconnected our call.

"Who was that?" my mother asked me.

"The detective that's investigating Jillian's murder," I lied.

"What did he say?"

"He wants me to come to the police station so that they can talk to me further about what happened yesterday."

"Are you up for it? Because if you're not, then you need to call him back and tell him you'll have to do this some other time."

"I'm fine with it. It's for Jillian."

"Want me to go down there with you?"

"No. I'm good. I can handle it myself."

"All right, well, if you change your mind, just let me know."

It didn't take me long to go home, take a shower, and get dressed to go to the DEA's main office downtown. DEA Agent Sims was waiting for me in the lobby. He stood up and greeted me when I approached him. "How was your drive?"

"It was okay," I responded nonchalantly. This is not a social visit, so I wanted to get in and get out as quickly as possible.

"How was the traffic?"

"It was okay," I replied once again nonchalantly. "Do you know how long I'm gonna be here?" I asked him. I wanted him to know that I wanted to be out of there as soon as possible.

"It shouldn't take more than a couple hours," he assured me. But I didn't believe him. Every word that came out of his mouth was a lie. Agent Sims lied about everything. I'm sure he built his career on lies. And now I've been added to his list of dummies.

He escorted me onto the elevator and took me up to the third floor. After we got off the elevator he took me into a small room with a wooden table and three chairs. We sat down. A few seconds later, Agent Montclair joined us. He smiled at me and said, "Hello." I spoke back.

"How's your grandmother doing?" he asked me.

"Oh yes, how is she?" Agent Sims chimed in.

"I'm not sure. She put me out of her house right after you guys left."

"I'm sorry to hear that," Agent Montclair stated.

"Yeah, I'm sorry too," Agent Sims agreed.

"So, what's going on now with the case? What do I have to do?" I changed the subject.

"Well, Amir was released from the ICU, so we formally arrested him today. He's currently handcuffed to his bed. We also have local police officers guarding his room around the clock."

"Has his family tried to visit him?" I wondered aloud.

"His wife and kids. His parents too. But neither Ahmad or any of the mafia family showed up."

"Think they left town?"

"Ahmad hasn't. We've been monitoring him very closely after you slipped the wire into his car. And speaking of which, he knows that you had a hand in the robbery. He also knows that Jillian was your cousin, so he may come after you."

"What do you mean, he may come after me?" I questioned. My entire body tensed up while my heart rate sped up.

"It means that you shouldn't ever be alone. Maybe stay at your mother's house. Anywhere but your apartment."

"So, you think he may hurt me?"

"We're thinking more on the level of murdering you."

Boom! My heart dropped into the pit of my stomach. It felt like my head was spinning around in circles. I couldn't tell if I was coming or going. "Murder?"

"Yes, murder," Agent Sims said.

I placed my right hand over my chest. "Do you think that if I go to my mother's house that I will be safe there?"

"We're not saying that you would be safe. But you would have a better chance of staying alive longer over there than at your own apartment," Agent Sims continued.

"So, that's it? You tell me that my life may be in danger and for me to go over to my mother's house because I may be safer than my own apartment? That's complete bullshit

and you know it!" I snapped because what they were saying sounded ridiculous.

"Just stay calm. We're gonna figure this thing out,"
Agent Montclair said.

"How can I stay calm when you tell me that there's a
possibility that I could get murdered by that mafia family?
Does that even make sense to you? Or am I overreacting?"

"Misty, if you cooperate fully with us, we'll take you
into protective custody," Agent Sims said.

"Protective custody? Isn't that a program for government witnesses?"

"Yes, as a matter of fact, it is," Agent Sims replied.

"So, I'm considered a government witness now?"

"Yes, you would be, especially if you testify against the
criminals we're prosecuting."

"What the fuck did I get myself into?" I snapped, and
then I stood to my feet. "Y'all motherfuckers trapped me
and you knew it way from the beginning."

"Have a seat, Misty. We're gonna work through this,"
Agent Sims said.

"Easy for you to say. You're not the one who has to give
up information and testify."

Agent Sims tried calming me down. "Look, we know
you're upset by the loss of your cousin and this case and
all, but if you calm down and go at this thing a little more
rational, then we would come out on the winning end."

I took a seat back in my chair and covered my face with
my hands. That didn't stop Agent Sims from talking. "Okay,
this is what we're gonna do," he started off. "We're gonna
get dates and details of illegal activities done at the hands
of Sanjay and Amir on the record. Whatever we don't
have on those recorders we got from the camera you wore.
And we're gonna take it from your statements today. After
that, I'm gonna type it up and have the US Attorney sign
it. Once that is done, we're gonna execute our federal war-

rants and then we're gonna start the ball rolling. Are you up for that?" Agent Sims continued.

"Do I have a choice?"

Before I answered his question, someone knocked on the door. Agent Montclair stood up and opened it. Everyone looked at the female agent named Gail Horn. She was the IT agent that monitored all the wiretaps on this case. "Ahmad must've discovered the wiretap and GPS because we lost his signal," she informed us.

My heart took another nosedive into the pit of my stomach. The likelihood that he knew that I placed the GPS device in his SUV moved up ten notches. There was no doubt in my mind that I was the first person on his list of candidates that could have done it.

"When did you lose him?" Agent Sims asked her.

"About five minutes ago and it looks like he was near the pharmacy when it happened," she told us.

"Shit!" Agent Sims cursed.

"Do we have Amir, Sanjay, and their other relatives' houses closely monitored if he decides to go back?" Agent Sims wanted to know.

"Yes, we do," she told him.

"Well, put an APB out on his car right now. We can't afford to let him slip out of our hands. I'm sure he's notified other members of his organization about the botched robbery and arrests we made."

"I'm sure he has too. But I'm gonna send out the APB now," she told him and then she walked away.

Agent Montclair closed the door and then he and Agent Sims turned their attention back to me. "I don't think it's gonna be a good idea for you to go back to your mother's house. He could be out there looking for you now, which is why we lost his signal near the pharmacy."

"He doesn't know where my mother lives, though."

"But what if he does?" Agent Sims questioned me.

"Trust me, he doesn't."

"So, you feel comfortable making that assessment?" Agent Montclair interjected.

"Right now, I am. Because I don't wanna be in a witness protection program. I heard that you won't be able to see your family members anymore if you go in one."

"Yes, that's correct," Agent Sims noted.

"Well, I'm good. I'll stay at my mother's house until I feel differently."

Agent Sims let out a long sigh. "As you wish," he told me.

After I made it clear that I wasn't going into a witness protection program, I gave them information about how the pharmacy was run while Sanjay was managing it and when Amir managed it.

"When was the first time you knew he was selling prescription drugs under the table?"

"It was around the time when I first started working there. A couple of times, he had me delivering prescriptions to people that lived in the hood. And when I say people, I'm talking about young guys that looked like they were heathier than purebred horses. But that only lasted for a couple of weeks. And then after that, I noticed that when he ordered certain drugs one day, we were out of them within three days' time. I knew something was off."

"When did you start taking drugs from the pharmacy without his knowledge?" Agent Sims asked.

"Right after my cousin Jillian had surgery and her doctor stopped prescribing her Vicodin."

"And when was this?"

"It started like three months ago."

"Was that around the time Sanjay was receiving his orders through the front door by UPS and then taking them through the back and piling them into his car?"

"Yes."

"Can you tell me when you first noticed mafia member Ahmad Ali come into the store?"

"It was two weeks ago. Sanjay's brother, Amir, brought them there."

"During that visit did you see Ahmad take any of the drugs from the pharmacy?"

"Yes, I did. He and another guy took several boxes out the back door."

"What was in those boxes?"

"One box contained huge bottles of Percocet and the other boxes contained high doses of Vicodin."

"Have you ever seen Ahmad carry a weapon of any sort?"

"Yes."

"And what weapon would that be?"

"On several occasions I've seen him carry a nine millimeter Glock."

"And how do you know it was a nine millimeter Glock?"

"Because I know what a nine millimeter Glock looks like," I told him. These questions lasted for almost two hours. And if I hadn't asked for a break I don't think I would've been given one. During that break, I was brought a sandwich wrap and a smoothie that tasted like crap. I didn't complain because I was going to be leaving out of there in the next hour, so then I'd be able to get the food I wanted.

On my way out of the meeting, Agent Sims asked me again if I wanted them to put me somewhere safe, according to their standards. Once again, I declined the offer, but I did assure him that I'd keep it in mind if my situation changed. He said okay and then he escorted me to my car.

39

NOT MY FAMILY

The moment I drove away from the federal building I kept my eyes on every car that drove behind me. I had to be on high alert to keep those guys from finding out where I was, or anyone that was close to me, like my mother and my grandmother. They were the only people I had left that I loved. God knows what I would do if I lost them too. It couldn't happen. *That's why I gotta stay on my toes. They can't have my family.*

I knew I needed to get more clothes to take to my mother's house, but I couldn't go home now. Not in broad daylight. So, I figured the best thing for me to do was to go by my apartment at night. That would be best. And in addition to that, I knew I needed to find out when and where my grandmother was going to have the funeral services for Jillian. No matter what, I had to be there. There's not a mafia in the world that could keep me from sending my cousin off in love.

On the way back to my mother's house I got up the nerve to call my grandmother. She didn't own a cell phone. The only mode of communication she had was a home phone. Yes, she had a landline. I blocked my cell phone number just in case she recognized it.

The phone rang five times before she answered it. "Hello," she finally said.

"Grandma, it's me, Misty," I said softly, hoping she wouldn't hang up on me.

"What is it?" she asked. I could tell that she was still a little salty with me.

"Grandma, I feel so bad about what happened yesterday at your house. And I'm sorry for what happened to Jillian," I started off, sobbing at the same time. "I love and miss her so much. And I don't know how I'm gonna function on this earth without her."

"Stop crying, baby. I know you miss her. Where are you?"

"Out driving around."

"Well, come on over here. I made a pot of chicken and dumplings. And then we can talk," she instructed me.

"Yes, ma'am," I said. I was so freaking happy that she invited me back over there. I don't know what I'd do without her sometimes.

After I got off the phone with my nana, I called my mother and told her about my conversation with my grandmother. "I'm so glad that she's not mad with me anymore."

"So, you're gonna run back over there just like that? She just put you out of her house last night. And you're gonna forgive her?" my mother asked.

"Mom, all I wanted from her was when and where the funeral would be. She's the one that apologized to me," I lied. I couldn't tell my mother how I was crying to her mother for her forgiveness. She'd call me a punk. And she'd call me a sellout. Now I'm really seeing that she liked it when my grandmother put me out of her house. She wants me to be at odds with my grandmother because this would cut off the time I spent with my grandmother. My grandmother already had to divide her time up with me

and Jillian. And now that Jillian was gone, she would prefer that I didn't speak with my grandmother so she could
get all the time with me. That might seem cool to other
people, but it's weird to me. It's actually called manipula-
tion.

"Mom, can we talk about this later? I've had a rough
morning and all I wanna do now is clear my mind of all
the negativity."

"Yeah, whatever," she said and then she hung up on me.

"Oh Lord, now she's mad at me. Can't we all just get
along? Shit!" I cursed while I turned my car in the direction of my grandmother's house, because I'm over it.

Covering my tracks while I was en route to my grandmother was something I truly had to do. I didn't want to
bring no drama to her. She's an old lady with some years
left on her life. So I'm gonna make sure that she gets them.

She opened the front door for me after I rang the doorbell. She gave me a warm embrace and it felt good. The
hug seemed genuine and she made me feel loved.

I started the conversation off as we walked down the hallway. "Have you talked to anyone down at the county coroner's office?" When we got to the den, Nana took a seat in
her favorite chair and I sat on the sofa across from her.

"Yes, I spoke with a gentleman and he's gonna release
her body to the funeral home today. I've taken care of all
the expenses so we can move this thing along," she explained.

"Have you decided what day to have her funeral? And
what time?"

"Yes, it's gonna be next Tuesday at eleven."

"That's in four days. Are you sure you wanna have it
that quick?"

"Why should I prolong it?"

"I don't know, Grandma. I guess I'm feeling this way
because I'm not ready to bury her. When you think about
burying people, it's like as soon as you put them in the

ground, you really know that you ain't gonna see them again."

"Well, I can understand that. But, once again, why prolong it? She's gone to heaven, so let's celebrate it that way."

I sighed heavily. "If you say so, Grandma."

While she and I were sitting there going back and forth about Jillian's funeral, my cell phone started ringing, so I took it out of my purse and looked at the caller ID. The number came up *Unknown* again. This unknown caller could be anybody, so I elected not to answer it. With everything going on, I couldn't allow anyone to get through to me. It's not that kind of party anymore.

"You don't wanna talk to whoever's calling you?" she blurted out.

"I don't know who's calling. Whoever they are, they blocked their number so I can't see it," I explained.

"Think it might be the cops that brought you here yesterday?"

"I know it's not them because I just left their office."

"What did they wanna talk to you about this time?"

"They talked to me about Jillian's killer and how they're really close to picking him up," I lied. I couldn't tell her that I was going to be a fucking government informant and that I was supposed to testify in a federal case.

"Well, you let me know when they do. Because I wanna be at that hearing. I'm gonna tell the judge to throw the book at him," she said with conviction.

"Me too, Grandma. I'm gonna do that same thing."

She changed the subject. "What is your mother saying about all of this?"

"She's upset and she says that she's going to miss her."

"Why hasn't she called me to say that? I was like Jillian's mother."

"I know, Grandma. But I told her that you were mad with me and that you probably didn't want to be bothered, so that's why she didn't call you," I lied once more. I couldn't tell my grandmother how my mother really felt about the situation. If I did, then they'd never bury the hatchet and move on from it. It was starting to get really draining. "Has Edmund called you since yesterday?" That stunt he pulled yesterday was grimy as hell and I couldn't wait to see him again to straighten his ass out about it. Jillian and my grandmother were my flesh and blood, not his loser ass's. So, he could keep all his lies and antics to himself. I would never let him cause another rift like that with my grandmother. Never!

"Yes, he called me this morning to see if I was all right."

Before I could respond to her statement my cell phone started ringing again. I looked down at the caller ID and saw that the caller had blocked their number again, so I placed my cell phone back into my purse and continued on talking to my grandmother.

"They still blocking their number?"

"Yes, ma'am, and as long as they do it, then they won't get through."

"Why don't you turn your phone off?"

"I wish it were that easy," I told her, while thinking about how the DEA needs to keep in touch with me through this device. My mother needs me to keep my lines of communication open for her too.

"There it goes again . . ." my grandmother pointed out when my cell phone started ringing again.

I looked at the caller ID and this time a number appeared. I hesitated because one part of me was telling me not to answer it. But then the other part of me told me to do it, so I answered it. "Hello."

"Is this Misty?" a woman said. But then her voice clicked in my head. It was Terrell's mother, Mrs. Faye, again.

"Yes, this is she," I replied.

"Have you heard from my son yet?"

"No, ma'am, I haven't."

"Are you sure? Because this is not like him. He wouldn't just up and disappear."

"Did he tell you that we broke up?" I asked, because she was beginning to get underneath my skin.

"Yes, he did."

"So, then why would I know where he is?" I replied sarcastically. She didn't like me and I sure as hell didn't like her ass.

"Don't get smart with me, girl! I know your mama taught you that you're supposed to respect your elders."

"Mrs. Faye, I don't know where your son is. Now is that all you called me for?"

"I'm telling you right now, Ms. Thang, if I find out that you know something or had anything to do with my son going missing, I'm gonna make sure you rot in jail," she threatened.

"Are you done?" I asked her.

"Yeah, I'm done, you slick-mouth bitch!"

"Okay, great. Have a nice day." I disconnected her call. I even blocked her number. I will admit that when she threatened to have me rot in jail if she found out that I had something to do with Terrell being missing, my heart rattled a bit. Just the thought of going to jail scares me. But I have to keep my composure if I wanna last out here on these streets. And I will say this too, I'm sorry that Tedo got murdered, but it was for the best as far as I can see it. Now I don't have to worry about him ratting me out. Oh, but wait, that chick April is still out there roaming around. Fuck! And I still owe her money for getting rid of Terrell's body. Damn, I hope she doesn't come out of the woodwork with huge demands. I just hope she didn't rear her ugly head. If she did, she would rock my world to the core. Fuck! Fuck! Fuck! God, please keep her at bay. At least until I can get out of this mess with the DEA. After that, I will see what happens.

"Who was that on the phone?" my grandmother wanted to know.

"The mother of my ex-boyfriend."

"What did she want with you?"

"She's been looking for him for two days. She thinks that he's gone missing."

"How old is he?"

"My age. She needs to be calling his other women. There's at least a dozen of them. So, wherever he is, I say good riddance."

My grandmother gave me more choice words about life and how I should be living. Aside from the hang-ups she has with my mother, she's a very wise woman. I knew she loved Jillian more than me, but it didn't matter to me because I knew that she still loved me.

40

WE HAVE A CRISIS

I left my grandmother's house later in the evening when it got dark. While en route to my mother's house, I decided to make a detour to my apartment. I wasn't going to go drive up to the building, so I decided to cruise the neighborhood to see if my apartment was being watched by Ahmad or anyone that looked like him.

I can't lie when I say that my anxiety level shot through the roof. I'd never been so fucking scared in my life until now. The thought of someone stalking me with intentions of killing me wasn't a nice feeling to have. In fact, it's killer on your heart and your mind. I just couldn't wait to get past it.

The streets that led to my apartment building were semi-quiet. But the anxiety inside of me intensified and roared like a lion the closer I got to my apartment. I wanted to drive slowly but I didn't want to bring any attention to my car so I drove at the posted speed and hoped that no one was out there looking for my car.

Once I was within twenty feet of the building, I was able to see my apartment, but I couldn't see any of the windows to my place, so I continued driving. Another few seconds into the drive, the windows in my living room became visible. It was dark in my apartment because I turned off the lights before I left that morning after changing clothes. So, another seven seconds, I was able to see my bedroom window. It was dark in there too. But then after I drove two more yards in, I saw the light of a flashlight bouncing off the walls in my bedroom. My heart nearly jumped out of my chest. "Oh shit! Somebody is in my fucking apartment," I said, my words barely audible while I continued to drive farther in. But then, I saw another flashlight bouncing off the walls in my living room too. "What the fuck is going on? There are two people in my freaking apartment." I cursed as my heart pounded.

Without thinking about it for another second, I sped out of there. I had to get away from my place as quickly as possible. And while I was driving away, I couldn't help but wonder who was in my apartment. Were they there to rob me? Or were they there to murder me? Whatever it was, I wasn't gonna stick around to find out.

As I drove to the opposite end of my street, I couldn't stop wondering who were those two people in my house. After narrowing it down to about three people, I still couldn't come up with a definitive answer, and that was driving me crazy. "Ahmad, you did say that you knew where I lived, so was it you and another mafia member from your organization?" I continued to speak low. "But then it could've been April and some guys she and Tedo knew, searching my spot thinking I had something of value to pay her for the work she put into getting rid of Terrell. So, was it you?" I mumbled.

Trying to figure out all the possibilities of who could be behind the break-in was starting to beat me up mentally, so I pulled out my cell phone. I needed to talk to someone. I knew it couldn't be my grandmother, because she's old-school. If I'd asked her for advice about this situation, she'd either tell me to call the cops or get on my knees and do some praying. And if I called my mother, she'd tell me to call the cops too. So, I guess that's what I was gonna do. I called Agent Sims's cell phone number first, but it went straight to voicemail. I called Agent Montclair second, and thank God he answered his cell phone. "Hi, Agent Montclair, this is Misty. Is Agent Sims around?"

"He just took off to go home. Did you call his cell phone?"

"Yes, I did. But it went straight to voicemail."

"Okay. Well, I'll try getting ahold of him and have him call you back. But let me ask you, are you okay? You sound a bit alarmed."

"I just drove my car by my apartment building and saw two people walking around in my bedroom and my living room in the dark with flashlights."

"How long ago was this?"

"Like a minute ago."

"Did you go inside your apartment?"

"No, I didn't get out of my car. I saw them from the street."

"Where are you now?"

"I'm on my way to my mother's house."

"Okay. Go straight there. And I will get Sims to call you back in a few minutes," he told me and then he disconnected our call.

When I pulled my car up to my mother's house, I saw two Caucasian detectives wearing cheap-looking suits standing at my mother's front door, talking to her. She must've told them that I was in the car because everyone turned around to look at me at the same time. Of course, I wondered who they were and why they were there, but I knew that I wouldn't get the answers to those questions until I talked to them.

While I was walking toward them I couldn't stop thinking about the two people that were looking around my apartment with flashlights. The feeling of not knowing, was driving me insane.

"What's going on?" I asked as soon as I stepped onto the front porch.

Both cops extended their hands and introduced themselves to me. "I'm Detective Hollings," the first one said.

"And I'm Detective Richards," the second one said.

"They're here because your ex-boyfriend Terrell is missing," my mother blurted out.

"Well, he's not here," I said.

"I told them that. But they still wanted to talk to you," my mother continued. I instantly noticed that she had to have had a couple of glasses of wine, because she was starting to be a little too talkative.

"Can we go inside?" they asked me.

"No, you can't. Whatever you gotta say, say it out here. Because I've got a lot of shit on my mind and you came at a bad time," I told them.

"Can we ask you when was the last time you spoke with Terrell?" Detective Richards asked me.

"Mom, please go in the house. I'll be there in a minute."

"As you wish," she said as she chuckled and closed the front door.

"Look, like I told Terrell's mother, I haven't seen or talked to him, so just please leave me alone."

"Can you tell us exactly when you last saw or talked to him? We need like a day and time, if you can remember," Richards asked.

"I don't know. Maybe a few days," I told him, trying to give him the right answer, but I couldn't concentrate. I couldn't get the images of those flashlights out of my head.

"Can you tell us when was the last time you two argued?" Detective Hollings interjected.

"I don't remember," I snapped. "Terrell and I broke up a while ago. I cannot tell you where he is, because when two people break up they go their separate ways. Now is that clear enough for you?"

"Well, can you tell us if he had any enemies? Or girlfriends that would like to see him dead?" Detective Richards started his questions again.

"No, I cannot."

"Would you tell us if you knew someone who would like to see him dead?" Detective Hollings interjected once again.

"Are you guys serious right now? I don't know shit. Now if you don't mind, I've gotta go." I walked by them onto the front porch.

"Did Terrell have a hand in that botched robbery that took place at your old employer's?"

I stopped in my steps and turned around. "You don't know shit! I lost my favorite cousin in that gun battle. Everyone else who lost their lives don't matter to me. So, get your facts straight." I gritted my teeth and then I walked into the house.

"Your mother has our card, so call us if you hear anything," one of them yelled after I closed the door in their face. Fucking bullies!

41

GET ME OUT OF HERE

Minutes after I walked into my mother's house, I found her sitting in the den watching TV with a glass of red wine in her hand. I started the conversation after I sat on the sofa across from her. "Mom, we need to talk."

"What's wrong now?" she asked me.

"Mom, are you drunk?"

"No, I am not. You always think I'm drunk. Did you get a chance to talk to the cops?"

"Yes, I did."

"Do they really think he's missing?" Her questions kept coming.

"Listen, Mom," I started off, and then my cell phone started ringing. I looked at the caller ID and saw that it was Agent Sims returning my call.

"Hi, Misty, this is Agent Sims. You need to talk to me?"

"Yes, I just drove my car by my apartment and from the outside I could see two people walking around my in bedroom and living room with flashlights. The shit scared the hell out of me. And I think it was Ahmad because he told me that he knows where I live."

"Where are you now?"

"At my mother's house."

"Okay, I'll check it out. Can you meet us back at the federal building downtown within the hour?"

"What's gonna happen?"

"We're gonna have to put you in witness protection."

"Why can't you just put me in a hotel out of town for a while until all of this blows over?" I suggested.

"Look, we'll talk about all of that after you get downtown."

"All right," I said.

"Who was that?" my mother asked after she took another sip from her wineglass.

"Mom, you can't stay here."

"Whatcha mean I can't stay here? This is my house. Your father bought this house for us."

"Mom, some bad people are looking for me. And I'm afraid that they may come here looking for me. So it would make me feel so much better if you would leave here for a few days or maybe a week."

"What's going on?" My mother's boyfriend walked into the living room while I was talking to her. He looked like he was on his way to work.

"Carl, I'm in a bit of trouble with some very bad people and I think that they are gonna come here looking for me. So if they come here and don't find me, they're gonna make you or my mom pay for the shit I got myself into. So will you please take my mom somewhere safe for a week or so? It would tear my heart apart if anything happened to her because of some dumb shit I did."

"What happened?" he wanted to know.

"I really don't wanna get into it right now."

"Does it have something to do with what happened at your job?" He pressed the issue.

"Yes, it does." I said.

"I'm not going anywhere. This is my house and I'm not letting anyone run me out of it," my mother protested.

"Carl, please talk some sense into her head. I'm getting ready to get out of here in a few minutes and it would make me so happy if you took her out of here too," I pleaded with him.

He stood there for a moment and then he said, "Don't worry. I will get her out of here."

After Carl promised to get my mom out of this house, I grabbed my purse and a bottle of water from her refrigerator and exited through the front door. My drive downtown would only take fifteen minutes, so I sped off toward the highway and headed in that direction. One minute into the drive, I remembered that I needed to call my grandmother. This situation with this drug case and murder case was becoming too much to bear. But I knew that I needed to get her to safety as well. So it relieved me when she answered my call. "Grandma, I'm gonna need you to leave your house for a few days until this case with the people who killed Jillian is over."

"Misty, are you out of your mind? I'm not leaving my house for nobody."

"But, Grandma, this could end up being a bad situation."

"Listen, honey, I know you're worried about a lot of stuff that's going on in your life, but I don't have that same testimony. I'm a child of God and I don't fear no one."

"Nana, I understand all of that, but would you do this for me? And for Jillian? Would you just come with me for a week or so until all of this blows over?"

Before she could answer, she told me to hold on because someone was at the front door. "Who is it?" I asked her. No one really visited my grandmother, so who in the hell could be at her front door?

"I don't know. But I'm about to find out," she told me.

My heart started jerking around in my chest while I heard each footstep walking toward the front door. "Who is it?" she yelled.

"It's me, Edmund," I heard him say on the other side of the door, so my heart rate slowed down a little.

I heard her open her front door. "It's Edmund and another fellow with him."

"Grandma, ask them what do they want?" I shouted through the phone. But she didn't reply. So I repeated the question.

"Misty, I can't listen to you and these two guys at the same time. Let me call you back," she told me and then she disconnected the call. Just like that, she hung up.

"Fuck! She hung up!" I growled and punched my steering wheel with my fists. "What the fuck does Edmund want with my grandmother? Jillian is not there anymore. So, why the fuck is he going to her house? And then he brings a plus one. What type of game is he playing? Was he there to rob her so he could buy himself some fucking prescription drugs, since Jillian wasn't around to purchase them for him? Whatever it was, I needed to stop it now.

I called my grandmother's number again. But she didn't answer. And I became furious. The fact that she didn't have a cell phone and only had a landline got underneath my skin because I knew that after she hung up the phone with me, she set the receiver down on the table in the foyer. "Ugghhh!" I snapped.

After calling her about five more times, I finally gave up. When I got down to the federal building, I walked straight into the office and didn't waste any time telling Agent Montclair what was going on at my grandmother's place. "I need you to send some agents there right now to put their asses out before they rob her. I need you to bring her down here so I can convince her to go with me."

Agent Montclair had to get approval from his and Agent Sims's boss before they could send agents out to my grandmother's house. It took about thirty minutes to do so, which was too long in my book, but at least he got it to happen. He also went along for the drive just so that my grandmother would be okay with speaking to him after she recognized who he was.

When Agent Sims walked into the large office, he asked me to go over what happened when I drove by my apartment, so I gave the story to him in more detail. And when he felt like I had given him enough information, he took it to his boss.

He returned a couple of minutes later and told me to grab my purse. "Me and a couple of agents will be taking you to a hotel until we can figure out our next course of action. Now are you ready for that?"

"Yes, I am."

"Have you spoken to your mother?"

"Yes, I stopped by there, told her and her boyfriend what happened, so he's taking her somewhere safe for a few days."

"Okay, great. Let's go," he said, leading the way.

42

MORE BLOOD ON MY HANDS

The drive to the hotel only took thirty minutes. I imagined that people going into witness protection would go straight to a halfway house or a house tucked away on a couple of acres, tucked away on some farmland. Agent Sims assured me that we wouldn't be there long. My time there didn't concern me. What did concern me was how quickly I could get my grandmother here to safety. I hoped that when the other agents got to her house that she'd be willing to come and join me.

The hotel room was spacious, but plain. I sat on the left side of the sofa bed and kicked my shoes off so I could . . . *relax* wasn't quite the word. I felt numb inside from Jillian's death and scared of what could come next.

"Is there anything in particular you want to watch?" Agent Sims asked me after he grabbed the remote control from the coffee table.

"I don't care what we watch," I told him and laid my head back on the sofa cushion.

I heard him sifting through the channels while I kept my eyes closed. My mind wasn't on anything that had to do with the television. The fact that I lost my cousin in a senseless robbery would always haunt me. I mean, how the hell did I let that happen? I told her to stay home and wait for the guys to bring the drugs to her. But no, she wanted to be the damn getaway driver, like they were committing a bank robbery. I also knew the other reason why she wanted to come with them. She wanted to make sure that the guys didn't take more drugs for themselves. Look what happened. She's gone. My favorite cousin is gone.

"Hey, Sims," I heard the voice of Agent Montclair say over their walkie-talkies.

Agent Sims grabbed his radio from his hip and pressed the Talk button. "Whatcha got for me?" Agent Sims replied.

"We got here too late," Agent Montclair said.

I had tuned out Agents Sims and Montclair's conversation until Montclair uttered the words *we got here too late*. I lifted my head up and looked directly at Agent Sims. His facial expression changed drastically. And when he looked back at me, he knew that I knew what those words meant. Without hesitation, I said, "Is he talking about my grandmother?"

Instead of answering my question, he told Agent Montclair to call him on his cell phone and that's when I knew that I was right. I jumped up on my feet and rushed toward Agent Sims and started attacking him. I brought up my fists and started hitting him over and over, because this was all his fault. "I knew I shouldn't a helped y'all. Now my grandmother is dead. She's dead! My cousin is dead. And neither one of them are coming back! This all your fault!" I yelled with rage. I knew that whoever killed my grandmother wasn't done with their killing spree.

43

HOPELESS

Losing my nana was the last straw. How could I go on? I loved my mother, but I loved my grandmother more. She was my rock, and the only woman in our family that held everyone down. I'd never be able to forgive myself for this. And to know that it all started from me stealing drugs from my job for Jillian. I didn't have to do that. I could've told her no every time she asked me to do it. But no. I was weak and did it anyway. And look where that got me. My hands were covered in blood. Sanjay was murdered first, Terrell was next. Then Jillian was gunned down. The guys that helped rob the pharmacy were all gone, and now my grandmother. Now I was worried about my mother. Thankfully, her boyfriend had enough sense to take her to his parents' house out of town after I asked him to. But I had other family and friends in my life, good people who were living their lives and didn't deserve to be gunned down over these drugs.

It hurt thinking about losing Nana and Jillian. Every time I thought about them, my heart got heavier and I could hardly breathe. With my family destroyed, I couldn't even think about the investigation. Or about the cops thinking I had something to do with Terrell's disappearance. None of those things mattered when I faced waking up tomorrow without my family.

Tears rolled down my cheeks as I looked around me at the drab, nearly empty room. The room's colorless décor seemed to suck away the little energy I had left. I'd lost my way for good this time. My life was doomed, no matter how you looked at it.

I grabbed a piece of paper and an ink pen from the hotel desk and started writing.

> *Dear Mom,*
> *I know you raised me the best way you knew how. I also know that you've been having a hard time coping with the death of my dad. You're a beautiful person inside and out, so you deserve to be happy. So that's why I've decided to go. Me not being here should stop the reign of terror from the mafia family I got mixed up with. And you'll be free to live a stress-free life without looking over your shoulder. Those men I got involved with are senseless murderers and they don't care about anything other than greed and death. Please understand that this is the best way to end this. I love you so much, Mama!*
> *Your daughter always,*
> *Misty*

I put down the pen and folded the paper in half. With one last look around me, I went into the bathroom and turned on the tub faucet. I was about to take my last long, hot bath.

DON'T MISS

Head Games
by Mary B. Morrison
New York Times bestselling author Mary B. Morrison
delivers a sizzling, twist-filled tale of four competitive
friends, a dangerous bet—and high-stakes consequences
no one can afford to win.

Dead on Arrival
by Kiki Swinson
Kiki Swinson's "tension-packed" (*Library Journal*) and
"unrelenting" (*Publishers Weekly*), bestselling novels
deliver startling twists, unforgettable characters—and a
stark, unforgettable portrait of life in the South. Now she
detonates an explosive tale about a couple who can't get
enough—and a risk that will exact a merciless price . . .

Collusion
by De'nesha Diamond
Framed for a high-profile murder, Abrianna Parker
finds herself hurtling down a conspiracy rabbit hole in a
desperate attempt to clear her name. Her only way out is
to go after the most powerful man in the country. But the
powers that be play dirty . . .

Turn the page for an excerpt from these thrilling novels . . .

PROLOGUE

THE CREWE

June 30

"Black women are easy, homies. Especially . . . the married ones." Trymm—pronounced "trim"—the most influential of the crewe, valet-parked his black Mercedes GLS at The Cheesecake Bistro. "Where y'all at?"

Females stood in clusters outside waiting to dine at the bistro that had some of the best dishes and drinks. Some held flat, square pagers. A few guys sprinkled throughout the crowd stared back and forth at Trymm's car, then at Trymm.

"Right behind ya, my brother." Blitz drove up in his midnight-blue BMW Alpina B7, responding to the group on their conference call. "I'm telling y'all, black professional women are easier." Handing the attendant his key, Blitz joined Trymm on the grimy sidewalk.

Standing on St. Charles Avenue, they watched two streetcars travel in opposite directions on the neutral ground paved with more dirt than patches of dried grass, more brown than green. Nawlins was a city that care forgot. True for local government and tourists in search of their wildest experience, but the crewe took pride in what they called home.

"Nope, under twenty-five. They're the easiest." Dallas backed his platinum Lexus LX into a space upfront, secured his gun in his side pocket, set the car alarm, and kept the keyless remote.

"Nah, D. The overweight ones. They give it up real quick." Kohl opened the door to his bronze Bentley Bentayga, retrieved his ticket from the guy wearing a red vest.

Valet parking at the bistro was for customers only. Kohl handed the guy his usual $100 tip, to keep his mouth shut.

En route to their destination, the crew walked side by side. A group of four women smiled back and forth among the guys. One woman complimented, "Nice cars, fellas."

A simple acknowledgment from Trymm as he held his wedding ring high, wiggling his finger. "Thanks, love," and the guys continued their stroll.

"Hold up. Where're y'all headed? Y'all not coming in here?" the woman inquired.

No one replied. Q and A with a female none of them were interested in was a waste of time.

"Women, women, and more women, my brothers." Blitz rubbed his hands.

"And all of 'em passing out free pussy." Trymm led the way across St. Mary Street.

A large oval sign, with THE TROLLEY STOP CAFÉ painted in bold green letters, was plastered under the flat roof, right above the door. OPEN 24/7 was displayed in caps on a white banner that stretched column-to-column, ten feet in front of the wooden green-painted wheelchair ramp. The red neon OPEN sign in the window was always lit. The twenty-two-year-old establishment, designed like a real city car—faded maroon framed windows gave the appearance diners were eating on the trolley—could easily be mistaken for being half a century old.

A staple in the community, the restaurant commanded a

hefty crowd all day during Essence Festival weekend. Too many badass females to count, the line snaked around the island centered in the parking lot, extending to the sidewalk. The all-too-familiar two-hours-plus wait wasn't for the crewe.

"Excuse us." Trymm opened the door.

The humidity welcomed the morning sunshine as four of New Orleans's finest eligible bachelors entered the standing-room-only café. At a glance, it was clear that beautiful, scantily dressed women outnumbered the men three to one.

"Glad you texted me, bro. Thanks for holding down the fort for us." Trymm patted his eldest brother, Walter, on the back as Walter and his three friends stood. Trymm, Kohl, Blitz, and Dallas settled onto four of the six barstools at the counter.

Walter placed his hand on Trymm's shoulder. "No problem. You know I got you."

A gentleman in a crimson buttoned-down shirt had three top buttons undone. A gold cross lay flat on his furry patch of gray chest hairs. His matching colored shorts were meticulously creased. Standing erect, he confronted Walter. "Man, no disrespect, but we been waiting to be seated for over an hour." He conspicuously clutched his Bible over his heart.

"None taken, but y'all gon' hafta wait a little longer. Ya heard me." Walter, a six-three, 250-pound former professional wrestler, wasn't asking.

Trymm, Kohl, Blitz, and Dallas pushed their stool toward the counter. Stood facing the man. Dallas eased his hand into his pocket, gripped the handle of his gun. The crewe knew the dirty South could get filthy without notice. Dallas was always strapped.

"Bay-bay, y'all sure looking extra fine today! Sit." Dana, the crewe's usual waitress, wiped away the food particles on the forest-green top, slapped menus in front of the fellas. "I got y'all in a sec, Trymm." Mixing orange juice and champagne into a plastic container, Dana stacked four red acrylic tumblers on her tray, then headed toward the main dining room.

The Trolley Stop Café had three areas—the bar was to the left upon entry; the street car section was to the right, up three stairs and another right; the interior was to the right up three steps, then left. Each square table was the same lacquer-coated cherrywood. Forty tables, 166 seats. Not one chair was empty.

Walter redirected his attention to Trymm. "I'll swing by and help Penny set up, but don't be chillin' all morning with these cats." Walter scanned the eyes of Trymm's friends. "Chasing pussy will leave you eating in the dark, gentlemen." Walter positioned his wrist in front of Trymm's face, pushed the start button on his stopwatch. "You've got two hours tops. See you at noon. Sharp. Not twelve-o-one."

Trymm clenched his teeth, braced himself. Being the youngest among ten children had benefits, and drawbacks. No need to respond. Walter wasn't asking, nor was he joking.

A wrestling competitor in high school and college, Walter, at the age of forty-five, had muscles solid as boulders. He bench-pressed three times his weight every morning before sunrise. "I have to make tracks to open my restaurant, and Penny can't manage this incoming Essence Fest crowd by herself. Shit gon' be busier tomorrow, so don't even bring your black ass ova here." He punched Trymm on the arm. Trymm leaned into Kohl, then sat up straight. "And don't forget to give me your twenty-five hundred for Mom and Dad's fiftieth anniversary party next month."

Trymm dug into his pants, peeled off twenty-five C-notes, slapped them in his brother's hand.

Walter stuffed the cash in his wallet. "Keep flashing. One of these fools gon' bust you upside the head and empty all your pockets. Your ass gon' get got too, Blitz. Let that Rolex rest. Y'all too old to say none of you have a wife. Trymm, what you holding out for? Disrespecting the family's last name and shit. Francine ain't going nowhere. Get the ring or I'ma get it for you. You're proposing at Mom and Dad's event. An hour and fifty-eight, Trymm." Walter followed his buddies out the door.

Trymm sat on the edge of his seat, planted one foot on the floor, the other on the bridge below, tightened his lips, looked at his crewe.

Blitz stared back at him. The watch was a family heirloom (from his grandfather) gifted to him by his father when he'd graduated from college. "What? You sour, nigga? At least you have a tribe of siblings. Wish big Walt was my brother for real. Being an only child is the worst. I still get blamed for shit I didn't do."

Sixteen years separated Trymm from Walter. Trymm was blessed to stand six inches taller than the brother who was like his second father. Disciplinarian was the role Walter assumed when they were kids. Mom, a housewife, and with their dad working sunrise to sunset each day of the week to make sure all of his kids had degrees and owned a business, Walter stepped up to help their mom, and he didn't hesitate to beat an ass or two when he felt it was necessary.

"Squash the monologue, Blitz. Man, I've been tripping all morning off of how weak black women are. They hawking us right now. Bet we could fuck a dozen each. That, and the fact that we're all about to hit dat big three-o this year. When we gon' slow our roll?"

People heading to and from the restrooms walked sideways, squeezing their way between the back of the barstools and the customers lined along the wall. One more row of twelve diners and no one would have enough space to move.

Unfolding the *Times-Picayune* newspaper Walter had left behind, Trymm Dupree adjusted the crotch of his gray, white, and black camouflage cargo shorts, giving his seven flaccid inches space to stretch out.

He stroked his freshly shaved head, where three-carat-diamond studs lit up both of Trymm's ears. Blackberry skin coated with coconut oil glistened on his flawlessly smooth face, thick lips, toned biceps, long athletic legs, all the way down to his pedicured feet, which rested in black leather open-toed sandals. Trymm scanned the front page of the metro section, slid the remainder one counter space over to Kohl.

"We should do some unforgettable shit!" Kohl peeled off the sport pages. "Let's take a thirty-day trip, dip to the DR, Jamaica, Puerto Rico, St. Martin, the Bahamas. Wherever it's hot, the chicks are freaks, and they won't hesitate to suck all of our dicks for the price"—nodding upward, he gave the crewe a tight smile that barely showed his teeth—"of a po'boy."

Blitz slapped Kohl on the nape of his neck. "The dime a dozen are in Brazil, nigga."

"Well, Rio de Janeiro, Ipanema, then," Kohl snapped back. "You ain't Walter. I'll take you down. You know what I meant."

Standing at six-two, tipping the scale at 270 pounds, Kohl was an only child. Unlike the rest of his crewe, Kohl's midsection was flabby and wide. From his hairline to his ankles, a stray bullet wouldn't hit him in the ass. Kohl's toasted-almond skin had red undertones from his Indian heritage. His jet-black hair was braided into a foot-long ponytail. Letting it down drew too much attention. Adopted son of a preacher man and a stay-at-home mom, Kohl wasn't permitted to pierce or tattoo any parts of his temple. His gold polo, with a fleur-de-lis logo, black slacks, and lace-up, hard-sole shoes were the most casual he'd dress.

"Fuck all that flight hopping, so it won't get back to Rev. and the First Lady. When I was stationed in Afghanistan, Dubai was my one-stop shop for all the pussy I wanted." Dallas smiled, lifted his left brow. "I had women from all the places you mentioned"—he pointed at Kohl, then touched each finger as he continued—"and add Africa, Asia, Australia, Russia. They were all within a few blocks' radius, and that's not half the list. And, hear me out, paying for pussy over there is legit."

Dallas didn't have an incentive to return to the United States while he was enlisted in the military, so he vacationed abroad. With two half-brothers by his father, Hawk, they might as well all have been dead, Dallas's combat buddies became his overseas family. The crewe was as close as he'd come to having brothers stateside. During deployment he'd gone eighteen months without seeing a woman he didn't have to kill.

Their section was packed. Squeezing had turned into pushing and shoving. A few verbal confrontations erupted. The newest owner, son of the original founder, yelled, "I need everyone to clear this aisle. *Now.* If you do not have a space to stand against the wall, if you're not going to the restroom, wait outside." Maroon dude with the cross secured his position in front of the window. None of the crewe inched their seats closer to the counter.

Kohl, as usual, had to prove he knew a lil more about the subject at hand. "And they let you have babes waiting in your bed when you check into your hotel room."

"Touché." Dallas didn't want to get into a pissing match with Kohl over the trivial when Dallas had more firsthand experiences than he could count. "It's hypocritical. Kinda like how your folks know you own that strip club and hookah lounge, but they take your tithes under the table."

The smallest of the crewe, five-ten, 180 pounds, 80 percent of Dallas's left side of his body, from his chin down, was covered in tattoos. There was nothing to fight for after his mother drowned in their house during Katrina.

The military trained him to kill the enemy. Problem now was determining who the real enemy was. Being raised in a Baptist church didn't save his soul. Dallas harbored animosity for God. Post-traumatic stress disorder was God's fault.

Blitz joined in. "All pussy taste different, but when I'm ready to bust a nut, smashing is the same. I don't care where's she's from, long as she ain't dumb. I'm gon' get mine, if that bitch doesn't get hers, that's on her." He snagged the front part of the paper leaving the classifieds for Dallas.

"Y'all see all the fine sistahs jam-packed up in here?" Kohl pointed out. "I'm not driving to the West Bank for a 'bj,' and that's five minutes away, ya heard me."

The ratio was now five females—high heels, hair flawless, makeup impeccable—to every guy as departing guests changed seats with new customers. Laughter and chatter drowned out the background music as men made new acquaintances with jovial women.

Trymm smirked at Kohl. "Second that, homey, but you keep leaving out your baby mama. The mere fact that she hasn't gotten a penny of child support outta your ass in ten—"

Kohl sang aloud, " 'If she only had a brain—' "

"Or took it to the head," Dallas tagged on.

Blitz remained silent. Stole away to his private fantasy of Kohl's alleged baby's mama. Ramona was a sexy motherfucker.

"My married sides crawl to me on their belly like reptiles." Trymm had an hour and a half remaining. He glanced across the room.

Dana rushed from a table of four guys to a group of twelve women, scribbled orders, then disappeared into the kitchen. Dana was light-skinned; short, tapered blond hair framed her full face. Her wide hips and round ass shifted side-to-side as she reappeared, balancing four plates on a tray.

Kohl frowned. "Nigga, they have to. What they supposed to tell their husband? 'Move over. Big-dick Willy coming through.'"

Blitz and Dallas laughed, nodding in agreement.

The boy, a fifth grader, was possibly Kohl's son. At nineteen, Kohl wasn't ready to become a father. Ten years later, nothing had changed.

Trymm twisted his lips to the side. "Don't hate, homies."

"Whateva. It's the Fourth of July weekend, which means it's a Black Mizz America pageant for the next three. . . ." Blitz paused, eyeing an Amazon chocolate woman heading toward them. "Contestant number one, come through."

Silence among the crewe ensued. Chatter from guests lined along the wall behind them, determined to grab the next available seats at the bar, conspicuously lowered.

The crewe's stares beamed like infrared lasers at the white halter dress that clung to the woman's voluptuous breasts, highlighting her perky nipples. As she passed, the guys' heads turned in unison, fixating on her curvaceous hips that seductively swayed like a gentle breeze kissing everything in its path. Her naked back blessed them with a gold lace thong peeping from underneath the white scoop that stopped right above her bodacious booty.

Trymm rotated his platinum band, showcasing the diamonds, wet his lips as he admired the wedding set the woman wore; then he gently grasped her hand. "Excuse me, goddess, you mind blessing me with your name?"

The crewe sat on the edge of their seats as the woman's gaze lowered toward Trymm's lap.

As she bat her lashes, her cheeks rose higher, and higher. "Kandy. Capital *k*, small *y*."

Slowly releasing her soft, slender fingers, Trymm returned the smile. "Stay beautiful, Mrs. Kandy."

Trailing the split wedged between her cheeks, Dallas's dick began to swell.

The conversation was mute until Blitz cleared his throat. "She came here for this." He slid his hand down his abs to his partial erection.

An even six feet, weighing 210 pounds, Blitz had a shadow-thin mustache and a neat, upside-down, triangular patch of hair, which was centered directly beneath the dimple in his naturally red bottom lip. The facial hair made him appear distinguished. His crystal-gray eyes pierced in an arrogant, confident way. When he was unsure of himself, he was the only one that knew it.

"You're disillusioned, homey." Trymm pulled up his left sleeve, flexed, then rubbed the horseshoe brand on his biceps. "You'd betta crunch that wallet if you want to eat," he sang, "Kan-dy."

Blitz lamented, "Every man isn't cheap like you and Kohl, my brother."

Trymm directed his response to the crewe. "I can charm a woman out of her pussy before she takes off her panties. They buy me shit. I bet all of y'all, one, Kandy with a *y* isn't her real name, and two, she wants to feel my Clydesdale slide on her clit and pound the bottom of that pussy till she's raw."

Dallas and Kohl nodded.

Blitz flicked his tongue. "Women don't require all that banging. Brothers like you"—he pointed at Kohl, then Trymm—"don't do shit for women. Dropping a few hundred or a designer bag on a chance to do the unforgettable, to come inside of that, man, that's chump change." Blitz's cell rang. He declined the familiar bill collector's call.

More diners exited into the parking lot, which was as filled with new faces. The guy in maroon stared at the crewe with discontent. Dallas noticed him. Long as dude didn't make a move in the crewe's direction, he'd live to see another day. Dallas placed his palms on the countertop, stared up at the purple, green, and gold Mardi Gras beads hanging high upon the wall among bottles filled with whiskey, tequila, rum, and vodka, then resumed reading the paper.

"Correction, homey. You mean the unimaginable. That's one-of-a-kind pussy right there. She's got her own money. She's not thirsty." Trymm smirked at Blitz. "You ain't gon' get with that for a few hundred dollars." Trymm held up his pinky. "I'm just sayin'."

Kohl held up the menu to Blitz, then pointed. "You speak out of sheer ignorance, my bruh. Why buy the cow when I can milk her with grits, eggs, bacon, toast, coffee, and orange juice, and have change left ova from a twenty to treat her girlfriend, and tip. Do the math. Oh, that's right, I forgot. That's your accountant's job."

"You've never worked a day in your life, Blitz." Dallas looked up from the newspaper, snatched the menu from Kohl.

"I object!" Blitz slapped the menu out of Dallas's hand. It slid behind the counter. "I've never worked a day in my life for anybody *else*. Must I remind you Negroes, my degree is in psychology? My mother is an oceanographer, and my father is a politician. I live off of my investments."

Dallas exhaled. "With the exception of Trymm and his tribe of nine, none of us have siblings. The two my sperm donor had after leaving my mom, y'all know how I feel about them. Blitz, your problem is you don't respect money. Run into the wrong bitch, you gon' end up broke."

Stroking his chin, Blitz nodded upward. "And what the fuck you call Dupree Seafood? Trymm riding on his daddy's legacy."

"What the fuck?" Trymm's brows drew closer. He knew his parents wanted to live to see all of their children have kids, and he was the only one single with no kid. But

Trymm wasn't ready for a wife or a baby. "Don't forget I played professional basket—"

Kohl interjected, "D, why you always starting nonsense? Your mama left you straight with that fat-ass insurance policy. Worse than disrespecting Blitz's cash flow, why you won't collect your retirement and disability checks from Uncle Sam? You earned that."

Dallas didn't respond. He rubbed his face really hard, rubbed his head, then stared at Kohl.

Blitz commented to the crewe as Mrs. Kandy retraced her steps behind their barstools. "I don't mind breaking off females—" He winked at Kandy.

She smiled at Trymm, winked at Trymm's dick as she kept walking, never acknowledging Blitz.

The crewe had no words as they each lusted, not for a chance to court the woman in white, but for an opportunity to feel what she felt like, outside and in.

"Y'all good?" Dana asked. "Trymm, I saw that. Don't start no shit up in here today with these married women. Take yo' ass 'cross the street where y'all park, or one betta, to Dupree's. I heard Walter. You got about an hour twenty to get your ass outta here."

Trymm caressed Dana's hand. "Line up our usual. I'm hungry."

"Don't talk yourself outta this tip, Dana." Blitz waved a $100 bill.

"Chump change, right, homey?" Trymm snatched the money, gave it to Dana.

Blitz watched as in one continuous motion Dana stuffed the cash in her bra.

"Thanks, Trymm. I got y'all in a sec." Dana mixed more mimosas.

"Yes!" resounded from the game room behind the double swinging doors. Inside the small game room, which was a few feet away from the bar, were two slot machines. A man parted the doors, dancing his way to the counter. "Pay me, baby!"

Wasn't as though there was a $1 million bonus. But if he'd won $1,000, that could potentially cover all of his bills for a month.

Trymm eyed his crewe. "I just came up with an outrageous challenge for y'all."

Blitz directed his attention to Dana. "I got a feeling whateva dat nigga fixina say is worth a setup. Make it a Hen."

Dana reached underneath the counter, retrieved an unopened bottle, plopped four empty red acrylic cups by Trymm, four more filled with ice, and the Hennessy. He poured equal portions until the bottle was empty, then dropped one cube in each cup, enough to chill, but not to dilute the alcohol content.

Dallas stared at Dana and wondered why she always gave Trymm preferential treatment. Wasn't like Trymm requested the setup.

"Give me your ticket, baby." Dana took the piece of paper from the overjoyed guy. "Wait for me by the kitchen."

Kohl tapped his waterproof GPS watch. "Dude, we can't get faded this early. You gotta clock in, and I have to open up my spot."

Dallas asked Kohl, "You been up since what? Six?"

Kohl shook his head. "Five-thirty."

"Give yourself the rest of the morning off, nigga. Drink. Your hookah-lounge-slash-strip-club ain't going nowhere. *Fuck*. It's not as though you served in the military. I did." Dallas took a huge gulp.

Kohl stood, stepped behind Blitz's stool, and saluted Dallas. "You still having them triggers? Flashing on women and stuff? Your problem is you've got too much time on your hands. When the last time you choked a chick?" Kohl flinched at Dallas, then quickly sat in his seat on the opposite side of Blitz.

"Aw, hell no." Being the fairest of them all, Blitz was not accidentally taking one on the chin. Blitz scouted back, granting Dallas direct access to Kohl's face.

Trymm's eyes grew large. He swallowed a mouthful of liquor.

"Not up in here! Sit y'all's asses down!" Dana yelled from across the room as she handed the guy who'd given her his ticket, fifteen $100 bills.

Glad to avoid having Dallas get out of his seat and whoop Kohl's ass, Trymm followed with, "She's right. Squash all that. How about, starting today, we fuck as many whores as we can?"

"Why they got to be whores?" Kohl inquired, sipping on his Hennessy.

"Okay." Dallas stared at Kohl. "Bitches. Like you."

Dana placed Trymm's plate in front of him. Dallas ripped his newspaper in half.

"Don't hate. You ain't never gon' be me, homey." Avoiding eye contact with Dallas, Trymm smiled at Dana. "Thanks, baby girl. Breakfast looks almost as delicious as you."

Dana wiggled her bare left ring finger before serving the others.

Dallas glanced across the room at all the pretty women, wishing one day he could have a relationship where he didn't scare a woman off. Maybe the thick one in denim shorts. Or the other one at the next table wearing a short dress. He could almost see everything she had to offer a man between her thighs. His dick became hard. His heart was good. It was his head that was fucked up.

Blitz's cell phone rang. He declined the "No Caller ID"

call. Consumed a portion of his drink. "Fuck them, then what?"

"Man, that's enough." Kohl glanced around the restaurant. "Yas lawd. I'm down. I'll start lining 'em up, and banging the juicy ones in the restroom right now."

Blitz narrowed his eyelids at Kohl. "Yo', ruthless, collar-wearing, Scorpio ass would."

Dallas laughed. "Ain't nothing wrong with calling the Lord's name. I do it every day."

Blitz wasn't talking about a priest collar. He was referring to Kohl's polo.

"Listen, we bet on tunk, dominos, every damn Saints game. Let's make the challenge the biggest gamble we've ever made." Blitz looked to his right at Dallas, then left at Kohl and Trymm. "Two hundred and fifty thousand dollars. Each."

"For pussy?" Kohl questioned. "You done lost all your damn marbles." He placed the rim of his glass on top of his bottom lip, then flipped the plastic cup upside down.

Trymm leaned on the green laminated counter, looked two seats down to Blitz. Kohl tilted backward.

"Chump change, homey. I'm in. Winner takes all." Trymm held up his glass.

"Dat's what's up." Blitz scanned the faces of Dallas and Kohl. "I know y'all not scared. This is our last rendezvous of this decade. We are all turning thirty this year," Blitz said, laughing.

"'Laissez les bons temps rouler,'" Dallas replied. "Fuck it. I can write a check today." If Dallas lost the bet, with all the money he'd saved not frivolously spending on females, he'd still have a net worth of over seven figures.

Shaking his head, Kohl thought about the money he'd stashed to open a second location for Kash In & Out. Winning would mean not having to use any of his funds. "It's not that I'm not in. It's too simple. I mean. How we gon' keep count? What about, in addition to banging the most chicks, you have to actually make them fall in love with you?"

"Y'all might as well cut me a check now," Trymm boasted, then told Dana, "Let us have another bottle."

Dana refilled each glass, placed the empty bottle next to Trymm, then left.

"And," Dallas interjected, "you have to dump her ass publicly in front of a whole lot of people."

Trymm added, "Or on social media. That's the ticket."

"Cool. But how are we to prove the love connection 'cause y'all niggas lie?" Blitz added, "Let's scrap that part. Toss in video footage and photos, and both have to be posted on social media."

The fellas eyed one another with excitement and certainty that they each would win.

Dallas insisted, "That shit that disappears in a snap doesn't count, either. Let's post pics or videos. We don't have to do both."

Kohl frowned at Dallas. "It has to disappear in a short time. I ain't tryna get sued. I have too much to lose."

Trymm raised his plastic cup. "Double points for live social videos that exceed an hour. Drink up. I'm not trying to get knocked upside my head today. I'm making time to secure my cashier's check, but one of y'all have to swing by Dupree's and get it."

Blitz quickly volunteered. "Tomorrow, July first, is the official start date. We end on July thirtieth."

"And I gets my mil soon as the bank opens the following business day." Trymm, self-assured he'd outdo the crewe, waved at Mrs. Kandy, who was walking toward the exit.

"She's a piece of work and waste of time. My bank is down the street." Dallas stuffed the last piece of his hot sausage patty in his mouth, then swallowed. "I'll cashier up my quarter of a mil soon as we're done."

"Me too," Kohl added.

"Y'all reconvene at my bank at two o'clock. Trymm, if you're good on time, I can meet you at your bank now." Blitz had to have control and full access to the million. Even if he didn't win, with the right short-term investment of the crewe's money, Blitz could skim enough off the top to pay off his debt.

"I'll get it to you, nigga. What's the rush?" Trymm stared past Kohl, focused on Blitz. "When y'all lose, I don't want to hear, 'No, I had too much to drink.'"

"I second that. We're settin' this up with a four-signature authority." Kohl wanted to close all the loopholes. "Wait, Trymm. Let's go over all the deets again, and oh, oh, Trymm, you've smashed too many vaginas, bruh. Exes don't count."

"*My* exes don't count." Trymm had never smashed any of the crewe's girlfriends, but qualifying for the grand prize might change all that.

Blitz grinned at Trymm. "So I can fuck fine-ass Atlantis? She's not married, but I heard she's engaged."

"Sure. Long as you can handle the ass whuppin' I'ma put on you, homey." Trymm didn't know the one he'd let get away was back in town. And she was engaged? If Blitz was telling the truth, Trymm couldn't let Atlantis walk down the aisle and into the arms of another man.

Kandy approached Trymm. Opened his hand. Wrote her number in his palm with a red marker, then walked away without saying a word.

Trymm adjusted his crotch. "Twelve-oh-one I'ma be all up in that. Ya heard me."

Anxious to secure the funds before any of the crewe backed out, Blitz dropped $200 on the counter. "Let's do this."

Everyone stood in unison.

"Wait," Blitz said, picking up his cup. "A toast. Let the head games begin."

"You a fool, boy." Trymm held his glass the highest. "I like that shit, though."

Kohl nodded. "Me too."

Dallas downed the last of his Hennessy, then saluted the others. "Laissez-faire, my brothers. Laissez-faire."

PROLOGUE

DAWN

Where the fuck was he?

I looked at the clock and noticed that I'd been sleeping for a couple of hours. I'd dozed off waiting for Reese to come home so we could talk about where we were going when we left town. He told me he was leaving his grandmother's house and was gonna make a quick stop at NIT. Then he was coming straight here. So, where the fuck was he?

Before I could grab my cell phone and dial his number, my phone started ringing. I picked it up from the nightstand next to my bed and looked down at the caller ID. I let out a sigh of relief when I saw that it was Reese calling me.

"Hello," I said.

"Did I wake you up?" he asked. He sounded kind of weird.

"Reese, where are you?" I asked, ignoring his question.

"I'm about to pull up to the house, so put on something and meet me outside," he instructed.

"Meet you outside for what? *Do you know what time it is?*" I screeched. He was making me angrier by the second because he was displaying some very odd behavior.

"Please don't ask me any questions. Just do what I said," he replied calmly.

"Bye," I said, and then I disconnected our call.

I was furious at the thought that I had to get out of my bed and meet him outside. What kind of fucking game was he trying to play?

I grabbed a sweatshirt and a pair of sweatpants from my dresser drawer and a pair of sneakers from my closet and got dressed. After I grabbed a jacket from the hall closet by my bedroom, I headed toward the front door. My adrenaline was pumping. I was already thinking of what I was going to say to him if he was making me come outside for nothing. He was going to feel my wrath.

Blinded by the headlights of Reese's car parked in our driveway, I blinked my eyes a few times and held up my left arm to shield my eyes. I saw the silhouette of Reese's body sitting in the driver seat, so I closed the front door behind me and walked over to his car. I was heading toward the driver side, until he rolled his window down halfway and told me to get into the car from the passenger side.

I obeyed his instructions and got into the car with him. As soon as I closed the door, I turned around and looked at him. "What the fuck is so important that I had to come outside and get into the car?" I asked him.

Reese wouldn't open his mouth to respond.

"What's wrong with you?" I questioned him.

A voice from behind me said, "He's dead!"

I turned my face slightly to the left and saw an Asian man with a gun and a silencer pointed directly at me. My heart dropped into the pit of my stomach. Anxiety and fear crippled me as I slowly moved my eyes away from the Asian man, back to my husband's face. At that moment, that's when I noticed the blood seeping from the hole in his head. I instantly froze. I knew then that this man was about to take my life too.

1

REESE

I knew Dawn was going to jump down my throat when I walked through the front door of our home. Not only did I not come straight home from work, I didn't answer my cell phone when she called me over a dozen times, and I didn't have the $800 I promised her I would have. Shit hasn't been going right for us these last six months, so she'd been breathing down my neck because of it. To be more candid, we'd been having some financial problems for the last couple of years. Our car payments were past due, our credit cards were maxed out, our light bills had more than tripled, and our home was in fucking foreclosure. Taking a boatload of flat-screen smart televisions, laptop computers, and fur coats here and there helped me pay a few of our bills. It also helped me get into a few poker games at my homeboy Edward Cuffy's spot, which was exactly where I was when Dawn called me earlier. Edward was one of the senior operators at the Norfolk International Terminal. So far, he's got twenty-four years under his belt. In other words, he had seniority, so nothing got by him. If anything was stolen out of the shipping containers and sold for a handsome profit, Ed definitely got his cut. No ifs, ands, or buts about it.

Edward was like a big brother to me. He wasn't a big guy, but he made up for it in height and walked around like he owned the world. He was like Samuel L. Jackson. Sixty-five percent of the longshoremen on the pier liked Edward, but the other thirty-five percent hated him. My wife, Dawn, was one of them. "Did you just come from Ed's house?" she didn't hesitate to ask as she walked toward me. I knew she had just come from the kitchen because I smelled the aroma of tomato sauce, she wore a cooking apron, and she held a plastic mixing spoon in her left hand.

"Why are you asking me that?" I instantly became defensive after I locked the front door.

"Because I called you over a dozen times and you kept sending me to your voicemail," she spat as she stood before me. Dawn and I got married two years ago. We dated for a year before I popped the question. When I first met her, she was gorgeous. She resembled the actress Toni Braxton. She was sexy too. Plus, she wasn't this fucking nagging. I remember when she used to walk around our house almost naked, on a daily basis. Now I can't get her to take off her terry-cloth robe. She went from looking like a Playboy bunny to a Catholic nun. She assumed on several occasions that I was cheating on her because I complained about her appearance, but my guilty pleasure was gambling.

"I was at the pier. This new guy named Nate needed some help with a few containers, so I stuck around and helped him," I lied as I passed her and strolled into the kitchen. She knew I was lying, so she followed me.

"So, if I call down to the office and ask Porsha' to check your time sheet, it's gonna show that you were still at work?"

I gave her a head nod and then I turned my attention toward the pot of boiling water. When I looked closer and saw spaghetti noodles, I knew I was having spaghetti for dinner.

I changed the subject. "When will the food be done?" Dawn knew that I wasn't confrontational. I'd do anything to stay away from an argument, especially with her. She was famous for backing me into a corner, and I hated it.

"As soon as you hand over the eight hundred dollars you promised to bring home to me," she answered as she stood two feet away from me.

Hearing her ask me for the money hit me like a ton of bricks. Anxiety consumed me. I literally felt like a fucking little kid who just got caught stealing money from my mother's wallet. I tried to think of a good excuse as to why I didn't have the money, but my mind went totally blank.

"Reese, where is the money?"

"I don't have it yet." I dreaded my own words.

"What the fuck you mean you don't have it yet?" she roared. I could tell that she was at her wit's end.

"Listen, Dawn, I've been working on a few things, so as soon as it comes through, I'll get the money," I tried to explain.

"You're still stealing from those shipping containers, huh?"

"Why are you concerning yourself with that?"

"Because I don't want you going to jail," she said. "Do you know that the port police are doing a lot more patrolling than usual?"

"Stop being so paranoid. I know what I'm doing," I assured her.

"So, how much longer am I gonna have to wait for the money?"

"Give me until tomorrow. I'll definitely have it by then," I told her, even though I wasn't sure. I needed to say something to get her off my back, at least for now.

"Reese, I'm telling you right now that if you don't have the money tomorrow, I'm taking your fucking Rolex watch down to the pawn shop and pawning it," she threatened, and then she turned around and walked to the stove.

I didn't comment one way or another because if she knew that I had already pawned my Rolex, she'd really be breathing down my neck. It was important to her to get this money from me because for one, she lent the $800 to me a couple weeks ago and two, she needed it for a fertility treatment. Having a baby was the most important thing to her. I had children from a previous relationship, but I didn't have any children with Dawn.

I've told her time and time again that if she and I don't ever have kids that I won't love her any less. But she doesn't believe it. She thinks that having a child with me will bring us closer together. I don't believe that. I think things are good the way they are. We don't need another mouth to feed. Shit! I bring home around $85,000 a year and Dawn about $50,000. But we're still in fucking debt. She pays the little things like the light bills, gas bills, and her $750 BMW car note. I pay most of the bills, like our $2,500 mortgage payment, $700 a month in child support for my other kids, my $1,300 truck payment, and then I gamble up the rest. So, tell me how bringing home another mouth to feed is going to bring us closer together? It won't.

I headed to the bathroom and took a quick shower. After I was done, I slipped on a pair of shorts, a white T-shirt, and then I headed back to the kitchen. Dawn had my plate of spaghetti on the kitchen table waiting for my return. She was already sitting down and eating when I walked in. "Looks good," I mentioned as I took a seat in the chair across from her.

Instead of thanking me for the compliment, she rolled her eyes and continued to eat. We sat there in an awkward silence for at least five minutes. I started to get up a few times and take my plate in the living room so I could watch a little TV, but I knew that would send her up the wall, so I decided against it. Thankfully, the doorbell rang.

I pushed my chair back to get up, but Dawn insisted that she answer the door while she got to her feet. So I scooted my chair back toward the table and continued to eat.

I heard Dawn as she walked across the hardwood floors to the front door. And when she yelled through the door and asked the person on the other side to announce themselves, I listened for their answer. "It's me, Alexia," I heard the lady say, and then I heard Dawn unlock the front door and open it. "What brings you by?" I heard Dawn ask Alexia.

"I was in the neighborhood," she replied.

Alexia was Dawn's older sister. She was five years older, to be exact. She closely resembled Gabrielle Union. She had this overly confident personality. When she walked in a room, she always commanded the attention of everyone there. I personally didn't like her because she always had something negative to say about Dawn's and my marriage. And to keep from cursing her ass out, I did my very best to avoid her.

"Wait, I smell food," she continued, and then I heard two sets of footsteps walking in my direction. I knew that at any moment I was going to come face-to-face with Alexia, so I needed to keep my composure. She knew how to ruffle my feathers, but I wasn't going to let her get to me today. I had too much other shit going on in my personal life, so I refused to let her add anything to it.

"Look at what we have here," she commented after turning the corner to enter the kitchen. She gave me this cunning look.

"What's up?" I said, and then I buried my face back into my plate.

"Nah, what's up with you? I see you got my sister slaving over the hot stove again," she replied sarcastically, as she sat down in an empty chair at the table.

"Isn't that what a wife is supposed to do when she has a family?" I told her.

"Speaking of family, Dad's been complaining about how he's been giving you guys money so you can make ends meet around here," Alexia said while she gave me the evil eye.

I got defensive immediately. "I don't know why you're looking at me. I don't owe your daddy shit!" I roared, firmly gripping my fork.

"Alexia, Reese didn't go to Dad to get the money, I did," Dawn chimed in.

"He might as well have gotten the money from Daddy, because if he was handling his business with the money he made from the terminal, then you wouldn't be in this situation."

"Bitch, why don't you just mind your fucking business!"

"You're the bitch! Got my sister around here running to my parents for money so y'all won't lose your house and cars. You aren't a real man. Real men take care of their family and make sure there's nothing lacking in the household. Not you. You rather throw your money away gambling while your wife does what she can with the money she makes and the money she gets from my parents."

"Alexia, you promised that you wouldn't say anything else!" Dawn yelled.

"He started it with me."

"Fuck her! She out of line, coming in my house talking all that fly shit out of her mouth."

"Nah, nigga, fuck you!"

"Reese, please stop. You too, Alexia. Y'all are about to give me an anxiety attack!" Dawn yelled once more.

"So, it's okay for her lonely ass to walk in here and start talking her shit to me?" I hissed.

"Stand up and be a man, and then I wouldn't talk shit to you," Alexia spat.

Dawn walked over toward Alexia and grabbed her by the arm. "Come with me, please." She led Alexia out of the kitchen. I realized that Dawn had taken Alexia outside after I heard the front door open and close. I heard bits and pieces of their conversation, with Alexia talking louder than Dawn, of course. Their spat only lasted a couple of minutes and then they came back in the house. This time when Alexia entered the kitchen, she focused on carrying on a conversation with Dawn, instead of me.

Alexia started talking about some bullshit-ass nigga she just started dating who wanted to have kids with her already. "We've only been dating for a month and a half and the nigga wants me to have a baby. I told him he was crazy."

"I thought you couldn't have any kids," I blurted out. I swear I couldn't let her slide by with that bullshit-ass statement, especially since she started running her mouth at me as soon as she walked into my kitchen. In my eyes, this was the perfect time to put her ass back in check.

"Don't worry about me. Worry about the fact that you haven't gotten my sister pregnant." Alexia hurled her words at me. I swear, I wanted to ignore her and not feed into her bullshit, but she started hitting nerves I didn't know I had.

Dawn jumped to my defense. "Come on now, Alexia, that's hitting below the belt. And besides, it's not his fault that I haven't gotten pregnant."

"Well, who's fault is it, my sister? He's a fucking loser." Alexia pressed the issue.

My blood was boiling. I wanted so badly to stand up and slap the shit out of her no-job, meddling ass. But I knew that putting my hands on her would be a huge mistake, so I got her where I knew it would hurt, and that was her personal life. All the niggas she fucked and continued to fuck.

"You got a fucking nerve coming in my house and disrespecting me. If you weren't Dawn's sister I would drag you by your hair and haul your ass out of here," I told her.

"Do it, nigga! Do it!" She stepped closer to me.

Dawn stepped between us. "You're a lucky-ass bitch!" I said.

"Nah, nigga. You're the lucky one because if I had it my way, I would file the divorce papers for my sister myself."

"Well, thank God you're not. Now mind your business before I call the cops and have your ass thrown out of here," I replied while clenching my teeth. I had so much other shit I wanted to tell her. For starters, she was a fucking unemployed high school dropout and a whore. Everyone down at Norfolk International Terminal had fucked her. Talking about Dawn not being able to get pregnant, she can't get pregnant either. So for her to come in my damn house and start stirring up drama between my wife and me is unacceptable. This bitch needs to know who's really in charge.

"I swear I can't believe that you married this nigga! You would've done so much better if you'd married that nigga Blake," Alexia continued.

"Well, she didn't, so deal with it," I snapped.

"I don't have to deal with that shit."

"Well, I'll tell you what, deal with the fact that you had to have over a dozen abortions because you were fucking two and three niggas at one time and you had no idea who the father was." I hissed like I had venom spewing from my mouth.

"Nigga, you don't know shit about me!" Alexia shouted.

"Reese, are you fucking kidding me right now?" Dawn said as she stood between us.

"I know you're a fucking ho! And I know every nigga you slept with. I mean, hell, every nigga at NIT know who you slept with," I continued. I was digging deep in my bag of information so I could humiliate the hell out of her. Judging from her facial expression, my tactic was working, but I could also tell that my words were hurting Dawn.

"Reese, stop it right now! I fucking mean it!" Dawn yelled at me.

I stood on my feet. "Tell *her* to stop it! She started this whole fucking thing!"

"Fuck him, Dawn! He's a fucking loser anyway!"

"Bitch, you're the fucking loser! That's why you can't keep a man! Nobody wants you," I roared.

"Oh, but you wanted me," Alexia said. She and I were standing at opposite sides of the kitchen table.

"Bitch, I never wanted you!" I protested, but she was right. About one month before I met Dawn, I met Alexia at the nightclub Upscale in Chesapeake. I was with one of my friends, who pointed out that he knew Alexia and that she was easy to get into bed. So, being the adventurous man that I was, I bought her a few drinks and then I tried to talk her into coming back to my apartment so I could fuck her. Now the only reason it didn't happen was because she was with two of her homegirls, and she drove. So she gave me her number that night. I can't tell you why I never called her, it just didn't happen.

"I want both of y'all to shut the fuck up right now!" Dawn roared as she stood between us.

"I'm not doing shit! This is my fucking house. Just send that bitch on her merry way."

"I ain't gotta go nowhere! This is my sister's house too," Alexia griped as she stood her ground.

"Dawn, get that ho out of my house right now! I'm not gonna say it anymore," I warned her.

Without saying another word, Dawn grabbed Alexia's hand and tried to pull her in the direction of the front door. "Come on, Alexia," she said.

But Alexia snatched her arm away from Dawn. "Are you scared of this nigga or something?" she blurted out.

"Nah, she ain't scared of me. She ain't got a reason to be," I told her as I took a step toward her.

"So, whatcha about to do?" Alexia asked me while Dawn grabbed her arm once again and started pulling her.

"I'm not about to do anything."

"So, why you walking toward me like you're about to do something?"

"Bitch, just get out of my fucking house! You're not wanted here," I concluded, and then I walked around her and Dawn. I started walking down the hallway toward my bedroom so I didn't have to hear Alexia's mouth anymore. I swear, if she were my woman, talking to me like that, I would've choked all the breath out of her body and gladly taken the thirty-year prison sentence to go with it.

I closed the door after I entered my bedroom. I heard Alexia utter a few more words to Dawn and then I didn't hear her voice anymore. I didn't hear Dawn's voice either. I figured she must've walked outside with Alexia, or even left for that matter. Either way, silence was something I needed to unwind. With the drama surrounding my relationship with Dawn, the bills we had and the gambling debt I couldn't get rid of, I needed this time to think. I needed to figure out how I was going to get things back on track. I needed a plan and I needed it right now. I just hoped that whatever I came up with eliminated my problems completely. If it didn't, then it would be a waste of my time.

PROLOGUE

Hay-Adams Hotel, Washington D.C.
Eight days ago

In the posh presidential suite of the five–star hotel, minutes from the White House, the new House speaker spent his celebration night in a luxurious den of debauchery. High off a potent designer street drug, Cotton Candy, he fulfilled a lifelong ménage à trois fantasy with an ex-lover and one of Madam Nevaeh's sexy escort girls.

When he woke, he was surprised to see his ex-mistress preparing to leave.

"Where are you going?"

"Home."

"What?" He struggled to detangle himself from the bed's soft linen. "No. Wait. Don't go."

"Why not? You still got company." Kitty referred to the gorgeous cocoa-brown woman lying in a cocaine high among a cloud of white sheets. "By the way, where did you find her? She's stunning."

"Yeah. What can I say?" Kenneth Reynolds boasted, his

eyes glassy and his nose swollen with pink dust under it. "I'm Mr. Lucky tonight. I'm going to talk to Madam Nevaeh about keeping Miss Abrianna here on an exclusive arrangement." He brushed strands of hair from the despondent girl's face.

"Madam?" Kitty arched one brow while she tightened the belt on her trench coat. "You're paying for pussy now? Hell. I thought she was some chick that you picked up from one of those sleazy clubs you like so much."

He laughed. "I don't mind paying for the best." He met Kitty's gaze. "Not that you're not."

"Fuck you, Kenny."

"Where are you going?"

"Home."

Reynolds stood from the bed and reached for her, but she dodged his touch. "Aw, now. Don't be like that. I thought we were putting our little spat behind us?"

"Behind us? How? Are you pretending not to know what happens to my nomination to the Supreme Court if you impeach the president?"

He groaned. "Politics, politics, politics. Can't we have one night that doesn't involve politics?"

Kitty stood still while Reynolds slithered his arms around her waist. "Tonight is supposed to be a celebration. You're looking at the third most powerful man in the country . . . and I'm gunning for the man at the top."

"And fuck me, right?" she clarified, brows arched.

"C'mon, Kitty. Why are you killing the mood? Hmm?" Reynolds snuggled his head in the crook of her neck. "Don't you feel how much I've missed you? What we had together?" Kenny's dick hardened against her. "Why don't you take off that coat and come back to bed? Hmm?" He nibbled on her earlobe.

"So you get what you want and fuck me. Is that it?"

Reynolds groaned. "Look. You're a good judge. You'll eventually get your seat on the court."

Kitty laughed. "Are you fucking kidding me? These are once-in-a-lifetime appointments. Lightning doesn't strike twice. If you remove the president, then it's bye-bye to my nomination."

"That's not true," Reynolds whined, backpedaling to the bed. "As soon as we remove that asshole from the Oval Office, the vice president will uphold your nomination. We can impeach him and then confirm you with no problem."

"Right." Kitty slid her hand into her coat pocket and wrapped it around a gun.

"Contrary to popular opinion, Congress can walk and chew gum at the same time."

"Bullshit—or it would have been done before."

Reynolds exhaled and leaned against the headboard. "I don't know what you want. The House doesn't confirm judges. That's the Senate's job."

"Majority Leader McCullough is following your lead on this."

Reynolds chuckled. "You're giving me way too much credit." He reached over and groped the unconscious woman lying beside him. "I'm still horny." He cast his gaze back toward Kitty, surprised to see a gun leveled at him. After a few seconds, laughter rumbled low in his chest. "Now what are you going to do with that?"

"I'm about to make sure that I end up on that court . . . by getting you out of the way." Kitty clicked off the safety.

Too high to realize how much danger he was in, Reynolds laughed more deeply. "C'mon, Kitty. It's only politics. It's not personal."

"Politics is always personal," she said and pulled the trigger.

1

In the rich suburbs of Alexandria, Virginia, drug lord and political insider Zeke "Teflon Don" Jeffreys had gathered his friends and valuable political D.C. clients at his lavish home to celebrate his thirtieth birthday.

While he mixed and mingled, a motley crew of party-crashers was kidnapping his business partner-slash-lover, Madam Nevaeh, right from under his nose.

"Hurry! Load her up." Draya, dressed as a server for La Plume's catering service, opened the back doors of the van.

"We are going as fast as we can." Abrianna Parker, disguised as a male server, complete with a mustache and padded chest, banged the madam's head on one of the doors.

"Easy," Kadir Kahlifa, in disguise as a man twice his age, whispered back.

Annoyed, Abrianna banged the madam's head again.

He frowned.

Abrianna shrugged. "I'm petty."

"Are you two for real?" Draya hissed.

Abrianna climbed up, still holding the front of Madam's body.

"Hey!"

Everyone froze.

"What are you guys doing over there?"

Abrianna, out of view, mouthed to Kadir, "Who is it?"

"Hey, I asked you guys a question!"

"Security," Kadir mouthed back.

Horrified, Abrianna glanced around for a weapon.

Draya spun. "Nothing. We're . . . grabbing supplies for the kitchen."

A large, lineman-shaped security guy waddled closer to the open van door.

Draya attempted to close one of the back doors to block his line of vision.

"But what the hell is that?" He gestured to the bag and leaned forward.

Panicked, Draya rammed the door into the nosy security guard's face, shocking him. However, she hadn't seen the drawn gun until it went off.

BANG!

Abrianna dropped Madam Nevaeh and screamed, "No!"

Instantly, the four-hundred-plus-pound man flew backward and slammed against the back of the house and then dropped like a stone.

Abrianna raced forward. "Draya, are you all right?" She gathered her friend into her arms. "Speak to me. Say something."

Draya lifted her shocked gaze. "How the fuck did you do that?"

Julian croaked, "Somebody tell me that I didn't see that."

Everyone stared at Abrianna, especially Kadir. "I, uh, uh—"

"It came from over there," a man shouted from the distance.

"Fuck. We gotta go," Kadir said, picking up Draya. "Get in the van," he ordered.

Everyone hauled ass.

Julian climbed behind Kadir and placed Draya in the back of the van along with Abrianna and Madam Nevaeh.

For a brief moment, Kadir's questioning gaze met Abrianna's, but then he slammed the doors shut—and raced to climb into the passenger seat. "Let's go!"

Julian jumped behind the wheel.

The van peeled off as an army of security goons rushed around the corner and found their unconscious colleague.

Rat-at-tat-tat-tat.

Bullets punctured the back of the van; a few ricocheted, forcing them to duck or dive for cover.

"What the hell?" Julian shouted, bringing everyone's attention to the police cars streaming onto the estate.

"Holy shit," Kadir said, incredulous.

Julian's foot lifted off the accelerator.

"Don't stop," Kadir shouted.

Julian hesitated on seeing the swarm of blue lights, but then slammed his foot back down on the gas.

The last two patrol cars swerved and blocked the van's exit.

"Don't you fucking stop," Kadir threatened again.

Julian tightened his grip on the steering wheel. When they blazed closer and made it clear that the van wasn't stopping, the cops scrambled to get out of the way.

It was too late.

"Hold on!" Julian cried, closing his eyes.

BAM!

Everyone and everything slammed forward.

The two police cars spun like pinwheels in the van's wake.

Draya groaned.

"You guys okay back there?" Kadir asked.

Abrianna, sprawled beneath pans and supplies, pushed herself up and crawled to Draya.

Draya rolled onto her back. "What the hell, Jules? Are you trying to kill me?"

"She's fine," Julian said. "If Draya is bitching, then she's okay."

"Are they following us?" Abrianna asked.

The guys checked their mirrors. "Not that I can tell," Julian said, relieved.

"Yeah. Well. We better get off this road just in case."

"How is our other passenger?" Kadir asked.

Abrianna turned and moved over to the insulated nylon bag and stopped short. "Uh, guys . . ."

"What?" everyone asked.

"There's blood," Abrianna announced.

"She was hit?" Kadir asked, coming out of his seat to climb into the back.

Abrianna pulled the zipper down and opened the bag. "Damn."

Blood bloomed across the center of Madam's white dress, but Abrianna was certain that it was the bullet lodged in the center of Madam's forehead that had killed her.

Draya shook her head. "Well, I guess she won't be telling us shit."

Zeke Jeffreys hid his humiliation behind a stony mask while former police lieutenant Gizella Castillo gloated as they shoved his large frame into the back of a squad car. Once he was tucked inside and the door slammed shut, his black gaze zoomed to hers and transmitted the message that this game wasn't over by a long shot.

She knew that he was probably right.

His guests were equally humiliated but more outraged at having to be loaded up in the back of police vans. Many of them had no idea of Jeffreys's double life. They had no idea that while they were mixing and mingling, he was trafficking the designer street drug Cotton Candy. However, this time he had done so with undercover cop Steven O'Day.

Castillo had wanted to bring the drug lord down for years but had never been able to scratch the surface. Police Chief Dennis Holder, an ex-lover and colleague, had clued her in about the planned raid and permitted her to be here to watch the whole thing go down. Other than a strange shoot-out involving someone jacking a caterer's van, the raid had gone down smoothly.

Now she wanted to see about putting the screws to Madam Nevaeh, Zeke's business partner and rumored lover, about Abrianna Parker. Castillo had learned from Abrianna's best friend, Shawn White, that Parker had been working for the infamous madam the night of Speaker Reynolds's death. The first time Castillo confronted Nevaeh about this, she stonewalled her.

But Castillo had a bad habit of never giving up. Holder had often joked that she was like a bloodhound. She never deviated from a trail. Never. Plus, Castillo had a history with Abrianna Parker. Six years ago she'd led a team that had rescued Abrianna, Tomi Lehane, and Shalisa Young from the basement of madman and serial killer Craig Avery. Back then, Parker was a tough but scarred teenage runaway, who didn't stick around long enough to answer questions about her abduction.

It surprised Castillo when Parker blipped on her radar while investigating the new House speaker for Tomi Lehane, who was now a Washington Post reporter. It shocked Castillo when she realized that Parker was actually running from a murder scene.

After a near forty minutes of threading through the handcuffed crowd, Castillo couldn't find any trace of the madam when she was certain that Nevaeh had been in attendance earlier. For a fleeting moment, Castillo wondered whether the madam had been the one who'd hijacked La

Plume's catering van, but then dismissed it when she overheard someone say they saw that it was a group of servers.

Suddenly a group of officers scrambled to their cars.

"What's going on?" she asked, rushing alongside Officer Donovan.

"They found the van," she told her.

"From the shoot-out?"

"Yeah. Apparently it crashed down an embankment. The driver is deceased."

"What about the others?"

Donovan frowned. "Others?"

"Wasn't it a group of servers?"

She shook her head. "Dispatch only mentioned the driver."

Castillo's hackles rose. "Male or female?"

"Female."

2

The Bunker

In an unknown place in an unknown location in the bowels of Washington D.C., Douglas "Ghost" Jenkins, lifelong political hacktivist, pulled open the metal door of his underground bunker to see his old friend.

"Well, if it ain't Bonnie and Clyde," Ghost said, blocking the entrance to his hideout. "Or should I say Clyde and Clyde?" He cocked his head at Abrianna and took in her outfit. "Nice disguise."

"Thanks."

Ghost's gaze darted to Julian and Draya. "Damn, if every time I see you, man, your ass don't multiply. What kind of place do you think I'm running here?"

"Really? You're going to do this now? I have an injured woman. She's been shot."

Ghost straightened and glanced at Abrianna. "What? Again?"

"Not me this time."

Draya raised her good arm. "It's me."

Interest lit Ghost's eyes. "Well, hello."

Draya frowned.

"You're hitting on an injured woman?" Kadir asked.

"Is it my fault that women are always getting shot around you?" Ghost stepped back, allowing the small group to enter.

Hunkered down behind a row of terminals sat a skeleton crew of millennial hackers. Ghost introduced them as "the fellas" to Draya.

"Uh, nice to meet you," she said and then looked to Abrianna like Who is this clown?

"C'mon." Abrianna led Draya toward the bunker's back cot room. "I'll fix you right up."

Ghost smiled as he watched them walk away.

Arms crossed, Julian stepped forward to block Ghost's view.

"Oh. My bad." Ghost looked to Kadir. "How many people are you planning to tell about this place?"

"Chill. They're cool," Kadir said. "So what happened to you the other night? I thought you'd still be waiting to post bail."

"C'mon, playa. Am I the sort of person to give the cops my real ID?"

"They were putting you in the back of a squad car."

"Some rookie busting my chops. You know how they do. Of course, I hope you got rid of the van. I had to report it stolen."

"Yeah. We traded that one in for another one and then filled that one with bullet holes too."

Ghost chuckled. "That straight and narrow path you swore that you were on isn't looking too damn straight, if you ask me."

"You don't know the half of it." Kadir looked around and leaned in close. "What do you know about . . . telekinesis?"

"What?"

"You know . . ." Kadir shrugged, inched closer. "The

ability to move shit with your mind. Have you ever known anyone who could—"

"KADIR!"

At Abrianna's shout, Kadir and Ghost took off toward the back.

In the cot room, Draya and Abrianna stood in front of a nine-inch TV.

When the guys couldn't see what the emergency was, Kadir asked, "Is everything okay?"

Abrianna shook her head and then pointed at the news broadcast on the screen.

"Federal Judge Katherine J. Sanders will be sworn in tomorrow as the eighteenth chief justice of the United States Supreme Court, enabling President Daniel Walker to put his stamp on the court for decades to come. Sanders's nomination had been slow walked, while the Republican Senate members waited to see whether the new speaker would pursue impeachment of the president. But with Speaker Reynolds's death, the Senate majority leader decided to move ahead with the confirmation."

Abrianna stared transfixed at the image in the corner of the screen. "That's her!"

"That's who?" Kadir asked.

She pointed. "That's the other woman from the hotel. That's Kitty!"

"Judge Katherine Sanders?" he thundered. "She's the one you think framed you for murder?"

"Yes! I'd know that face anywhere. It's her!"

"But why?" Kadir asked, puzzled.

"Didn't you hear the reporter?" Draya asked. "That speaker guy was going to impeach the president. An impeachment meant no confirmation. No Supreme Court."

Ghost slapped a hand across his forehead and whistled. "Holy shit. The same judge who sent you to the clink," he said. "The new chief justice of the Supreme Court. Ha! Good luck taking her down."

"We're going to need more than luck," Kadir grumbled, ripping off his fake mustache. "We're going to need a miracle."

Ghost shook his head. "Yo, dawg. That road you are on just got more crooked than a muthafucka."

"No shit," Kadir hissed, staring at Judge Sanders's image on the screen until the telecast cut to a commercial.

Defensive, Abrianna glanced around the eclectic group and read doubt and disbelief. "You guys believe me, don't you? I'm not making it up. She's Kitty—the other woman at the hotel that night."

Draya pressed a hand against Abrianna's shoulder. "I believe you."

"Yeah. I believe you, too," Julian added, curling up only one corner of his lips. His eyes, however, avoided her gaze.

Abrianna's jaw hardened.

Julian explained, "It's just that . . . well, this is huge, Bree. The fucking chief justice of the Supreme Court? What the fuck are we going to do?"

Abrianna's body slumped. "I have no idea."

"Well. How about that?" Ghost said. "We're all on the same page with our heads up our asses. Great!"

Kadir cut his friend a hard look. "Chill."

"What? I'm stating facts. It's a miracle that every Uncle Sam soldier isn't pouring into this bitch and hauling our asses to jail right now. You're wanted for bombing the damn airport, and your new chick here is wanted for killing the third most powerful man in America. Firing squads were made for terrorists like you two." He held up a hand and added, "I'm just telling you how the media is going to spin it."

"And don't forget the dead bitch we left back in the van," Draya reminded them.

Shut up, Abrianna mouthed.

"Come again." Ghost cupped his ear and leaned toward

Draya. "Dead body? What dead body?" He looked to Kadir. "What the fuck is she talking about?"

Kadir hedged.

"Mutha—come here! Let me holler at you for a moment." Ghost spun his boy by his shoulder and then shoved him out of the door.

Sighing, Kadir went along. Deep down he knew that he was wrong for springing this situation on Ghost. If the roles had been reversed, he would have gone apeshit.

Ghost hustled Kadir to the bunker's break room and slammed the door. It took another minute to calm down and choose his words carefully. "There is no point in my asking whether you've lost your damn mind because I already know that since you've laid eyes on that suicidal stripper, you've completely checked the fuck out of reality."

"Ghost, calm—"

"Ah, ah, ah." Ghost held up a finger and shook his head. "You've lost any right to tell me to calm down. I'm not the one whose face is plastered on the news as a domestic terrorist."

"Hold up," Kadir interjected. "You're wanted by the federal authorities too for political hacking."

"For questioning . . . and for something that they can't prove and, more importantly, my mug shot hasn't debuted on a single wanted poster or news broadcast."

Kadir cocked his head. "Are you jealous?"

"Jealous? Who? Me?" He waved the notion off. "Don't be ridiculous."

Kadir squinted and read the truth in his face.

Ghost swung the conversation back to the matter at hand. "Who is the corpse?"

Kadir sighed.

"Please, please tell me it's not the president of the United States."

"Don't be ridiculous," Kadir said.

"Then who?"

"Remember the madam we raced across town to talk to?"

"You're shitting me," Ghost said. "She killed her?"

"No. Abrianna didn't kill her," Kadir snapped. "We . . . sort of kidnapped her."

"Oh. Well. That makes more sense. What's a little kidnapping every now and then?" Ghost shrugged with a straight face. "What the fuck, man? Snap out it!"

"We didn't have much of a choice since the woman cleared out of her estate. A friend of Abrianna was catering a party for the woman's boyfriend, so her other friend, Draya, created these disguises and we crashed the joint."

"To kidnap the madam?" Ghost clarified, following along.

"Right. Only . . . there was a hiccup."

Ghost crossed his arms. "That tends to happen when committing federal crimes."

Kadir glared.

"What happened?" Ghost asked, rolling his hand, wanting to get to the end of the story.

"Bruh, I'm still not sure. This guard showed up when we were loading the body up and I think . . ." Kadir glanced at the closed door and then crossed over to stand in front of it, to make sure that no one entered. He lowered his voice. "I think . . . Abrianna threw this four-hundred-pound guy up against the side of the house—without laying a finger on him."

Ghost stared.

"You think I'm crazy, don't you?" Kadir tossed up his hands. "I don't blame you. If I hadn't seen the shit for myself I wouldn't believe it either, but . . . there's no other explanation. I saw what I saw."

"Catering?"

"Yeah. We—"

"Never mind. Finish the story."

"Like I was saying. The guy startled us, and when he

approached the van to see for himself what we were doing, Draya slammed the van door into his face and his gun went off."

"So that's how she got shot?"

"Right. But when the gun went off"—Kadir voice went even lower—"Abrianna screamed and . . . this huge guy flew backwards. I mean literally up in the air and slammed into the side of the house, knocking him out cold. I've never seen anything like it."

Silence.

Kadir's hands fell to his sides. "You don't believe me."

"Believe what? That your hooker girlfriend out there has super powers? Sure. Of course, I believe you. Why wouldn't I?"

Kadir's gaze leveled on his friend. "I'm not bullshitting you, man."

Ghost evaluated Kadir and then took a deep breath. "Okay."

"Okay? So you believe me?" Kadir checked, surprised.

"I believe that you believe what you thought you saw."

Kadir ran that sentence back through his head. "But . . . you don't believe it happened?"

"Is it important that I believe it? Does it change anything?"

Kadir sighed. "I guess not."

A few minutes later, they returned to the cot room where the group waited.

"I'm not crazy," Abrianna Parker insisted.

Ghost folded his meaty arms while his black gaze centered on her. "I've only known you for a few days; I hope you don't take offense but I personally think you're batshit crazy and I don't want anything more to do with this nonsense." His lethal gaze sliced toward Kadir. "Look, bruh. We go way back, but this mess right here? I want no part of it."

Kadir squared his shoulders at the curt tone. Emotions

warred across his face and, despite his own visible doubt, he defended Abrianna. "Why don't we hear her out?"

"Hear her out? She just said that the new chief justice of the Supreme Court—and your mortal enemy, I may add—murdered the House speaker of the U.S. Congress, the second man in line to the presidency. Do you know how fucking crazy that shit sounds?"

"No crazier than half the conspiracy theories that you've entertained over the years. All of which has you huddled down here in this underground bunker, hiding from the feds in the first place. Is what she saying really that hard to believe?"

Ghost opened his mouth but words never tumbled out.

Kadir arched a brow and cocked his head.

Ghost closed his mouth and then speared Abrianna with a look. "What happened to the madam? Wasn't she supposedly behind the conspiracy theory when y'all left here the last time? Who is it going to be next? The president?"

"Hey!" Kadir shoved Ghost, sending him careening into the nearest wall.

"Yo, dude!"

"Watch it," Kadir warned.

Julian crowded behind Kadir, ready to tag into the fight.

Tension layered the room while everyone else held their breaths.

Ghost backed down. "All right, man. My bad." He clamped his mouth shut.

Kadir glanced back over at Abrianna. "Please. Continue."

Abrianna battled her pride to get the rest of her story out. "Look, you guys already know the rest. It was my first night as an escort working for Madam Nevaeh. That woman showed up and introduced herself as Kitty. My john was happy when she arrived. They knew each other. We . . . partied . . . and when I woke up my client was missing part of his head and that Kitty bitch was nowhere to be found. I got out of there, but then gunmen showed up at my apartment. My best friend Shawn, who's still laid up in the hospital right now, took a hit, but I kept running until I jumped into your car, Kadir."

"Where they shot up my car and I brought you here the last time," Kadir finished the story for her.

"Right." She huffed. "Now. What are we going to do?"

Everyone's eyeballs ping-ponged around the room again. Clearly, none of them had a clue to what to do next.

Ghost sighed.

"Great," Ghost moaned.

Their gazes shifted around the room again.

Roger, one of Ghost's hackers, cleared his throat and drew everyone's attention.

Ghost's brows climbed to the center of his forehead. "You got something to say? Speak up."

Nervous, Roger cleared his throat. "Well . . . I take it that the media received the image of Abrianna from the Hay-Adams Hotel security surveillance."

Ghost shrugged. "Yeah, and?"

"Then Kitty, er, Judge Sanders should be on surveillance, too," Abrianna said, grinning.

Roger smiled. "Exactly."

Hope, the last emotion in Pandora's box, filled the room.

"But how are we going to get our hands on their surveillance footage?" Draya asked.

Kadir's handsome grin stretched. "How else? We hack."

However, hacking the luxury hotel turned out to be a more difficult job. Ghost and Kadir ascertained that it would require physical access to the hotel's security server.

"How are we going to manage to do that?" Abrianna asked.

"My guess is that someone is going to have to pose as

an employee and break into their security department. Once in there, upload a custom malware to give us access to their digital files."

"That sounds simple, which means it's anything but," Abrianna said.

Ghost smiled. "Smart girl. I'd imagine posing as an employee would be difficult. Something as small staffed as a hotel, everyone would know everybody. Don't you think?"

"Well, it's a pretty big hotel with shops and restaurants—but getting near security . . ." Abrianna shook her head.

"Right."

Julian spoke up. "What if someone was applying for a job?" He had everyone's attention and continued, "I worked security once at a hotel, and our security department was near the human resources office. New hires passed by our department every day."

Ghost and Kadir smiled. "You're hired."

Julian blinked. "Me?"

"Yep. You're not on anybody's radar. And you have the expertise to get in the door." Kadir slapped Julian on the back. "First thing tomorrow you're applying for a job."

Julian looked sick.